100
Guitar Accompaniment
Patterns

by
Abe Mandelblatt
Malká Ackerman Mandelblatt

Amsco Music Publishing Company
New York • London • Sydney • Cologne

Acknowledgments

There are many, many good people, relatives and friends alike, who spiritually supported us, and thereby contributed to our creating this book. Their efforts to help, their understanding, and their ability to endure a temporary "stage of neglect" that we occasionally inflicted upon them, will always be considered a major contribution to this effort and our sanity! This is especially true of our daughter and resident-philosopher, Aviva, who has been, and continues to be our greatest inspiration.

But since it's not feasible to thank 160 people, no matter how terrific they might be, we'll just have to thank them all here, collectively, as a group. . . . Thank you, group!

We would however like to mention those who directly affected this book's production.

First to Anne Mandelblatt (not only a mother but a friend), for typing nightly until the most absurd hours of the morning, all the love and appreciation she richly deserves.

And our loving respects to the Ackermans, Giordanos, Harveys, Kabuses, Mandelblatts, Sheffs, and Spilkias who literally and figuratively provided the seeds for our growth and nourished our development . . . especially to the parental contributors: Ida Sheff-Giordano ("Little Hawk") whose 4 feet 10 inches of towering talent was a model of musical professionalism; Billy Kay Ackerman, who combined laughter with song to exemplify the entertainment value in the musical experience; and Sol Mandelblatt, whose high artistic standards and social conscience were profoundly influential.

Our fondest homage to Herb Wise whose unique vision of publishing encourages humor and humanity. His support has enabled creative dreams to become realities.

To Jean Hammons, who encouraged us from this book's conception, and who continued to give of her ideas, energies and patience until its completion, our gratitude and affection.

To Ira Haskell and Jason Shulman who could have been merely helpful but chose instead to become invaluable . . . thank you for caring.

To Jack Baker, Andria Barzilay, Fred Sard, Bert Snyder, Iris Weinstein, Eugene Weintraub, Gordon Williams, and Chana Yachnis whose time, interest and efforts we most gratefully acknowledge.

Photographs

Diana Davies	82
David Gahr	30, 40, 44, 76, 98
Lou Garbus	back cover
Howard Kalish	84
Abe Mandelblatt	104
Dominique Tarle'	108
Herbert Wise	front cover, 68

International Standard Book Number: 0-8256-2812-1
Library of Congress Catalog Card Number: 73-92398

Distributed throughout the world by Music Sales Coporation:

799 Broadway, New York 10003
78 Newman Street, London W1P 3LA
27 Clarendon Street, Artarmon, Sydney, NSW 2064
Kölner Strasse 199, D-5000, Cologne 90

Contents

Song Section

Chords   182

Appendix

Foreword

Basically, an Accompaniment Pattern is a short, rhythmic unit of various right hand motions. The overall quality of most patterns are greatly affected by the touch, technique, mood and timing of each particular guitarist. For a beginner, a pattern unit may be repeated throughout an entire piece, and can easily create and carry the musical mood of the song. For the experienced guitarist, patterns can be used interchangeably with compatible or contrasting patterns, and seasoned with various special techniques.

The Accompaniment Patterns presented here reflect a variety of styles to accommodate a broad range of musical tastes. The patterns and strums are ordered into a comprehensive system to include a cross-section of guitar styles. Included is a repertoire of songs to be used in conjunction with the Accompaniment Patterns. These 100 songs will be found in a special section in the back of the book. The 100 pattern pages include:
1. the actual strum
2. a discussion of that strum
3. ten song possibilities
4. background of the specific song illustration with its corresponding page number.

The first 20 patterns are graded according to their levels of difficulty. The remaining patterns are grouped and graded according to type. Every pattern name has two or more parts: The first part indicates the type of strumming or plucking motion that begins or characterizes the pattern. The last part of the pattern name gives you its time signature. Any terms used in between further describe the style or the textural qualities of the pattern. This nomenclature tells you clearly which accompaniments are related to each other, where they can be used, and when they can be played interchangeably. Once you're familiar with the system you'll be able to choose patterns and pattern combinations suitable for most music you'll want to back yourself with. You'll just have to establish a song's meter, tempo, and it's regional considerations. In the case of short pattern units, 2 units are given in order to complete the measure.

There's a lot of material here to learn and grow with. It's really up to you how far you want to go. Enjoy the musical trip.

Reading Accompaniment Patterns in Tablature

The notation directs the right hand to pick or strum the indicated strings as the left hand frets a chord.

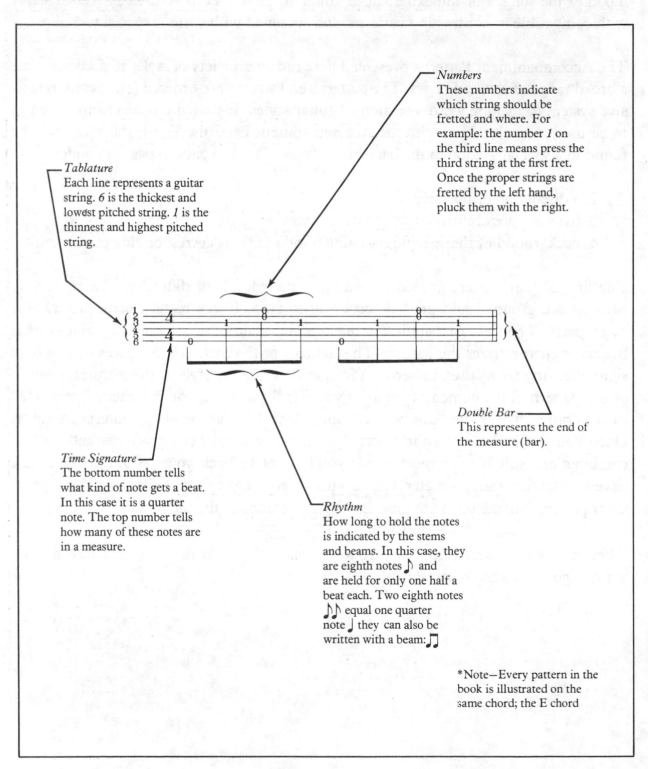

Numbers
These numbers indicate which string should be fretted and where. For example: the number *1* on the third line means press the third string at the first fret. Once the proper strings are fretted by the left hand, pluck them with the right.

Tablature
Each line represents a guitar string. *6* is the thickest and lowest pitched string. *1* is the thinnest and highest pitched string.

Double Bar
This represents the end of the measure (bar).

Time Signature
The bottom number tells what kind of note gets a beat. In this case it is a quarter note. The top number tells how many of these notes are in a measure.

Rhythm
How long to hold the notes is indicated by the stems and beams. In this case, they are eighth notes ♪ and are held for only one half a beat each. Two eighth notes ♪♪ equal one quarter note ♩ they can also be written with a beam: ♫

*Note—Every pattern in the book is illustrated on the same chord; the E chord

Reading An Accompaniment Pattern in Standard Notation

The notation directs the right hand to pick or strum the indicated strings, as the left hand frets a chord; in this case, the E chord.

Using this chart, along with your knowledge of tablature, you will be able to read the Accompaniment Patterns in standard notation.

Tablature

Corresponding notes in *Standard Notation.*

The notes in standard notation are identical to those in tablature. The tab example on the previous page is the same as the music example below:

Staff
The system of 5 lines and 4 spaces used to house the music symbols.

The Stem, Beam and Note Body.
All contribute to indicating the time value. (They tell you how long to hold the sounded tone.)

Notes
A note is the symbol that tells which tone to play, and how long it should be held (2 or more notes attached to one stem are played simultaneously).

Accidental
A symbol used to alter the original sound of a note by ½ a tone. Here, the sharp (♯) *raises* the tone ½ step. A flat (♭) would lower the tone ½ step. To play a sharp on the guitar, you would raise the pitch of the note ½ step by moving your finger one fret toward the body of the guitar. To play a flat, you would *lower* the pitch by moving your finger one fret toward the tuning pegs of the guitar.

Ledger Lines
The lines added to the staff to accommodate notes that are either too high or too low to fit into the 5 line staff.

*NOTE: *Every* pattern in the book is illustrated on an E chord.

Pattern Code Chart

SYMBOL	DESCRIPTION, RIGHT HAND DIRECTIONS
1	1st finger plucks, index finger plucks the 3rd string; it's a lifting rather than striking motion.
2	2nd finger plucks; middle finger plucks the 2nd string.
3	3rd finger plucks; ring finger plucks the 1st string.
2 + 3	2nd and 3rd finger pluck; middle and ring fingers pluck the 2nd and 1st strings simultaneously.
1 2 3	1st, 2nd and 3rd finger pluck; index, middle and ring finger pluck the 3rd, 2nd and 1st strings simultaneously.
↓2	2nd finger sweeps down; middle finger sweeps only the top 4 strings, from the 4th to the 1st.
2*	2nd finger catches; middle finger pulls-up, "catching," and sounding *only* the 1st string.
↑1	1st finger sweeps up; index finger sweeps back up the top 4 strings (from 1st to 4th).
T	thumb plucks; thumb sounds *single* bass string.
↓T	thumb sweeps down; thumb sweeps down across 4, 5 or 6 strings depending on the bass string for each chord. From low to high.
↑T	thumb sweeps up; thumb sweeps back up over 4, 5 or 6 strings, depending on the bass string for each chord. From high to low.
T–1	thumb and 1st finger pinch; thumb and index finger pinch together simultaneously, as they "press toward" each other.
T–2	thumb and 2nd finger pinch; thumb and middle finger pinch together simultaneously, as they press toward each other.
T–3	thumb and 3rd finger pinch; thumb and ring finger pinch together simultaneously, as they press toward each other.
↓F	fingers sweep down; the index, middle and ring fingers sweep down across 4, 5, or 6 strings, depending on the bass string for each chord, from lowest to highest.
↓R	fingers Rasgueado; spray the fingers (4, 3, 2, 1) rapidly one at a time diagonally across the strings.
P	palm muffles; the sweeping percussive motion of the fingers is followed by the palm which muffles the first sounded strings. The fingers and the palm are two parts of one continuous motion.
S	hand slaps; palm slaps strings as the fingers simultaneously strike the guitar face.
B	2nd and 3rd fingers tap bridge; middle and ring fingers tap bridge for drum effect.
/	accent; placed *over* a motion symbol to indicate a heavy stress on the beat of that motion.

Pattern Code Reading

Introduction: This Pattern Code has been devised for those people who haven't "gotten around" to learning either Standard Music Notation or Tablature. It's a system of letters, numbers and easy to remember symbols that are used in marking out just how a strum or picking pattern should be played.

It should be noted that this code illustrates a rhythmic pattern unit to be played by your right hand. It does *not* in any way help you to read music. Before we actually detail the system, here is a chart that should help you get the overall picture:

Reading Accompaniment Patterns in Code

The symbols used direct the right hand to pick or strum the indicated strings as the left hand frets a chord; in this case, the E chord.

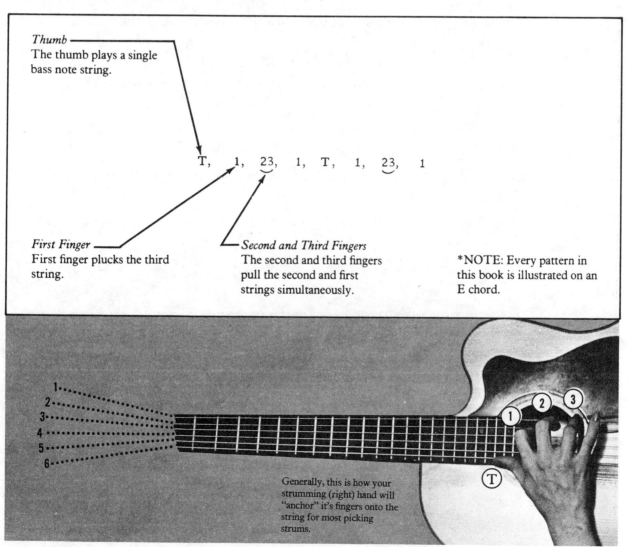

Thumb
The thumb plays a single bass note string.

T,   1,   23,   1,   T,   1,   23,   1

First Finger
First finger plucks the third string.

Second and Third Fingers
The second and third fingers pull the second and first strings simultaneously.

*NOTE: Every pattern in this book is illustrated on an E chord.

1.
2.
3.
4.
5.
6.

Generally, this is how your strumming (right) hand will "anchor" it's fingers onto the string for most picking strums.

pull $\frac{4}{4}$

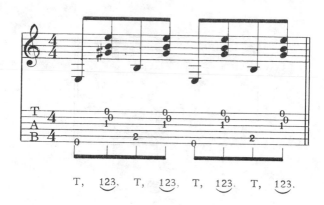

T, 123.   T, 123.   T, 123.   T, 123.

See key to Pull Patterns, page 32.

Although the Pull $\frac{4}{4}$ is the easiest of all the plucking-type $\frac{4}{4}$ patterns, it is still an effective accompaniment for a surprising number of songs. When you begin, play only the Root Bass Note String where the thumb motion T is indicated. Later, as you feel more confident, try using the *alternate bass string*. (See alternate bass string table on page 188.) Remember, the Pull $\frac{4}{4}$ (as well as a few other introductory strums), is a very simple, uncomplicated unit. Once learned, you can make it sound full, bouncy, or even kind of chunky. Given a little energy and patience, this, your first strum, could be the start of something incredible...your own music!

He's Got The Whole World In His Hands is a perfect song for beginners. There are only two chords in the whole piece! That in itself would be enough to recommend it, but it also has a catchy, spiritual quality, making it even more comfortable to work with. You might want to add your own verses if you're feeling creative. Use two pattern units for each measure.

Other Song Possibilities

Maxwell's Silver Hammer / Those Were the Days / Salty Dog / Michael Row The Boat / When the Saints Go Marching In / The City of New Orleans / I Rode My Bicycle Past Your Window / Hava Nagila (Hebrew) / All I Ever Need Is You / Don't Be Cruel

(See song on page 168.)

pull waltz $\frac{3}{4}$

T,   123,   123,

Here, as you may have guessed, is the easiest of all the $\frac{3}{4}$ patterns. The Pull Waltz $\frac{3}{4}$ pounds out the beat solidly. It would generally be more appropriate as a background for songs with a heavy dance rhythm, rather than those songs with a ballad feeling; but it can be used for either, if played with an appropriate touch.

Grand and Glorious Feeling is a short, gentle song that can become forceful when it's sung as a round with three or more voices. If it is done as a round, have each voice begin its part on a new line. Use one pattern unit for each measure.

Other Song Possibilities

Greensleeves / Que Sera Sera / Around the World / Sunrise Sunset / Little Boxes / Until It's Time For You To Go / Santa Lucia (Italian) / Chim Chim Cheree / Otchi Tshornyia (Russian) / What the World Needs Now

(See song on page 151.)

slow $\frac{4}{4}$

T, 1, 23, 1, T, 1, 23, 1,

See key to Slow Patterns, page 42.

The Slow $\frac{4}{4}$ seems to be the most widely used $\frac{4}{4}$ pattern of all the possibilities, and for very good reason. You'd really have to try hard not to sound good when you use this. Whenever you back yourself with it, your listeners will relax and assume you are in full control, and you may even believe it yourself. The Slow $\frac{4}{4}$ is simple yet full, and gives a decided feeling of motion. It should also give you a decided feeling of confidence. Incidentally, it is also one of the most versatile $\frac{4}{4}$ accompaniment patterns you will come across, which is probably why it is heard so often in records of almost every music style and character.

Kumbaya is an old gospel song called *Come Thy Here Lord*, brought over to Africa by missionaries. It was later brought back by song collectors as an African piece. One of the lovliest versions of this song was recorded by Judith Durham and The Seekers during the folk revivals of the early 1960's. It has been played in both $\frac{3}{4}$ and $\frac{4}{4}$ timing. Here, used in $\frac{4}{4}$ time, each measure gets two pattern units.

Other Song Possibilities

Yesterday / Changes / Misty / Four Strong Winds / Cruel War / Both Sides Now (Clouds) / I'd Like to Teach the World / Blowin In The Wind / Will You Still Love Me Tomorrow / As Tears Go By

(See song on page 163.)

slow $\frac{3}{4}$

T,   1,   23,   1,   23,   1

This is the $\frac{3}{4}$ counterpart of the Slow $\frac{4}{4}$ pattern. And, like its counterpart, the Slow $\frac{3}{4}$ gives you the same rich sound and an intense feeling of motion. It is also equally versatile and can be used with dance or ballad type songs. Both of these patterns have an elastic character that enables you to fit them into an amazing number of musical settings.

Scarborough Fair is a lovely old ballad which was re-popularized recently by Simon and Garfunkle. We've included all the verses we could find. Pick out the ones you like best. Use one pattern unit for each measure.

Other Song Possibilities

Mr. Bojangles / Try To Remember / Jerusalem Of Gold / The Joys Of Love / Greensleeves / Strangest Dream / Where Are You Goin' / My Father / Scarlet Ribbons / I Never Will Marry

(See song on page 173.)

fast $\frac{4}{4}$

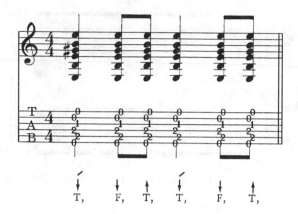

See key to Fast Patterns, page 95.

Assuming this will be your first attempt at a *wall of sound* type strum, prepare to loosen up. Your right hand is about to get some exercise. Here, as the Pattern Key indicates, the strings are hit, with a sweeping motion, either by the thumb alone or by all the fingers (their nails). The Fast $\frac{4}{4}$ is solid and sometimes chunky. It is best suited to bright, or up-tempo songs but can handle slower songs that call for a heavy beat.

Sinner Man—This turbulent old spiritual is ideally suited to learning your first Fast Strum because the chords change so infrequently. It affords time to ponder the new swiftness of your strumming hand as you change chords. Use two pattern units for each measure.

Other Song Possibilities

This Land is Your Land / All My Loving / If I had A Hammer / Kodechrome / Georgy Girl / Feeling Groovy / Go Tell It On The Mountain / Freight Train / The Beat Goes On / What Have They Done To My Song, Ma

(See song on page 177.)

slow bass note $\frac{4}{4}$

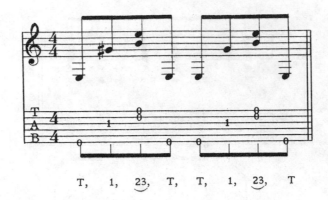

T, 1, 23, T, T, 1, 23, T

This is a surprisingly effective variation of the Slow $\frac{4}{4}$. A small change can make such a big difference! Instead of ending the unit as you did for a Slow $\frac{4}{4}$, by returning with your first finger, plucking the 3rd, (rather high-pitched) string, you now close with a thumb motion, playing the deeper *root bass string*. Because a bass string is heard at the end *and* at the beginning of your unit, it seems as though a bass line has been added by another instrument! Later on, when you're feeling more adventurous (and are in control of playing the pattern with the *root base string*), try using *alternate bass strings;* that will effect an even more pronounced moving bass line.

The Cruel War—Peter, Paul & Mary have, among other performers, recorded a lovely arrangement of this beautiful old ballad. In the process, they brought it renewed popularity. Play two pattern units for each measure.

Other Song Possibilities

Sunny / Yesterday / Hey Jude / Something / Will You Still Love Me Tomorrow / You've Got a Friend / By the Time I Get to Phoenix / Bridge Over Troubled Waters / El Condor Pasa / Love Story

(See song on page 176.)

fast rock $\frac{4}{4}$

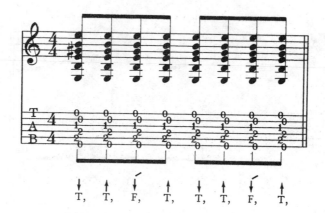

This is a useful and versatile variant of the Fast $\frac{4}{4}$. In the Fast Rock $\frac{4}{4}$, you will fill in the "unsounded" motion of the Fast $\frac{4}{4}$ by *sounding* the strings with a sweeping thumb motion. Most important to remember is that you should forcefully accent the 3rd motion (F), in order to "imitate" the rhythm of a rock drummer. He accents the 2nd and 4th beat of each measure. Accenting the 3rd motion of your strum gives the same effect. This is one of the easiest rock strums and is very popular. It lends itself to a large number of songs. Played slowly it can even be used for a ballad.

This Train has been sung in both major and minor keys. We chose a version in a minor key that seems in keeping with the spirit of the lyrics. Use two pattern units for each measure.

Other Song Possibilities

Light My Fire / Spinning Wheel / Proud Mary / Joy To The World / Comin' Into Los Angeles / Get Back / Rockin' Robin / Satisfaction / Shambala / Get Together

(See song on page 144.)

arpeggiated triplet $\frac{4}{4}$

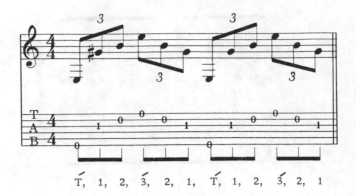

See key to Arpeggiated Patterns, page 48.

This ringing busy pattern resembles the triplet rhythm that rock drummers use on ballads; the tempo is slow but it has a heavy beat. The two accents that should be played by the thumb and the third finger are the essence of the rock ballad style you are trying to create. The accents will break the pattern unit into 2 parts, each containing 3 motions. It will also no doubt carry you off, deep into the solid gold sounds of the 50's.

House of the Rising Sun—A beautiful old folk song that had several fruitful revivals. Two of the best known more recent recordings were the rock version by the Animals and the folk version done by Joan Baez. Use two pattern units for each measure.

Other Song Possibilities

Cuando Caliente El Sol / Maybe / In the Still of the Night / Sixteen Candles / The Great Pretender / You're A Thousand Miles Away / I Only Have Eyes For You / A Million To One / Happy, Happy Birthday Baby / Donna / Maybe

(See song on page 145.)

fast latin $\frac{4}{4}$

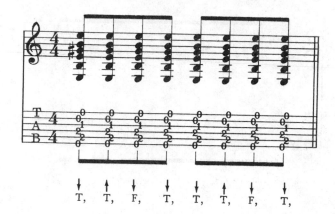

T,   T,   F,   T,   T,   T,   F,   T,

This is a variant of the Fast Rock $\frac{4}{4}$. In the Fast Latin $\frac{4}{4}$ the last motion of the thumb now sweeps *down* instead of up. This change is similar to the Slow Bass Note $\frac{4}{4}$ (in its relationship to the Slow $\frac{4}{4}$) where the first *bass* motion is repeated at the end of the pattern. It has rhythmic force and is equally effective with latin or rock tunes.

La Bamba—A Mexican wedding song with a contageous beat, this song has been popularized by both Richie Valens and Trini Lopez. Use two pattern units for each measure.

Other Song Possibilities

Que Bonita / Sunshine (Go Away Today) / I Feel the Earth Move / California Dreamin' / Comin' Home Baby / Spanish Harlem / Aquarius / Sunny / Put Your Hand in the Hand of the Man from Galilee / The Letter

(See song on page 157.)

arpeggiated $\frac{4}{4}$

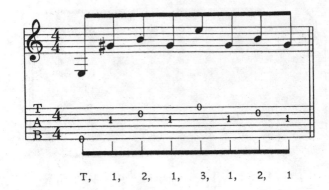

T,   1,   2,   1,   3,   1,   2,   1

The Arpeggiated $\frac{4}{4}$ is a genuine attention getter. It is a long flowing ballad pattern, extremely effective on songs where you have no less than one chord to a measure. Because the unit has eight motions, only one pattern unit for each measure should be needed. (With the previous $\frac{4}{4}$ patterns 4 motions—four eighth notes—or two strum units were needed to fill the measure.)

Where Have All the Flowers Gone is Pete Seeger's classic anti-war song. Joe Hickerson added the last verse to complete the cycle. It's the kind of song that serves to remind us of how powerful and potent a simple lyric and song can be. Use one pattern unit for each measure.

Other Song Possibilities

Sounds of Silence / If I Were A Carpenter / Suzanne / Cruel War / There's a Kind of Hush / Everybody's Talkin' / Traces / Let It Be Me / As Tears Go By / Will You Still Love Me Tomorrow.

(See song on page 167.)

pinch slow $\frac{4}{4}$

T,   1,   T23,   1,   T,   1,   T23,   1

See key to Pinch Patterns, page 54.

With the addition of the Pinch Motion on the 3rd beat (which effects the simultaneous sounding of 3 strings), the Slow $\frac{4}{4}$ undergoes a metamorphosis; you now have a very full sound that provides an even more marked contrast to the single bass string heard at the beginning of a Slow $\frac{4}{4}$. Try alternating the second bass string (the thumb motion that is played as *part* of the *pinch* motion). This pattern has a crisp and commanding sound; use of *alternate bass* strings gives it movement.

Rose—An old piece most often sung as a round. It can be done in four parts. Unlikely as it may seem, if you sing this with three other friends (who can stay even reasonably in tune), you will sound like a chorus! Use two pattern units for each measure. Also, you can try our new words.

Other Song Possibilities

I Don't Know How to Love Him / Liverpool Lullaby / Dona Dona / Sealed With a Kiss / Love Is Blue / He's Not Heavy, He's My Brother / Somewhere / God Bless the Child / Brother Can You Spare a Dime / Both Sides Now

(See song on page 165.)

arpeggiated $\frac{3}{4}$

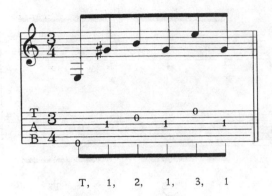

T,   1,   2,   1,   3,   1

The Arpeggiated $\frac{3}{4}$ is derived from the Arpeggiated $\frac{4}{4}$ unit. Leaving off the last 2 motions of the Arpeggiated $\frac{4}{4}$ brings it into $\frac{3}{4}$ time. It is as rippling and appealing as its $\frac{4}{4}$ counterpart. This unit is a simple, clear ballad pattern which can be used interchangeably with the Slow $\frac{3}{4}$ quite nicely.

River of My People—This was originally a Russian song. *Stenka Razin* is about a sailor who throws his lover overboard in order to prove his independence to the crew. But Pete Seeger, with his great forsight, realized that this was far too good a melody to waste and wrote some new words. Use one pattern unit a measure. You might also try the Slow $\frac{3}{4}$ on this song for a different textural approach.

Other Song Possibilities

Where Are You Going / Strangest Dream / Scarlet Ribbons / Greensleeves / Moon River / Today / I Can't Help Falling In Love With You / Scarborough Fair / Yarushalayim Shel Zahav / Mr. Bojangles

(See song on page 163.)

pinch extended slow $\frac{4}{4}$

T,　1,　T23,　1,　T23,　1,　T23,　1

In the Pinch Extended Slow $\frac{4}{4}$, as the name implies, the basic Pinch Slow $\frac{4}{4}$ unit has been extended. With additional motions, the effect becomes flowing and gentle, like an understated ballad. This is ideal for implying an underlying suggestion of the beat. Remember to use *alternate bass* strings for the last three bass notes.

Man of Constant Sorrow—A ballad heard in various parts of the Southern Mountains. The first line is often changed to "I am a maid (or girl) of constant sorrow." Use one pattern unit for each measure.

Other Song Possibilities

Something / Could You Ever / Suzanne / Umbrellas of Cherbourg / You've Lost That Lovin' Feelin' / The Water Is Wide / Traces / Yesterday When I Was Young / If I Was a Carpenter / Windmills of Your Mind

(See song on page 174.)

fast $\frac{3}{4}$

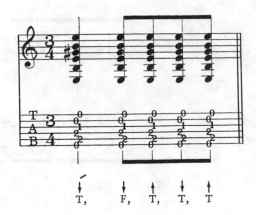

The Fast $\frac{3}{4}$ is a very important strum. All the preceding $\frac{3}{4}$ accompaniment patterns were for slow or ballad type songs; the Fast $\frac{3}{4}$ is for heavier, more energetic $\frac{3}{4}$ songs. The Fast $\frac{3}{4}$ is derived from the Fast $\frac{4}{4}$ and is performed by repeating the last 2 sweeping motions of the Fast $\frac{4}{4}$.

The House-Wife's Lament—This song is copied from the diary of Mrs. Sara A. Price of Ottowa, Illinois. She had seven children and lost them all (some during the Civil War). Walt Robertson has recorded the tune. It would be very funny if it weren't so pathetic. Use one pattern unit for each measure.

Other Song Possibilities

Norwegian Wood / The Times They Are a Changin' / The Lonesome Death of Hattie Carroll / Beans in My Ears / Die Gedanken Sind Frei / Sweet Baby James / La Firolera / I've Got to Know / Song of the Deportees / So Long It's Been Good To Know You

(See song on page 143.)

slow bass pull $\frac{4}{4}$

T,   1,   23,   T,   T,   123,   T,   123

You won't believe how sophisticated a simple strum can sound until you've tried this one. Although it is very easy to play, it can be used to create a Bossa-Nova-like effect! Because of the variety of sound textures it combines, listeners inevitably assume that it is very complicated. The results will amaze you!

All My Trials is an old spiritual with a West Indian inflection, and lends itself beautifully to Bossa-Nova treatment. Use one pattern unit for each measure.

Other Song Possibilities

Killing Me Softly / Girl From Ipanema / The Wheel of Life / Here's That Rainy Day / Let it Be Me / Carnival / I Am Woman / You've Got a Friend / If I Was a Carpenter / Light My Fire

(See song on page 160.)

fast calypso $\frac{4}{4}$

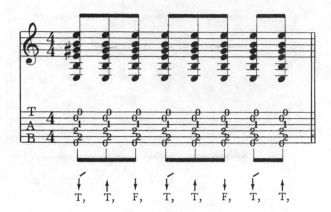

The Fast Calypso $\frac{4}{4}$ is an unmistakable winner. It is so versatile and fluid, it will probably become one of your favorites within minutes. Most Calypso and Latin American rhythms utilize syncopation which results when you play $\frac{3}{4}$ time against $\frac{4}{4}$ time. This (and other) Calypso patterns take eight eighth notes and divide them into 3 unequal groupings: 123, 123, 12. In this pattern, you repeat one three motion section of your unit two times, then begin again for the third section, but this time you end abruptly *without* playing the last expected motion. The heavy accents pound out the first motion of each section and add to that strongly syncopated feeling. Oddly enough, this strum is used on surprisingly uncalypso-like songs by many people. It can give mild spice to ballads that have infrequent chord changes.

Jamaica Farewell—Recorded by Harry Belafonte in the 50's, this original by Lord Burgess hit the top of the charts, thus making it a favorite in pop as well as folk circles. Use one pattern unit for each measure. The song also works well with the Moving Bass Ballad $\frac{4}{4}$.

Other Song Possibilities

Ob-La-Di / Maryanne / Sloop John B / Guardian Beauty Contest / Love Alone / Day-o / Brown Skin Girl / Man Smart Woman Smarter / All My Trials / Bamboo

(See song on page 169.)

moving bass pinch ballad $\frac{4}{4}$

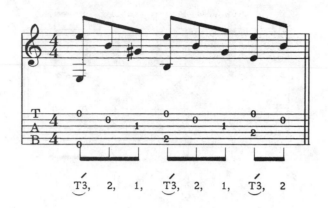

T3, 2, 1,   T3, 2, 1,   T3, 2

See key to Moving Bass Patterns, page 62.

This is one of the most lyrical and active of any of the ballad strums. It ripples with its crisp, ringing *pinch motions* and has movement and interest because of the moving bass strings. When you've got the Slow $\frac{4}{4}$, Fast Calypso, Arpeggiated $\frac{4}{4}$, Rock $\frac{4}{4}$, and this, you'll be just about ready to go on the road!

What Have They Done to the Rain—Like its folk-singer-composer author, Melvina Reynolds, this song is ageless. It is perhaps one of the most gentle and beautiful protest songs ever written. It can be viewed as either a song concerning the nuclear fall-out threat, or as a protest to the ever increasing pollution problems we must face. Use two pattern units for each measure. This song also works well with the Arpeggiated Slow $\frac{4}{4}$, or, later, Travis Picking $\frac{4}{4}$.

Other Song Possibilities

Hey, Mr. Tambourine Man / Changes / Four Strong Winds / Liverpool Lullaby / More / Everybody Talkin' (Midnight Cowboy) / Little Green Apples / I Can See Clearly Now / Comin' of the Roads / Jamaica Farewell

(See song on page 153.)

fast folk $\frac{4}{4}$

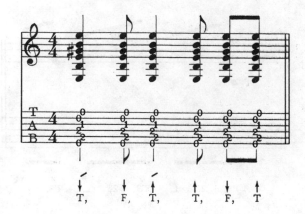

This is a very lively and useful strum. Sprinkle it liberally over your spirited folk songs and you will be very happy with the results. They rhythm should sound "Boom chick Booma chicka."

Everybody Loves Saturday Night is a West African song written in response to a curfew that was lifted only on Saturday night. In 1950 some Los Angeles school children translated the words into as many languages as they could. Maybe you can add a verse in another language. Use one pattern unit for each measure.

Other Song Possibilities

Me & Julio Down by the School Yard / Down by the Lazy River / Midnight Special / The Lion Sleeps Tonight (Wimaweh) / Aquarius / Me and Bobby McGee / Twelve Gates to the City / This Land Is Your Land / Done Laid Around / Cotton Fields

(See song on page 174.)

moving bass arpeggiated calypso $\frac{4}{4}$

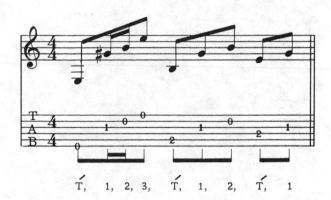

This pattern combines the three essential rhythmic divisions most calypso strums use (123, 123, 12) with a *moving bass* technique. In the first rhythmic division, where we usually have three motions, we now have 4 motions. The thumb and third finger each get one-half beat while the second and third fingers together are squeezed into one half beat. The rhythm should sound "Bom, chick-a-chick; Bom chick chick, Bom chick."

Sloop John B—Carl Sandburg, in his book The American Songbag, reported that this was actually a classic Calypso song from the Bahamas brought here more than fifty years ago. Use two pattern units for each measure. When there are two chords in the first half of the measure, the second chord gets the last two motions of the strum.

Other Song Possibilities

Jamaica Farewell / Come Back Liza / Delia / The Big Bamboo / Island in the Sun / Pay Me My Money Down / Will His Love Be Like His Rum / Take Me / Bonsoire Dame / All My Trials

(See song on page 166.)

travis pattern picking $\frac{4}{4}$

T2,   T,   1,   T,   2,   T,   1

See key to Pattern Picking Patterns, page 78.

This pattern is most often associated with Merle Travis, the well known Country-Western performer. Although he didn't actually create the style, Travis's technical virtuosity in this area was instrumental in widely popularizing it. Actually, this three-finger type picking was an old Black style. It evolved from an attempt to imitate the sound of ragtime piano music on the guitar. It might be best to practice this pattern in two parts. First, get comfortable alternating the bass strings with your thumb; then, add the treble notes with your fingers. The rhythm should sound "Boom, Bom-a, Bom-a, Bom-a."

Freight Train—This is an Elizabeth Cotton classic. After working for the Seeger family for several years, one day she surprised them, not only by playing the guitar beautifully, but by holding the instrument in a most unusual way. Like a few "lefties" she held it "backwards," but unlike these players, she never reversed the strings! She still performs, so if she gives a concert near your area, you might well want to treat yourself to a piece of history. Use one pattern unit for each measure.

Other Song Possibilities

I am a Pilgram / Helplessly Hoping / Puff the Magic Dragon / Don't Think Twice / Oh, Babe It Ain't No Lie / Alice's Restaurant / All I Ever Need Is You / Gentle On My Mind / Thirsty Boots / Reason to Believe

(See song on page 144.)

Pull Patterns

The *Pull Pattern* units are easy to play and control. They can give even beginners the feeling that they have something substantial going for them. Most *pull patterns* will provide a very manageable, solid accompaniment. They have a full, clear and often ringing sound. Certain patterns using the pull motion lend themselves to a mellow touch while others can be quite forceful.

Each of the accompaniment patterns in this grouping, regardless of their meter or the total number of motions used, will always begin its basic unit with the following 2 motions in this fixed sequence:

1. The thumb plays a *single* bass note string first. (For a clear, supportive, tone, a rest stroke is effective.) That *bass string* is determined by the chord being played.

2. Then, your first, second and third fingers *simultaneously* pluck the third, second and first strings, respectively. (This triple plucking action effects the pull motion, which can also appear in other pattern groupings.)

As you play a pull motion, try to bring out your first string. The third finger is usually not very strong, so exaggerate your effort on that finger in order to compensate for this weakness.

After the core is played some of these motions may be repeated, or other motions from different groupings may be added; but the beginning of each *pull pattern* unit is always the same. Remember, although your thumb can change *bass strings,* your three fingers always work the same top three strings as long as you are playing first position chords (i.e. chords played within the first three frets which utilize open strings). Later, when using bar chords, a few adjustments will be necessary.

When the use of *alternate bass strings* is suggested or desired for strums in this grouping, refer to this table:

	A-B-C	D-F	E-G
Root Bass Strings	5	4	6
Standard Alternates			
1. Primary	5-4	4-5	6-5
2. Supplementary	5-6	4-5	6-4

pull slow bass rock $\frac{4}{4}$

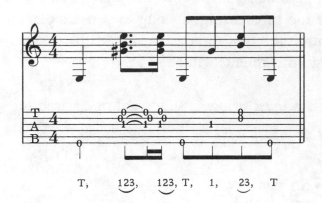

T,   123,   123, T,   1,   23,   T

The Pull Slow Bass Rock $\frac{4}{4}$ uses motions from two parent groups. The first three motions are pull pattern motions while the last four motions create a Slow Bass $\frac{4}{4}$ pattern. Together they create the rhythmic figure rock drummers of the 70's. Play on slow songs and ballads. It should sound: "Bom, chick, a-Bom-a-chick Bom."

Swing Low, Sweet Chariot is one of the better known spirituals that has stood the test of time. It will swing very nicely if you use one pattern unit for each measure. In measures with two chords, give the first chord the three *pull motions* and the second chord the last four *slow* motions.

Other Song Possibilities

Delta Dawn / My Foolish Heart / Doodlin' / Hey Jude / Comin' Home Baby / The In Crowd / How Deep Is the Ocean / The Days of Wine and Roses / Con Alma / Sunshine of My Life

(See song on page 143.)

pull mid-east $\frac{4}{4}$

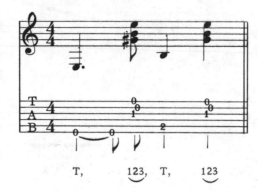

Here you have a rhythmic variation of the Pull $\frac{4}{4}$ that really changes the character of the original strum. The Pull Mid-East $\frac{4}{4}$ still has fullness and clarity from its multi-toned *pull motions,* but the rhythmic change creates a nice bite. Alternate your bass strings for maximum effect.

Erev Shel Shoshanim—The title, translated from Hebrew, means "Evening of the Roses." It is a beautiful Israeli love song that is well-known in folk circles far beyond the borders of its own land. It became a classic of its country in less time than it takes most songs to become popularized. Use one pattern unit for each measure.

Other Song Possibilities

Erev Ba (Hebrew) / Miserlou (Greek) / All My Trials / Mustafa (Arabic) / Yellow Bird / Nad Elan (Hebrew) / Never on Sunday (Greek) / El Condor Pasa (South American Indian) / To Treno Yermaneos Athenen (Greek) / Nigun Atik (Hebrew)

(See song on page 173.)

pull arpeggiated $\frac{4}{4}$

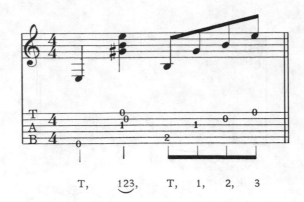

Here we have combined elements of two pattern groupings: the *pull patterns* and the *arpeggiated patterns*. The arpeggiated section of this pattern is held for *one* beat, so we've really got to move our little digits in order to finish the unit in time. For the song illustration the unit should be played very slowly, but it's also effective at much faster tempos.

Sakura (pronounced *Sakulah*) is a delicate Japanese song about cherry blossoms. It's traditional melody is probably the oriental song most familiar to Western ears. In order to create a feeling of an Eastern accompaniment, we've provided 3 alternate chord fingerings for Dm, Gm and A. First, try these new chords, then work the strum into the chord progression, and then sing the melody; if you still want something to keep you busy, play a pair of finger symbols on the alternate beats of each measure (with your toes of course). Seriously though, it's not difficult only different. Use one pattern unit for each measure.

Other Song Possibilities

Kisses Sweeter Than Wine / Playboys and Playgirls / Raindrops Keep Falling on My Head / The Fox / Country Roads / Alone Again / Power and the Glory / Michael / Something Must Be Wrong / The Night They Drove Old Dixie Down

(See song on page 144.)

pull folk Chasidic $\frac{4}{4}$

T, 123, 123, T, 123

This is a somewhat stocky variation of the Pull $\frac{4}{4}$. It seems to rock back and forth rather heavily on it's two bass notes. The rhythm is "Boom, chick chick, boom, chick," and you should feel yourself nodding your head knowingly from side to side. This strum is mainly for tunes with an implied Chasidic Dance feeling. If you don't know any chasidic tunes, try this on any chunky dance music you do know. Chances are this strum could make the Tarentella sound chasidic.

Zum Gali Gali—An Israeli song about the life of the pioneer. The two melodies can be sung against each other. Use one pattern unit for each measure. In measures with two chords, the second gets the last two strum motions.

Other Song Possibilities

A Fiddler on the Roof / Az Der Rebeh Tanzt / Hine Matov (Chasidic version) / I'm Hashachar / Ootzu Etza / If I Were a Rich Man / Yibaneh HaMigdash / David Melach Israel (Chasidic version) / Yamin Usamol / Hana' ava Babanot

(See song on page 167.)

pull jazz $\frac{3}{4}$

With the Pull Jazz $\frac{3}{4}$, the object is to squeeze 4 motions into three beats. At first glance, it looks remarkably like the Pull $\frac{4}{4}$. This is probably because the motions for both patterns are identical. The trick is the em-*PHASIS!* If you haven't been exposed to much jazz music, you may feel a little stiff with the rhythm initially. But if you relax and give it some time, you'll eventually fall into the groove.

Something Borrowed—This was patterned after a Chopin Prelude which sustains a single tone in the melody while keeping the harmony shifting below it. Use one pattern unit for each measure.

Other Song Possibilities

Bluesette / Charade / Lover / What the World Needs Now / Someday My Prince Will Come / West Coast Blues / Gravy Waltz / African Waltz / My Favorite Things / Greensleeves

(See song on page 152.)

pull jazz $\frac{5}{4}$

The Pull Jazz $\frac{3}{4}$ pattern is the foundation for this unit, to which you add two bass notes. Within each unit, four bass note strings will be played; the first two are *root bass strings*, the second two are *alternate bass strings*. (See Alternate Bass Strings for Pull Patterns.) The thought of playing $\frac{5}{4}$ time may seem a bit scary, but it doesn't have to be. Just give it a little time. In order to feel $\frac{5}{4}$ time comfortably, divide the measure into: 1 2 3, 1 2.

Take Five—This Jazz classic achieved the almost impossible. It took its strange rhythm and sound outside the confines of the jazz world, and found love and acceptance. Since $\frac{5}{4}$ time is quite foreign to most people, the overwhelming (and well deserved) popularity of *Take Five* was impressive. Try an E minor *bar chord* (7th fret) and play the 1st two bass notes on the 5th string. Then move your 1st finger across to the 6th string 7th fret (B) for the 3rd *bass note* and your pinky up to the 10th fret 6th string (D) for the 4th and last *bass note*. Use one pattern unit for each measure, except on the bridge, where there are two chords in a measure; there, play the first half of the strum unit as usual. On the chord change, however, simultaneously pinch your thumb and 1st, 2nd and 3rd fingers together twice instead of using the original bass note. We wish you the best of luck.

Other Song Possibilities

Jesus Christ Superstar / Everything's Alright / Something for Django / Baile De Pandero (Spanish) / Searching for the Lambs (Greek) / Dance from Isakonia (Greek) / Uchima, Maycho, Nayuchi (Bulgarian) / Bass Reflex (Hi-Fi Suite) / Mission Impossible Theme / Fun Time / Castillian Drums

(See song on page 151.)

pull bass note rock $\frac{4}{4}$

T,   123, T, T, T, 123, T

The Pull Bass Note Rock $\frac{4}{4}$ is a rock strum that can be used for rock ballads and for songs that go well with an active accompaniment and treatment. Because of it's many bass tones, there is a soft insistent feeling of movement as though a bass player is churning away underneath, even though the tempo is slow. The rhythm should sound "Boom, chick bom, bom bom, Chick bom."

Oh Mary Don't You Weep—Although usually sung as a rousing gospel song, here *Mary* gets more of an underplayed rock feeling. Use one pattern unit for each measure.

Other Song Possibilities

There Goes My Baby / Hey Jude / Dock of the Bay / The Wind Cries Mary / Maggie May / Sunshine of My Life / You Won't See Me / Walk On By / Like a Rolling Stone / You've Lost That Lovin' Feeling

(See song on page 156.)

Slow Patterns

Accompaniments from this *slow pattern* grouping have a great deal to offer, yet demand relatively little. They generate a feeling of gentle activity, and blend ringing single string tones with fuller, tempered simultaneously plucked strings. Once you've used one of these strums, you'll wonder how you ever managed without it! Some strums require great energy and direction from the guitarist to get them off the ground. These strums kind of carry you along in their momentum!

Each of the accompaniment patterns in this grouping, regardless of their meter or the total number of motions used, will always begin its basic unit with the following 3 motions:

1. The thumb plays a *single bass string* to start each pattern unit. That string is determined by the chord being played. (For a clear, supportive tone, a rest stroke is effective.)

2. Next, your first finger follows by plucking the third string.

3. Then, your second and third fingers *simultaneously* pluck the second and first strings (respectively).

After this core is played, some of these motions may be repeated, or other motions from different groupings may be added; but the beginning of each *slow pattern* unit is always the same. As with the *pull patterns*, the thumb can change the *bass string*, but the fingers always work the same top three strings.

When the use of Alternate Bass Strings is suggested or desired for the strums in this grouping, refer to this table.

	A B C	D-F	E-G
Root Bass Strings	5	4	6
Standard Alternates			
1. primary	5-4	4-5	6-5
2. supplementary	5-6	4-5	64

slow syncopated $\frac{4}{4}$

This pattern has the same motions as the Slow $\frac{4}{4}$ unit, only here the rhythm is syncopated. The first and third motions are held longer than the second and fourth motions. This rhythmic alteration gives the pattern a lilting feeling. Most people find this change fairly easy to get into. The only real problem to watch out for is: don't end up syncopating all your rhythms once you've learned how.

I Know Where I'm Going—This is an old love song that finds its way into innumerable rock repertoires and anthologies. Use two pattern units each for each measure.

Other Song Possibilities

Raindrops Keep Falling on My Head / Daydream / A Little Help from My Friends / Heart and Soul / Goodnight Sweetheart / King of the Road / Do You Want to Know a Secret / Pennylane / All You Need Is Love / Your Mother Should Know

(See song on page 166.)

slow bass note $\frac{3}{4}$

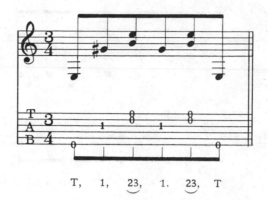

T,   1,   23,   1.   23,   T

For this pattern, take the Slow $\frac{3}{4}$ unit and substitute a thumb rest stroke on the bass string for the last motion (in which the 1st finger plucked the 3rd string). This change creates a new, somewhat heavier feeling of motion. As the two bass strings begin and end each unit, it sounds as though there is a moving bass line. This produces a subtle, driving under-current, rhythmically and harmonically.

Greensleeves—This beautiful English ballad dates back to 1548. It's still going strong after more than 400 years! Play two pattern units for each measure. You might like to try it again with the Jazz $\frac{3}{4}$ strum.

Other Song Possibilities

Jean / Brandy Leave Me Alone / Until It's Time For You To Go / Try to Remember / Joys of Love / Birmingham Sunday / River of My People / How Can We Hang On to a Dream / Scarlet Ribbons / My Father

(See song on page 175.)

slow multiple bass $\frac{4}{4}$

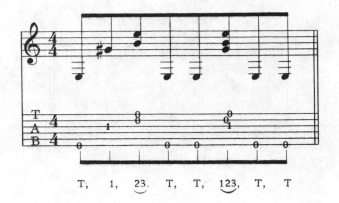

T, 1, 23, T, T, 123, T, T

This strum uses a Slow Bass $\frac{4}{4}$ with a *pull motion* and three more single string thumb motions. This combination yields a veritable plethora of bass strings which we can sprinkle around quite freely! The strum can be used to evoke a resolute feeling (with its bass strings pounding along like heavy feet), or used to create an accented feeling that contrasts with the other tone qualities of the pattern.

Zog Nit Keinmol—A powerful song in Yiddish that came out of the Vilna Ghetto during the second World War. Hersh Glick, who wrote the words, was killed while fighting the Nazis. Use one pattern unit for each measure.

Other Song Possibilities

As Tears Go By / Changes / Everybody's Talkin' / Hey, That's No Way to Say Goodbye / More / Dock of the Bay / Can't Take My Eyes Off You / Come Softly to Me / Circle Game / Diana

(See song on page 159.)

slow bass pull $\frac{3}{4}$

T, 1, 23, T, T, 123

The Slow Bass Pull $\frac{3}{4}$ is a delicious strum. It provides a blend of textures and activity that is bound to give any song a varied, full, polished sound.

The Lass from the Low Country is a classic English ballad about un-requieted love. Use one pattern unit for each measure.

Other Song Possibilities

Scarborough Fair / What the World Needs Now / Chim Chim Cheree / Matchmaker / The Girl That I Marry / She's Like the Swallow / Always / Irene / Someday My Prince Will Come / Mr. Bojangles

(See song on page 170.)

Arpeggiated Patterns

An *arpeggiated pattern* generally provides a clear, ringing sound. Its rippling quality can be peppery, cutting, or surprisingly delicate. This sound depends largely on what other motions are contained in the total pattern unit and the individual touch of the guitarist. Most patterns in this grouping tend to carry you on their natural momentum.

Each of the accompaniment patterns in this grouping, regardless of their meter or the total number of motions used, will always include in its basic unit four specific motions. Unlike the *pull* or *slow patterns,* most of the motions that form the core of the *arpeggiated patterns,* need not be played consecutively. Only the first motion listed must be played first:

    1. Your thumb plays a *single* bass string to start each pattern unit. The string will be determined by the chord being played. (A rest stroke or free stroke can be used.)

Once the single-string thumb motion has played the bass string, three plucking motions follow; their sequence varies and will depend on the particular Pattern Units.

    2. Your first finger plucks the 3rd string.

    3. Your second finger plucks the 2nd string.

    4. Your third finger plucks the 1st string.

The only constant that applies to these motions is that a specific finger will always pluck a specific string. As with the *slow* and *pull patterns,* the thumb changes its bass string, but the fingers will remain working the top three strings.

When the use of *alternate bass* strings is suggested or desired for patterns in this grouping, these are the recommended possibilities:

	A-B-C	D-F	E-G
Root Bass String	5	4	6
Standard Alternates			
1. primary	5-4	4-5	6-5
2. supplementary	5-6	4-5	6-4

arpeggiated triplet $\frac{3}{4}$

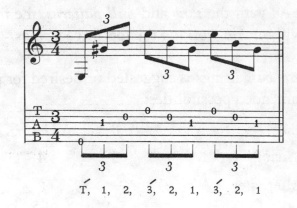

The Arpeggiated Triplet $\frac{3}{4}$ is a good strum for songs that need a very active accompaniment that will contrast but not conflict with a slow tempo song. Don't forget to accent the third finger to get the most out of this pattern.

Suliram is a most unusual and haunting Indonesian lullaby. We've re-arranged it and written English lyrics for those who are not confident about singing in languages you've never heard. But don't worry about your pronunciation; it's the thought that counts. Use one pattern unit to a measure. Try Suliram with the Slow $\frac{3}{4}$ for a simpler treatment.

Other Song Possibilities

The Joys of Love / Where Are You Going / My Father / Greensleeves / I Never Will Marry / Scarlet Ribbons / Try to Remember / Until It's Time for You to Go / Un Canadien Errant / Clementine

(See song on page 162.)

arpeggiated double bass triplet $\frac{4}{4}$

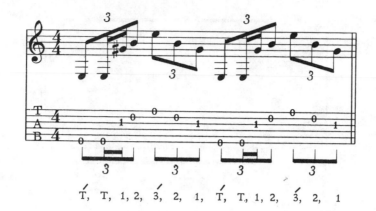

T, T, 1, 2, 3, 2, 1, T, T, 1, 2, 3, 2, 1

This is a cousin of the Arpeggiated Triplet $\frac{4}{4}$. However, for some reason, some students confuse this with the Slow Bass $\frac{4}{4}$ pattern. They begin this unit on it's second bass string, but it should begin on it's first bass string. Try saying "Bom Chicka Bom Boom chick chick," and fit the unit in. It helps to listen to old 1950's Slow Rock tunes! This pattern has the rhythmic figure that every drummer (we repeat, *every)* played on his ride cymbal. To be an instant 50's rock star, play 2 pattern units on each of the following chords: G, Em, C, D⁷, G.

Every Night When the Sun Goes Down is a soulful ballad with a blues inflection. Use two pattern units for each measure.

Other Song Possibilities

House of the Rising Sun / The Great Pretender / Debaer Ali Bifrachim / Tears on My Pillow / Over the Mountain / Catch the Wind / Maybe / Silhouettes / Impossible Dream / Daddy's Home

(See song on page 178.)

arpeggiated bass $\frac{4}{4}$

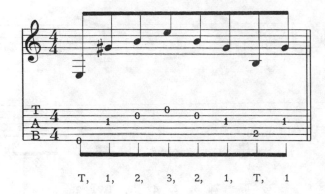

T,   1,   2,   3,   2,   1,   T,   1

This long rippling pattern flows outward from the first *bass string* only to be suddenly contained by the second *bass string*. It is most effective when used with easy, soft ballads where the feeling of the beat is suggested rather than pronounced. It moves along nicely when used interchangeably with the Pinch Slow Extended $\frac{4}{4}$. Try alternating the bass strings where you want even more activity.

They Looked a Lot Like We—This a New York love song which, with only slight modification, can be sung equally well in Liverpool or Paris. Use one pattern unit for each measure.

Other Song Possibilities

For No One / Let It Be Me / The Cruel War Is Raging / One Less Bell to Answer / In the Heat of the Summer / Comin' of the Roads / Yesterday When I Was Young / I've Got to Get A Message to You / Love Story / Unchained Melody

(See song on page 177.)

arpeggiated pull $\frac{4}{4}$

T, 1, 2, 3, T, 123

First, invert the order of an Arpeggiated Pull $\frac{4}{4}$ pattern. Then, pick up the tempo; you now have this bright, pushing little strum. It's a perfect dance type rhythm…if you're into polkas, jigs or reels. But if you are not, it is still useful for many up-tempo songs. For this pattern, alternating your bass strings is strongly recommended.

Michael—There are islands off the coast of Georgia called the Georgia Sea Islands. Apparently, at one time there were island slaves who were required to row large boats of various goods to the mainland and back. *Michael*, with its Biblical references and repetitive spiritual qualities, was one of their work songs. Richie Havens does a powerful version of this song. Use one pattern unit for each measure.

Other Song Possibilities

Bottle of Wine / The Beer Barrel Polka / Turkey In The Straw / Irish Jig / The L and N Don't Stop Here Anymore / Deep River Blues / Don't Think Twice / Five Hundred Miles / Mr. Tambourine Man / Groovin'

(See song on page 169.)

Pinch Patterns

These patterns are characterized by their use of the *pinch motion*. There are several types of *pinch motion strums* and they vary in fullness and voicing qualities. The variety of rhythmic and tonal textures that *pinch patterns* can produce is really amazing. The selection given here just scratches the surface. Whatever the differences, all *pinch patterns* share in common an insistent, busy quality and a feeling of motion.

Each of the accompaniment patterns in this grouping, regardless of their meter or the total number of motions used, will always include at least one *pinch motion* somewhere in this basic unit. A *pinch motion* is the simultaneous playing of two or more notes, in which the thumb and finger (or fingers) *pluck* individual strings by pressing toward each other.

These are the various forms of *pinch motions* that appear in this grouping:

1. The thumb can play a single *bass string* as the first finger plucks the 3rd string simultaneously. (Two tones are sounded.)

2. The thumb can play a single *bass string* as the second finger plucks the 2nd string simultaneously. (Two tones are sounded.)

3. The thumb can play a single *bass string* as the 3rd finger plucks the first string. (Two tones are sounded.)

4. The thumb can play a single *bass string* String as the 2nd and 3rd fingers pluck the 2nd and 1st strings simultaneously. (Three tones are sounded.)

5. The thumb can play a single *bass string* as the first, second and third fingers pluck the 3rd, 2nd and 1st strings simultaneously. (Four tones are sounded.)

You'll undoubtedly find it most comfortable for your thumb to use a *free-stroke* when it's playing as part of a *pinch motion*.

The thumb changes its *bass* string depending on the chord being played, while the 1st and 2nd fingers always work the top 3 strings.

The unit may be built with motions of any of the following pattern groupings:

1. The Slow Patterns

2. The Pull Patterns

3. The Arpeggiated Patterns

4. The Moving Bass Patterns

5. The Accented Patterns

The order in which the motions appear will depend on the particular pattern. There are *pinch* patterns where only one out of the five possibilities is used; but unless there is a more dominant motion (i.e. an accented one), the *pinch motion* is enough to classify a pattern as part of this grouping.

When the use of *alternate bass strings* is suggested for patterns in this grouping, refer to the following table:

	A-B-C	D-F	E-G
Standard Alternates			
1. Primary	5-4	4-5	6-5
2. Supplementary	5-6	4-5	6-4

pinch slow $\frac{3}{4}$

T, 1, T23, 1, T23, 1

For the Pinch Slow $\frac{3}{4}$, you add two bass notes to a Slow $\frac{3}{4}$ unit on the third and fifth motions of the pattern. Remember, as you simultaneously pluck your 1st and 2nd strings (with your 3rd and 4th finger), you also press your thumb down on the *bass note string*. As you "pinch" these strings together, you get a clear, yet mellow sound.

Down in the Valley is a well known Southern Mountain version of a song originally from the British Isles. Use one pattern unit for each measure.

Other Song Possibilities

How Can We Hang On to a Dream / Green Leaves of Summer / Wagoner's Lad / Fifteen (Theme of The World, The Flesh and The Devil) / Scarborough Fair / Coming of the Roads / Suliram / Annemarieke (Dutch) / Barbara Allen / Birmingham Sunday

(See song on page 170.)

pinch slow bass $\frac{4}{4}$

T, 1, T23, T,   T, 1, T23, T

This strum is ideal when you're looking for that ol' bass line feeling and yet want a little more fullness than some of the lighter patterns with bass string repeats. It's especially good for bringing out bass lines in songs that change chords frequently.

Two Brothers: This is a powerful song about a family during the Civil War. Use two pattern units for each measure.

Other Song Possibilities

Lean on Me / My Funny Valentine / Do You Want To Dance / The French Girl / Misty / Bridge Over Troubled Waters / Let It Be Me / Urge For Going / When Sunny Gets Blue / Close To You

(See song on page 174.)

pinch blues triplet $\frac{4}{4}$

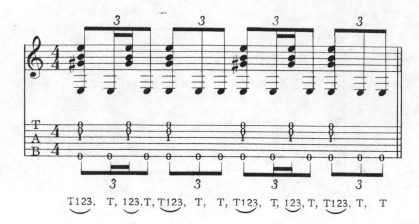

The Pinch Blues Triplet $\frac{4}{4}$ consists of two triplet groupings. The first triplet has an extra motion which provides a dash of syncopation. Keep the thumb droning away on the bass note for the maximum blues effect. The rhythm should sound "Bom chick-abom, bom bom bom."

Sportin' Life—We first heard this song sung by Bob Carey (then with the Tarriers) on a very old ten inch Folkways records. It was played so often that you could almost feel your fingers on the other side when you held it. This is another great eight measure blues. Use two pattern units for each measure. In the last two measures, each chord will receive half of a strum.

Other Song Possibilities

Since I Met You Baby / Just Like a Woman / Drownin' In My Own Tears / Tears On My Pillow / If We Only Have Love / When a Man Loves a Woman / Fools Paradise / Unchained Melody / Sunday Kind of Love / I Got You Babe

(See song on page 178.)

pinch folk Israeli $\frac{4}{4}$

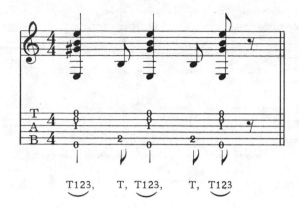

T123,   T, T123,   T, T123

And now the strum you've all been waiting for; the perfect strum to whip out at your next Bar Mitzvah or perhaps as you pass through the Catskills. Keep it as lively as possible to counteract its somewhat hefty tendency. Don't forget to alternate your bass strings. The rhythm should sound "Boom, bom boom, bom boom."

Hava Na Gila—Probably the most popular Hora dance (a circle dance) of all. The words simply invite everyone to join the dance. Start out with the Pinch Folk Israeli, but when you get to the second section ("u-r uruachim"), switch to the Pull $\frac{4}{4}$. Use one *pinch* pattern unit for each measure.

Other Song Possibilities

Eretz Zavat Chalav (Hebrew) / V'David Yafeh Aynayim (Hebrew) / Havanu Shalom Alechem (Hebrew) / Rad Halayla (Hebrew) / Yismachu (Hebrew) / Lamidbar (Hebrew) / Yesusom (Hebrew) / Hatov (Hebrew) / (We Kiss) And The Angels Sing / Kiss of Fire

(See song on page 149.)

pinch samba $\frac{4}{4}$

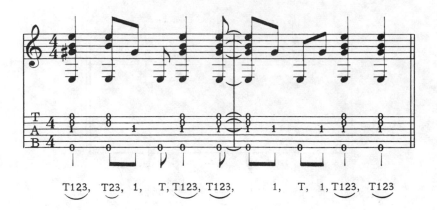

T123, T23, 1, T, T123, T123, 1, T, 1, T123, T123

Bossa Nova is thought to be a hybrid of the lively South American Negro Samba, and the restrained coolness of Progressive (West Coast) Jazz. This Brazilian Samba rhythm is favored by many Bossa Nova guitarists. It's generally played faster than the other two Bossa Nova strums in this book. Notice that this pattern unit extends for two measures. To get into these rhythms, break the measure into two halves and nod your head on the first and third beats. It may seem strange, but its a small price to pay for success. The rhythm should sound; "Boom Bom Chick Bom Boom Boom Chick Bom Chick Boom Boom."

Nava—In the 1940's and 50's, jazz musicians would often take the chord changes from a standard (established pop song), and totally re-write a melody to work with it. In this way, they could improvise on progressions they liked, and could use the song as their own. Examples are Charlie Parker's "Ornithology," Dizzy Gillespies "Groovin' High" and Sal Moscas "Sal's Line." Inspired by such a challenge, Nava was written. Sing it on a comfortable syllable like "ba" or "la." See if you can guess which standard the chord changes were based on. Most chords only get one measure, so you have to change the pattern in the middle, a half a beat before the end of the first measure.

Other Song Possibilities

One Note Samba / Wave / O Gouso (Portugese) / All the Things You Are / Summer Samba (So Nice) / Samba De Orfeus (Sweet Happy Life) (Portugese) / Aruando (Portugese) / Samba Do Aviao (Portugese) / O Pato (Portugese) / Samba De Minha Terra (Portugese)

(See song on page 150.)

pinch bossa nova $\frac{4}{4}$

T23, 1, T23, T23, 1, 23, 1, T

The Bossa Nova is a Brazilian dance rhythm that combines incredibly subtle and complex polyrhythms with impeccable delicacy and taste. The Bossa Nova Patterns you'll find in this book can be contained within one measure, but there are many Bossa Nova rhythms that extend for 2, 3 and 4 measures! Here, there is the teasing feeling that you have lost a beat, only to find it a second later. Listen to the playing of Joao Gilberto, Antonio Carlos Jobim and Luiz Bonfa (among others) to get a good idea of the feeling.

O Solo Mio is one of the best known and best loved Italian songs. It has been performed by singers with such differing styles as Ezzio Pinza and Elvis Presley. And it even sounds good as a Bossa-Nova. Use one pattern unit for each measure.

Other Song Possibilities

The Shadow of Your Smile / Fly Me to the Moon / Here's That Rainy Day / Rosa Morena / Meditation / Carnival / The Gentle Rain / How Deep is the Ocean / Bim Bom / Desafinado

(See song on page 149.)

Moving Bass Patterns

The *moving bass* patterns create an intense feeling of motion and have good tonal variety. They can be turbulent, grinding, florid, biting or playful. Whatever the character of the specified *moving bass* pattern you're playing, one thing will seem certain: Both you and the strum are going somewhere! Just who is driving and who is riding may be unclear occasionally, but the guitarist usually ends up taking the lead.

Each of the accompaniment patterns in this grouping, regardless of their meter or the total number of motions used, will always include the following core of motions somewhere in its basic unit:

1. At least three *different* bass strings: (A *rest stroke* may be used if you want volume for your bass sound. A free stroke is helpful if you are working for speed.)

2. At least one motion of the following groupings:
   a. Pull Patterns
   b. Slow Patterns
   c. Arpeggiated Patterns
   d. Pinch Patterns

Remember, no matter which groupings are used to build a *moving bass pattern,* there must *always* be at least three different *bass strings* used in each unit.

As with the *pull, slow, arpeggiated* and *pinch patterns,* when the first, second and third fingers are used, they always work the 3rd, 2nd and 1st strings, respectively.

The *alternate bass string* possibilities recommended for use with patterns in this grouping are listed in order of preference, in the following table:

	A-B-C	D-F	E-G
Moving Bass Alternates:			
1. Primary	5-4-4	4-5-5	6-5-5
2. Supplementary	5-4-6	4-6-5	6-5-4

moving bass pull Spanish $\frac{4}{4}$

This strum is effective not only with Latin American songs but also with Mid-Eastern and Eastern-European songs. Many students have even admitted to using it to spice up various folk and pop songs. It's also good for any Rhumba's you happen to have dancing around.

Que Bonita Bandera—A Puerto Rican folk song extolling the beauty of their flag. It sounds great if you can get someone to sing harmony in 3rds with you. Use one pattern unit for each measure. Also try *Que Bonita* with the Fast Latin $\frac{4}{4}$.

Other Song Possibilities

Carnival (Portugese) / Brazil / Miami Beach Rhumba / Bonsoire Dame (Crede) / Historia De Un Amor (Spanish) / Perfidia (Spanish) / Erev Shel Shoshanim (Hebrew) / Mustafa (Arabic) / Miserlou (Greek) / Besame Mucho (Spanish)

(See song on page 163.)

moving bass
pull (folk) Greek $\frac{7}{8}$

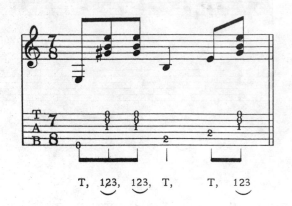

T, 1̣2̣3̣, 1̣2̣3̣, T,   T, 1̣2̣3̣

Frankly, we do not know how often you will have occasion to play a song in $\frac{7}{8}$ or $\frac{7}{4}$ time. This is considered an unusual rhythm for most Western music; but it really is very exciting if you give it half a chance. Most of our music is in $\frac{2}{4}$, $\frac{3}{4}$ or $\frac{4}{4}$; oddly enough, this can be the secret to feeling $\frac{7}{8}$ time. If you break it down into 3 familiar groups, you will get into $\frac{7}{8}$ easily. One group of 3 beats, and two groups of 2 beats each should sound "Bom chick chick, bom bom chick."

Yerakina is a lovely Greek Folk song about a girl who fell in a well and could only be rescued by promising to marry the crafty life guard. Use one pattern unit for each measure. In measures with two chords, the second chord gets the last 4 pattern motions.

Other Song Possibilities

Dance of Zalongou / I Had One Love / Three Young Men from Volos / Haralambis / Three Sisters / I Stole Me Se Ozeni / Little Sea / A Dark Beauty / Samiotissa / Vengelio

(See song on page 168.)

moving bass inverted pinch $\frac{4}{4}$

T2, 1, 3, T2, 1, 3, T2, 1

We start this pattern by pinching the second finger and thumb together; as a result, our highest tone (the first string) is played twice on what appears to be off beats. So, it turns out to be an offbeat variation of a pattern (Moving Bass Pinch $\frac{4}{4}$) which was syncopated to begin with. It's a rather mind boggeling thought, but the strum is soothingly effervescent.

Could You Ever—If you've ever been discouraged by someone you loved (or thought you loved) this could be your song. We've provided an alternate set of chords in the key of C, if you're not ready for an F♯ chord. Use one pattern unit for each measure.

Other Song Possibilities

In the Heat of the Summer / What Have They Done to My Song / Jet Plane / You've Got a Friend / Sealed With a Kiss / Something / Universal Soldier / Hushabye / Morning Morgantown / Michele

(See song on page 181.)

moving bass slow $\frac{4}{4}$

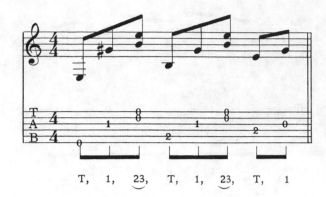

T, 1, 23, T, 1, 23, T, 1

This is actually a calypso pattern, and as with most calypso strums, eight eighth-notes are divided into a three section unit; the first two sections use the same three motions, and the third section will unexpectedly leave out the very last motion. This is counted: 1', 2, 3–1', 2, 3–1', 2.

Delia is an American honky-tonk song which found it's way to the Bahamas. Use one pattern unit for each measure.

Other Song Possibilities

Ya Ya / Lemon Tree / Shimmy Shimmy Ko Ko Bop / Sloop John B / Water Come To Me Eye / Urge For Going / Traces / Jamaica Farewell / This Guy's In Love With You / Come Softly To Me

(See song on page 177.)

moving bass displaced $\frac{4}{4}$

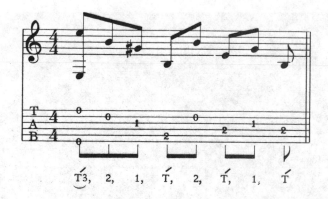

T3, 2, 1, T, 2, T, 1, T

This is an unusual pattern because the accents diffuse the feeling of $\frac{4}{4}$ time. This strum is especially effective when a kind of floating, quietly syncopated quality is desired. And it can be used as an alternative to the Arpeggiated $\frac{4}{4}$, Extended Slow $\frac{4}{4}$ and Moving Bass Pinch Ballad $\frac{4}{4}$, among others.

Far Far Away—If you've ever spent a great length of time away from the place you grew your roots in, you may remember yourself suddenly viewing that old world in a new light, no matter how much it seemed to have lacked in the past. You might even feel that perhaps you too lacked something in the past. Use one pattern unit for each measure.

Other Song Possibilities

The First Time Ever / Laura / The Trees They Do Grow High / When I'm Gone / Mary in the Morning / The Fool on the Hill / Killing Me Softly / All My Trials / Sounds of Silence / Will You Still Love Me Tomorrow

(See song on page 165.)

moving bass pinch $\frac{4}{4}$

T,   1,   T2,   1,   T3,   1,   T2,   1

This is a flowing strum where the pinched bass and treble notes climb in the same direction while the index finger alternates between each new bass string. This pattern can be used interchangeably with the Moving Bass Pinch Ballad $\frac{4}{4}$ and also the Pinch Extended $\frac{4}{4}$. It is best suited to slow gentle ballads, and is perfect for conjuring up images of water lapping against the shore.

The Water Is Wide is thought of as an Anglo-American Ballad. That probably means that in England it's an English Ballad, and in North America it is called an American Ballad. In any case, it is lovely. Use one pattern unit for each measure.

Other Song Possibilities

And I Love Her / Morning, Morning / Fools Rush In / The Party's Over / God Bless The Child / Society's Child / Little Girl Blue / My Foolish Heart / I Wish You Love / How Deep Is The Ocean

(See song on page 180.)

moving bass pinch $\frac{3}{4}$

T, 1, T2, 1, T3, 1

This is a delicate strum with an undulating feeling. Try it first with the thumb playing the Root Bass String all the time. After you're comfortable, try the strum with the moving bass strings.

Scarlet Ribbons—This long time favorite was popularized by Harry Belafonte some years ago. It's so beautiful, so classical in its appeal, we believed it was an old traditional folk-song! Use one pattern unit for each measure.

Other Song Possibilities

Dona Noblis / Un Canadien Errant / Lass From the Low Country / My Father / Rozhinkes Mit Mandlen / Father Along / River Of My People / Strangest Dream / Hiroshima / Green Leaves of Summer

(See song on page 153.)

Accented Patterns

These patterns have a subdued excitement. The *accented motion* used is a *fingers-down* motion, where the fingers sweep down across the strings much like the F motion in *fast pattern* units. Only here, the driving quality creates a decisive contrast. This is, in part, because the other motions used to build *accented* patterns are comparatively delicate or subordinate. Each *accented* unit will utilize motions from one or more of such contrasting groupings, and add the uncharacteristic *accent motion*, providing textural variety and a defiant rhythmic emphasis.

Each of the accompaniment patterns in this grouping, regardless of their meter or the total number of motions used, will always include, somewhere in its basic unit:

1. At least one emphatic downward motion with the fingers (here, called the *accented motion*)

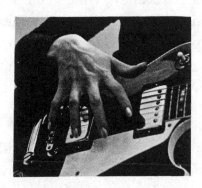

and
2. One or more motions of the following pattern groupings:
   a. Pull Patterns   (see page 32 for details)
   b. Slow Patterns   (see page 42 for details)
   c. Arpeggiated Patterns   (see page 48 for details)
   d. Pinch Patterns   (see page 54 for details)
   e. Moving Bass Patterns   (see page 62 for details)

The *bass strings* used will be determined by parent pattern groupings that make up a particular unit. For instance, if the second term used in the name of an *accented pattern* is *"pull,"* then use the set of *alternate bass strings* given for *pull pattern* units. If the second term used in the *pattern* name is *"moving bass,"* use the set of *alternate bass strings* given for that pattern grouping.

accented moving bass pinch $\frac{4}{4}$

For the Accented Moving Bass Pinch $\frac{4}{4}$, you are building on the first 2 sections of a Moving Bass Pinch $\frac{4}{4}$ unit. The 3rd section, which completes the pattern unit, uses the heavy *accent motion*. This motion abruptly changes the feeling created by the first two sections and provides a surprisingly fitting percussive complement. This accompaniment pattern will work well with soft ballad-like songs that lend themselves to a lightly percussive treatment, or to moderately peppery numbers.

When I Wake—This song is perhaps somewhat less strident than many women's lib songs. It poses the same realizations, and frustrations of women in our present society, however, and may reflect similar thoughts of other minority groups. Use one pattern unit for each measure.

Other Song Possibilities

The Circle Game / Hey Jude / Get Together / All My Trials / Mr. Tambourine Man / Yesterday When I Was Young / As Tears Go By / Tonight / Where Have All the Flowers Gone / Jet Plane

(See song on page 158.)

accented bass note rock $\frac{4}{4}$

T,   F,   123. T,   T,   F,   T

This pattern is quite good for slower rock songs that have an insistent beat. On the second and third sections of the unit we accent the motion of the fingers. Combined with the plucking finger motions, you have a unique blend of techniques which are rarely combined. Just remember that as soon as you spray out your fingers for the accent motion, you then have to quickly bring them together and pluck the top three strings.

Easy Rider is a popular 16 bar blues also known as C. C. Rider. Use one pattern unit for each measure. In measures with two chords, the first chord receives the first three motions while the second chord gets the last four motions.

Other Song Possibilities

Nowhere Man / A Hundred Pounds of Clay / He's Not Heavy He's My Brother / San Francisco (Wear Some) Flowers / See You In September / Just Like a Woman / Volare / One Two Three / Puppy Love / I Only Have Eyes For You

(See song on page 176.)

accented folk rock $\frac{4}{4}$

This is an active strum for active songs. The pattern keeps pinching and churning underneath, pushing even the most sluggish song to a triumphant ending. It is very effective for adding a little tension to any otherwise tedious tempo.

Study War No More—A wonderful Black Spiritual that is always made relevant by the seemingly unchanging, misguided energies of man. Use one pattern unit for each measure.

Other Song Possibilities

Ode to Billie Joe / Sunshine Go Away Today / Unchain My Heart / Spanish Harlem / Don't Bother Me / She's a Woman (W-o-m-a-n) / Gotta Travel On / Take Good Care of My Baby / (Last Night) I Didn't Get To Sleep At All / I'll Never Fall In Love Again

(See song on page 160.)

accented pinch blues triplet $\frac{4}{4}$

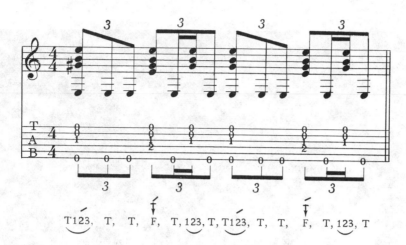

This is a very effective slow Blues pattern which should be approached with tender care. The strum consists of two sets of triplets; the second set of triplets is slightly syncopated and starts with an accented motion. All other motions involve pinching and pulling (watch those hands!). The rhythm should sound: "Bom bom bom, chunk bom-a bom!"

Come Back Baby is a soulful 8 Bar Blues with some really interesting chord changes. Dave Van Ronk does a beautiful arrangement of this one. Use two pattern units for each measure.

Other Song Possibilities

I Been Living With The Blues / Number Twelve Train / The House of the Rising Sun / Down and Out Blue / Since I Met You Baby / In the Evenin' When the Sun Goes Down / Trouble In Mind / Sportin' Life / Careless Love / Corinna

(See song on page 172.)

accented pinch bossa nova $\frac{4}{4}$

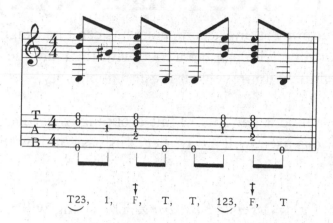

T23,　1,　F,　T,　　T,　123,　F,　T

As with the Pinch Bossa Nova, the feeling is created by putting accents in where you least expect them. Yet the time is sustained by the subtle drive contained within these motions. This and most Bossa Nova strums sound best when used with bar chords. The rhythm will sound "Chick-a Chick Bom Bom Chick, Chick Bom."

Night Boat—This love song glides along gently when played with the Bossa Nova rhythm. Many people like the second chord change in the song very much, but there have been a few who found it more unusual than impressive. Don't let them bother you. Just keep insisting that they are simply not hip. Use two pattern units for each measure.

Other Song Possibilities

Girl From Ipanima / I Wish You Love / Who Can I Turn To / Stella By Starlight / How Insensitive / Quiet Nights / Watch What Happens / Um Abraco NoBonfa / Green Dolphin Street / A Felicidade

(See song on page 173.)

Pattern-Picking Patterns
(Three Finger Style)

The popularity of Pattern-Picking accompaniments can't be exaggerated. They seem to turn-on just about anyone who can tap a foot, with their unique hypnotic sound. Pattern-Picking will definitely improve your musical popularity.

Each of the accompaniment patterns in this grouping, regardless of the meter or the total number of motions used, will always begin its basic unit with one of the following two motions: Either

    1. the thumb can play a *single bass string*. The string will vary depending on the chord,   or

    2. the thumb and second finger can play a *pinch motion*. In that *pinch motion,* the thumb plays the *bass string* of the chord as the second finger plucks the first string.

Once the first *bass string* has been played (whether it was sounded individually or within the *pinch motion),* the rest of the unit will be built with the following two motions:

    1. The first finger will pluck the second string.

    2. The second finger will pluck the first string.

The sequence of these two motions will depend on the particular *pattern-picking* unit.

Pattern-picking units are different from any of the preceding "single-string-plucking" patterns that we've presented. Here, we have an entirely different concept of alternating *bass strings*. In *pattern-picking*, the *bass note strings* are the essence of the strum, and they provide the *patterns* with their distinctive sound as well as their structure.

There are always four *bass notes* to each measure of $\frac{4}{4}$ music, and three *bass notes* for each measure of $\frac{3}{4}$ music. These *bass notes* alternate between the *root note string* of the chord being played, and the 3rd or 4th string.

The Bass Strings are played solidly, on each beat of the measure; they absolutely carry the strum. The first and second fingers will tend to provide off beat accents between the bass strings.

Notice the position of the right-hand strumming fingers. Unlike all the previous plucking type patterns, in Pattern-Picking only the first and second fingers will work the 2nd and 1st strings, respectively. (Before, your first three fingers worked the top three strings.)

The Alternate Bass Strings recommended for this grouping are as follows:

	A-B-C	D-F	G-E
Pattern-Picking Alternates			
a. Primary	5-3	4-3	6-3
b. Supplementary	5-4	4-3	6-4
c. Optional	5-3-4-3	4-3-5-3	6-3-5-3

inverted pattern picking $\frac{3}{4}$

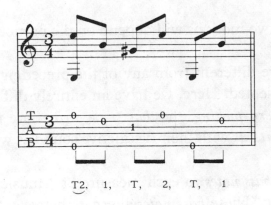

T2, 1, T, 2, T, 1

This pattern is an abbreviated, inverted variant of the Travis $\frac{4}{4}$. The Travis $\frac{3}{4}$ is effective where activity and speed are desired without the heavy quality of one of the Fast wall of sound strums. Keep the bass strings alternating solidly.

Un Canadien Errant—This French Canadian traditional ballad had its words added by a young student, A. Gerin-Lejoie after the Mackenzie Papineau Rebellion of 1837, in which many rebels were exiled and fled to the United States. It appears that history repeats itself. In 1973 America has her own exiles; ironically, many are in Canada. The melody alone has its own sadness. Use one pattern unit for each measure.

Other Song Possibilities

I'm a Rambler, I'm a Gambler / El Paso / Ballad of Addie Carol / Taste of Honey / Irene / Roll On, Columbia / Inchworm / Try To Remember / Who's Gonna Shoe Your Pretty Little Foot / So Long It's Been Good To Know You

(See song on page 172.)

inverted pattern picking $\frac{4}{4}$

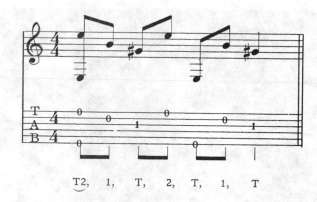

T2, 1, T, 2, T, 1, T

Here we add a bass note to the Inverted Pattern Picking $\frac{3}{4}$. It now sounds "Bom-a, Bom-a, Bom-a, Bom." Keep the alternating bass strings driving and heavy. This inversion produces a surprisingly marked distinction from the original pattern. It is quite useful when used on the bridge of a song where you're playing the original Travis $\frac{4}{4}$ pattern on the verses.

Good Boy—This music was written to a poem from Carl Sandberg's collection, *The American Songbag*. The song is playful, and lends itself to diverse treatments. Here it comes across somewhat impish and coy. Use two pattern units for each measure and play briskly. Although written in the Key of G, the chords are also provided in the Key of C for those of you who are intimidated by quick changes to a Bm chord.

Other Song Possibilities

Go Tell It On The Mountain / Thirsty Boots / Danny's Song / Don't Think Twice / Pack Up Your Sorrows / That's What You Get For Lovin' Me / Puff The Magic Dragon / I Ain't Got No Home / In The Heat of the Summer / Bye, Bye Love

(See song on page 150.)

inflected pattern picking $\frac{4}{4}$

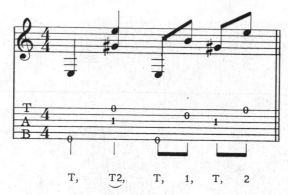

Play the first *bass string* by itself, then use a *pinch motion* in which the thumb plays the second *alternate bass string* as the second finger plucks the 1st string. This creates an inflected rhythm. It should sound "Bom, Bom, Bom-a, Bom-a."

Make Me a Pallet conveys a very special kind of loneliness. It speaks of gratitude for a friendship in a way that only one who has once been forgotten could express so well. Use one pattern unit for each measure.

Other Song Possibilities

Lookin' Out My Back Door / On The Trail Of The Buffalo / Oh Babe It Ain't No Lie / Early Morning Rain / You Were On My Mind / Carry It On / Will The Circle Be Unbroken / Tomorrow Is A Long Time / Banks Of Marble / Long Lonesome Road

(See song on page 162.)

The Guitar Player by Howard Kalish

complex pattern picking $\frac{4}{4}$

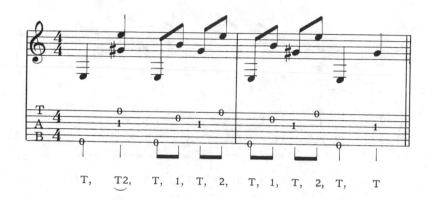

T,   T2,   T, 1, T, 2, T, 1, T, 2, T,   T

Now we've taken a relatively uncomplicated one measure pattern (the inflected Pattern-Picking $\frac{4}{4}$) and expanded it to a more involved two measure pattern. Play it through a few times until you feel the rhythm as a whole. Keep those bass strings pounding away unmercifully. The rhythm should sound: "Bom, Bom, Bom-a Bom-a, Bom-a, Bom-a Bom, Bom."

Hobo's Lullaby—Cisco Houston used to sing this mournful piece. It evokes memories of the 1930's and the homeless men of the Depression. We've altered the melody, and provided some new text. Use one complete pattern unit for every two measures.

Other Song Possibilities

Candy Man / My Creole Belle / Wabash Cannonball / Sinner Man / Colours / Pastures of Plenty / Weary and a Lonesome Traveller / Come and Go With Me to That Land / Cotton Fields / Spike Driver Blues

(See song on page 162.)

extended complex pattern picking $\frac{4}{4}$

T, T2, T, 1, T, 2, T, 1, T, 2, T, 1, T

Again we have a two measure picking pattern to deal with. The rhythmic flow has been increased by adding a single string finger motion just before the last *bass string*. The rhythm should sound "Boom, Boom, Bom-a, Bom-a Bom-a, Bom-a, Bom-a, Bom."

Hard Ain't It Hard—There was a time when it seemed that everyone within a two mile radius of Washington Square in New York City was singing this popular old-country song. Unfortunately, they were all singing in different keys, but the spirit was great and will long be remembered. Use one strum for every two measures generally, but here, use one full two measure unit for each measure in the song.

Other Song Possibilities

Silver Dagger / Goin' Down That Road Feelin' Bad / Freight Train / Aunt Rhody / Little Darlin', Pal of Mine / Good News, Chariots Comin' / Darlin' Corey / Hobo's Lullaby / Candy Man / I'm On My Way

(See song on page 171.)

Full Pattern Picking
(Four Finger Style)

Full pattern picking is a gold mine of combined tone colors, contrasting textures and well-balanced percussive spice.

Each of the accompaniment patterns in this grouping regardless of their meter or the total number of motions used will include motions from either the *slow* or *pinch patterns* and they use the *alternate bass string* of regular *pattern picking* units. A *full picking pattern* always begins its basic unit with one of the following motions:

Either

   1. The thumb can play a single Bass String. (The string varies depending on the chord)   or

   2. Thumb together with the second and third fingers can play a *pinch motion.* (In it, the thumb plays the *bass string* of your chord as the second and third fingers pluck the 1st and 2nd strings respectively.)

Once the first *bass string* has been played, whether it was sounded individually or within the *pinch motion,* the rest of the unit will be built with the following three motions:

   1. The first finger can pluck the 3rd string.

2. The second and third fingers can simultaneously pluck the 2ⁿᵈ and 1ˢᵗ strings.

3. The thumb and third finger can play a *pinch motion.*

These motions appear in different sequences, depending on the particular pattern unit.

As with regular *pattern picking,* in the 3 finger style the construction and character of the *full pattern picking* unit is based on the *alternate bass strings* it uses.

Unlike regular *pattern picking* where the first and second fingers work the top 2 strings, *full pattern picking* uses the first, second and third fingers to work the top 3 strings. So actually, in regard to right hand strumming positions, *full pattern picking* units use the same form as *slow* or *pinch pattern* units.

The *alternate bass strings* recommended for *full pattern picking* units are as follows:

	A B C	D-F	E-G
Full Pattern Picking	5-4	4-5	6-4

full pattern picking $\frac{4}{4}$

T23,   T,   1,   T,   23,   T,   1

First, establish the new right hand position. It should resemble the hand position used in the *slow* and *pinch patterns*. This strum has rich tonal variety, and a punch that comes from a pulsing bass motion that is interspersed with mellow picking motions.

Please Don't Lay Your Trip on Me—Although the catalyst that inspired this piece was admittedly frustration, it is really a very loving, optimistic song. It was directed toward two groups of people, but we're told it sometimes takes a few singings before you can figure out who's on first (which people are represented as "Lady Guilt & Shame, and which group is addressed as "Mr. Hate and Fear"). Use one pattern unit for each measure.

Other Song Possibilities

Someday Soon / I've Got a Lot of Living to Do / The Fool on the Hill / I Can't Help But Wonder Where I'm Bound / San Francisco Bay Blues / Bottle of Wine / The Best Thing For You Would Be Me / Just a Closer Walk With Thee / One Man's Hands / When I'm Gone

(See song on page 156.)

full inverted pattern picking $\frac{4}{4}$

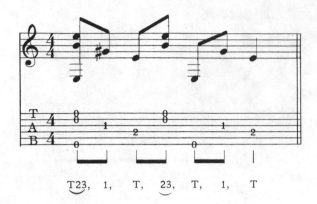

T23, 1, T, 23, T, 1, T

Here, you reverse the rhythmic order of the Full Picking $\frac{4}{4}$ so that you now have "Bom-a, Bom-a, Bom-a, Bom." This is one of the shorter *pattern picking* units, and can therefore be used with songs in which the chords change often.

Silver's Really Grey—It would be hard to imagine anyone who hasn't suffered some disillusionment in life. This song should serve to comfort you, as it reminds you that you aren't alone.

Other Song Possibilities

Hey, What About Me / Wasn't That a Time / Last Thing on My Mind / Long, Lonesome Road / You Were on My Mind / Early Morning Rain / Passing Through / Run Come See Jerusalem / First Girl I Loved / Home In That Rock

(See song on page 159.)

full inflected pattern picking $\frac{4}{4}$

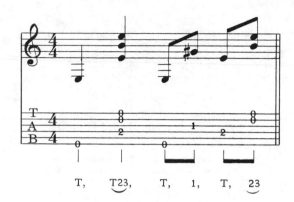

T,   T23,   T,   1,   T,   23

Although this name may conjure up visions of Calomine Lotion and cotton swabs, it is really the name of a mild mannered strum. Use sparingly on all songs whether they be inflected or infected with joy and good will.

Wabash Cannonball—This old hobo song has a feeling of bubbling over with life. Use one pattern unit for each measure. Also try this with the Snap Back Carter $\frac{4}{4}$.

Other Song Possibilities

Take This Hammer / I Am a Pilgrim / Round the Bay of Mexico / Just a Closer Walk With Thee / The Desperado / Oh, Freedom / Lonesome Valley / Careless Love / Puttin' On the Style / Go Tell It on the Mountain

(See song on page 148.)

full complex pattern picking $\frac{4}{4}$

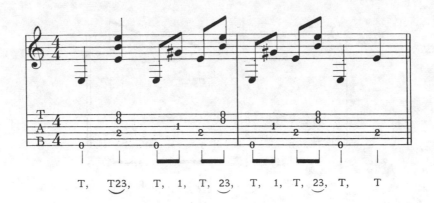

T, T23, T, 1, T, 23, T, 1, T, 23, T,   T

We now have a two measure strum that will require a fair share of energy to sustain its activity. Your efforts will be well rewarded. It will provide contrast and movement for songs where the chords change infrequently.

Miners Life—Originally this was the hymn *Life Is Like A Mountain Railway,* adopted by miners at the turn of the century. It sounds great when sung by a cast of thousands, but if you sing it with spirited determination, you can almost create that same feeling. Use one pattern unit for every two measures. Also try this with the Snap Back Nashville $\frac{4}{4}$ or the Pull Bass Rock $\frac{4}{4}$ for different treatments.

You might also try playing all D chords from the sixth string. In order to do this, fret the 6th string on the 2nd fret with your left hand thumb. It may smart a bit at first, but it's worth the effort.

Other Song Possibilities

Ghost Riders in the Sky / The Crawdad Song / Long Chain On / Bury Me Beneath the Willow / Skillet Good and Greasy / Rocky Racoon / Banks of the Ohio / Polly Von / Reuben James / I'll Cry Instead

(See song on page 147.)

full extended complex picking $\frac{4}{4}$

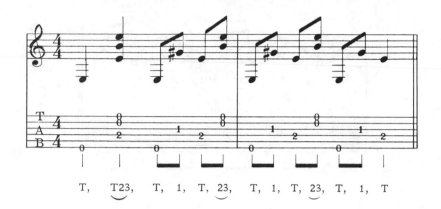

T,   T23,   T, 1, T, 23,   T, 1, T, 23,   T, 1, T

With the addition of a single-string finger motion right before the last *bass string,* this rambling pattern becomes the longest, fullest strum to appear in this book. Don't let it go to waste! Play it at every opportunity. It works best with songs in which you generally hold each chord for at least two measures.

Worried Man Blues—A bit of Americana that became a piece of Tin Pan Alley. The Kingston Trio brought this thoughtful prison song to radio with their somewhat bouncy arrangement in the 1950's. Use one pattern unit for each two measures. This song works equally well with both the Snap Back Carter $\frac{4}{4}$ and the Fast $\frac{4}{4}$.

Other Song Possibilities

The Great Mandella / Happy Together / Me and Bobby McGhee / Goin' Down This Road Feelin' Bad / Help! / Pack Up Your Sorrows / Walk Through The Valley / My Creole Belle / We Are Crossing Jordans River / Gilgarry Mountain

(See song on page 154.)

full pinch pattern picking $\frac{4}{4}$

T, 1, T2, 1, T, 1, T3, 1

This pattern is a softer, less busy variety of the *full picking strums.* As with all *full-picking* units, the thumb alternates the bass strings while the fingers provide textural variety.

Go Tell Aunt Rhody is an old folk favorite, especially popular with young people. The simple melody and story are made even more appealing by the easy chord accompaniment—an accompaniment requiring only two chords! Use one pattern unit for each measure.

Other Song Possibilities

Mary in the Morning / Comin' Through the Rye / Where Does It Lead / Red Rosy Bush / Katy Cruel / Coming of the Roads / Times a Gettin' Hard / Go Down You Murderers / In Contempt / Anne Boleyn

(See song on page 150.)

Fast Patterns

If you're into the heavier sounds, this is definitely the type of strum for you. These patterns have enough starch to hold up almost any music with a driving quality. Fast Strums are usually loud and spirited, but it should be mentioned that a few of them, if played with a light touch, can provide a somewhat mellower accompaniment for certain slower songs (i.e. Fast Calypso $\frac{4}{4}$). In any case, when you want to make your (musical) presence known, any of these strums should do the job. In this grouping are the patterns that lay the foundation for many rock, pop and other similar accompaniments. Because individual tones (single-string plucking) are not played here, *fast patterns* create a strong, reverberating quality called a Wall of Sound effect.

Each of the accompaniment patterns in this grouping, regardless of their meter or the total number of motions used, builds its basic unit with different types of "hitting" motions; these motions evenly sweep down (or back over) several strings consecutively. (They do this so quickly that the strings ring out together, almost as if they'd been hit simultaneously.)

To begin every unit:

   1. The thumb sweeps down, hitting all the strings that are in agreement with the chord being played. Try to aim the the sweeping motion so that only the strings from the chord's *root bass string* and the notes below are sounded (i.e. aim for the top four strings when playing a D chord, or the top 5 strings for an A chord, etc.).

Then, in a sequence determined by each particular pattern, the following motions may appear in different combinations:

   2. The thumb comes up, sweeping across the strings from the first (the highest) string up to the *bass string* of the chord being played. Relax the thumb and don't fight or "dig" into the strings. This should be a light brushing motion.

3. The hand circles back over the strings (passing from the 1st string to the 6th string) but does not touch the strings! This is a "silent motion;" the action does not produce any tone, but is accounted for in the time value of the strum. In certain strum units, noting this motion with a symbol can help you keep the rhythm and prepare you for the next motion.

4. The hand forms a loose fist and then simultaneously shoots the fingers down across the strings. (The fingers move perpendicular to the strings.) Only the finger nails actually touch the strings.

Scooping into the strings is a no-no. So spray the fingers straight out from the palm. Again, these motions may appear in different numbers, and in a variety of sequences. In summing up, these are heavy, driving, loud strums, which for the most part should be used accordingly. Although there are no *bass strings* isolated as such, an effort should be made to strum only those strings that belong with the chord being played.

fast rock $\frac{3}{4}$

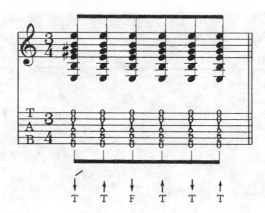

Here we are building on a Fast Rock $\frac{4}{4}$ by adding a thumb down-up sweeping motion at the end of the pattern. Now you have a heavier alternative to the Fast $\frac{3}{4}$ strum. Don't forget to accent the finger motions, because that's what gives us the rock feeling.

Mangwaini Mpulel is a very catchy Zulu song from Africa. It was recorded by The Kingston Trio and Theodore Bikel among others. Use one pattern unit for each measure.

Other Song Possibilities

You've Got to Hide Your Love Away / African Waltz / Roll On, Columbia / Copper Kettle / Norwegian Wood / The Times They Are a Changin' / Beans in My Ears / Los Cuatro Generales / Venga Juleo / Song of the Deportees

(See song on page 152.)

fast back beat rock $\frac{4}{4}$

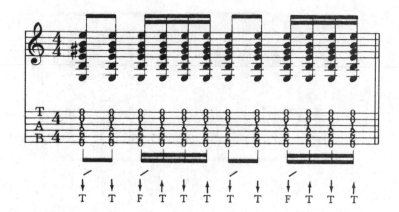

When you talk about the "back beat" you are referring to the second and fourth beats in a measure of $\frac{4}{4}$ time, which are heavily accented in order to give you a rock feeling. In this strum, accent the down motion with the fingers; this will give you that heavy back beat sound you've always wanted. Make sure that the second group of four motions takes up the same amount of time as the first group of two motions.

We Shall Not Be Moved is Spiritual adopted by the Union Movement in the 1930's. This song, and generally this type of song, easily lends itself to the addition of some of your own verses. Use two pattern units for each measure.

Other Song Possibilities

I Want to Hold Your Hand / Get Back / Light My Fire / Get Together / Sunday / Handsome Johnny / Crockodile Rock / Ticket to Ride / I'm Happy Just to Dance With You / Long Train Comin'

(See song on page 161.)

fast twist $\frac{4}{4}$

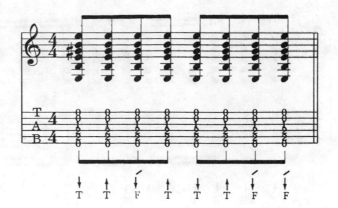

This is a happy, bouncy strum which is built on the Fast Rock $\frac{4}{4}$. The first and the second half of this strum starts like a Fast Rock $\frac{4}{4}$ but then changes its mind and uses not one, but two emphatic down motions with the fingers to close the unit! The overall effect achieved by these additional accents is to recreate, more closely than any other strum, the rhythm played by rock drummers when playing 1950's Twist Music. The rhythm should sound "Bom-a chick-a, Bom-a chick chick."

Let's Twist Again—Chubby Checker belted this one in the 50's and started a social phenomenon (separate dancing). Sing it with a smile. Use one pattern unit for each measure.

Other Song Possibilities

The Twist / Why Do Fools Fall in Love / Blue Suede Shoes / Twist and Shout / Rock Around the Clock / Crockadile Rock / Rockin Robin' / Little Darling / What I Say / Peppermint Twist

(See song on page 158.)

fast rhythm and blues shuffle $\frac{4}{4}$

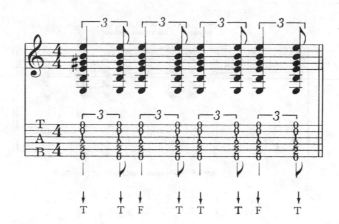

This is another one of those saucy 1950's rhythms. The pattern unit consists of two triplets. The first motion of each triplet is always longer, so the rhythm will sound "Bom-pa chick-a."

Twelve Gates to the City, although not technically a rhythm and blues song, is nevertheless saucy, rhythmic and responds very well to Percussive strums. We've added some of our own verses, but try to listen to versions of this song by Sonny Terry and Brownie McGee and also by the Weavers. Use two pattern units for each measure.

Other Song Possibilities

Blueberry Hill / Kansas City / Chantilly Lace / I'm In Love Again / Stagger Lee / Night Train / Tossin' and Turnin' / Personality / Maybelline / Let the Good Times Roll

(See song on page 148.)

fast $\frac{6}{4}$

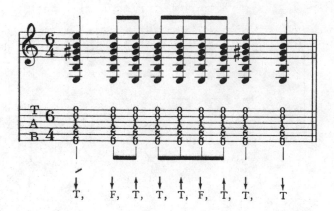

This is such an active strum that one of your main concerns will be simply to contain it within the boundaries of each measure. The rhythm will sound "Bom chick-a chick-a chick-a Bom Bom;" once you've got the feeling, it's time to work on the speed. It should be played briskly, even when you are backing a slow song.

Asikatali, a very unusual and powerful South African freedom song, was brought back to the states by Mary Louise Hooper. We include our arrangement with some new text. This is one of our favorite songs; off hand, we can't remember one performance or TV show we've done that didn't include *Asikatali.* Use one pattern unit for each measure. Where two chords exist, the last chord gets the two thumb motions at the end of the strum unit.

Other Song Possibilities

African Waltz / Irene / La Llorona / Forbidden Games / Bring Flowers / Mongwaini Mepuleli / Viva El Matador / Coplas / On Top of Old Smokey / Scandal in St. Thomas

(See song on page 165.)

fast r & b Bo Diddley $\frac{4}{4}$

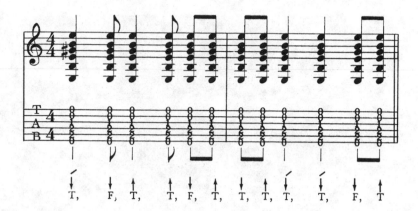

The rhythm used in this strum was Bo Diddley's trademark in the 1950's.

The only other performer who comes to mind as having had a specific rhythm so closely associated with him was Chubby Checker, with his Twist.

The rhythm extends for two measures and should sound: "Bom-chick bom a chick a chick-a-Bom Bom-chick-a." Bar chords work best on this strum. On the third thumb motion of the second measure, move your chord down two frets for one beat and then move it back to the original chord for the fourth thumb motion.

We Are Crossing Jordan's River is a traditional spiritual which bears a striking resemblance to I've Got a Woman by Ray Charles. Use one complete two measure pattern unit for each measure of the song.

Other Song Possibilities

Bo Diddley / Limbo Rock / Flute Diddley / I'm On My Way / We're Gonna Get Married / Who Do You Love / Quit Your Low Down Ways / Spike Driver / Long Time Man / Hey, Bo Diddley

(See song on page 170.)

fast merengue $\frac{4}{4}$

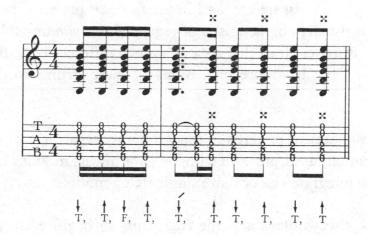

If you've ever considered being a club date musician, this is for you! You won't be at your first wedding job 20 minutes before they hit you with "merengue time!" This is a very distinctive Latin strum. The uniqueness of the merengue rhythm is that it begins on an upbeat (fourth beat of the preceding measure). To be most effective, dampen the motions marked with an **X** by slightly releasing the pressure of your left hand fingers from the chord. Bar chords sound best with this pattern because you can control all the strings that should or should not be sounded.

Aviva's Merengue was written with an assist from the delightful young lady whose name is unabashedly a part of the song title. She was less than 3 years old at the time of her contribution. The lyrics include several of her notable comments and descriptions that have been worked into this somewhat unusual musical setting. Use one pattern unit for each measure.

Other Song Possibilities

Universal Merengue / Compadre Pedro Juan / Al Compas del Merengue / Maryanne / St. Thomas / Tropical Merengue / Poco Pelo / Quando, Quando / Jamaica Farewell / La Cruz Merengue

(See song on page 152.)

Fast Bass Patterns

The individually played *bass strings* used in the *fast bass* patterns, break up the wall of sound effect that is usually characteristic of regular *fast strum* units. Here, you'll have a kind of cutting, textural contrast that creates a much different overall quality. The new sound is still heavy, but has more bite. Many of these strums work well on hard or funky-type songs.

Each of the accompaniment patterns in this grouping, regardless of their meter, or the total number of motions used, are built with the same hitting motions used for *fast pattern* units, but will also integrate one or more single string motions into its basic unit.

    1. The *thumb* always plays a single *bass string* to begin each *fast bass* unit. The string used will vary depending on the chord. A rest stroke is helpful where you want a very loud or strong bass. Try a *free stroke* where you need to move quickly.

Once the single *bass string* is played, the following motions can be used in varying number and combinations to build the rest of the unit:

    1. the *bass strings* may be individually played by the thumb.

    2. any of the hitting motions from the *fast pattern* grouping may be used.

Generally, these strums sound best when used with Bar chords. Bar chords help you to control all the strings that you cover, which, in turn, enables you to control the sound quality. You can also better direct the rhythm of the chords by either exerting or releasing the pressure on the strings that you are fretting.

When the use of *alternate bass strings* is desired for strums in this grouping, refer to the following table:

Root Bass Strings	A-B-C	D-F	E-G
Standard	5	4	6
Alternates	5-4	4-5	6-5

fast bass hard rock $\frac{4}{4}$

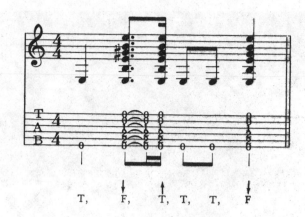

This rhythm is immediately identifiable as the one used by the late Jimi Hendrix in the song *Foxy Lady*. (Incidently, the chord he used to get that unusual sound is a Dominant 7 + 9.) Using this chord, you can practice the Fast Bass Hard Rock $\frac{4}{4}$ strums and fantasize being on stage, amazing throngs of greatful fans. It's important to note that the second motion is slightly longer than the third. The rhythm should sound "Bom, chick, A bom bom chick."

Can't Beat That Roach is a two part blues (the melodies should be played against each other) that was written in commemeration of New York's number one household pet: the cockroach. It appears, however, that some people have misconstrued the words to mean something else entirely! Use one pattern unit for each measure.

Other Song Possibilities

Foxy Lady / Sunshine for Your Love / I Dig Rock and Roll Music / The Word / Fire / Purple Haze / Spinning Wheel / I Just Want to Celebrate / Woodstock / Hey Jude

(See song on page 166.)

fast bass rock $\frac{4}{4}$

T, T, F, T, T, T, T, F, T, T

The first two bass notes in this unit provide a springboard for what follows. The rhythm should sound "Bom bom chick chick a." This strum can be played on open string chords, but you'll find the style more effective when played with *bar chords*. The last two motions should be damped with the left (the chording) hand.

Work Up This Mornin'—An old spiritual, re-written during the early 1960's by the Freedom Movement. We've provided our own arrangement which utilizes new text and some syncopated phrases. The rhythm helps to emphasize the line "stayed on freedom" very effectively. Use two pattern units for each measure.

Other Song Possibilities

Piece of My Heart / I'm So Glad / High Heel Sneakers / Twist and Shout / Half Moon / Hang On Sloopy / Ticket to Ride / Lay Lady Lay / Louie, Louie / Combination of the Two

(See song on page 175.)

fast bass Motown rock $\frac{4}{4}$

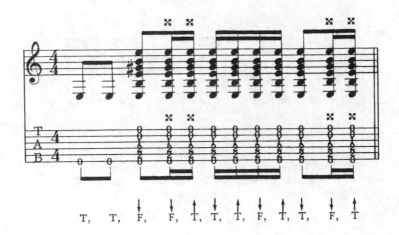

T,   T,   F,   F,   T,   T,   T,   F,   T,   T,   F,   T

"Motown" is the name of the Detroit Record Company that began what is now called *the Motown Sound*. This sound uses a heavy electric bass-line as its foundation, then builds layers of intricate, syncopated counter-rhythms on top. These rhythms are played by percussion instruments, electric guitars, various distortion devices, and sometimes an assortment of horns. Given the fact that we've only got two hands and six strings to work with, we start with a slight disadvantage. But you can come closer than you might imagine! Remember, no matter how many off beat accents you have, keep the pulse going with your foot as the undercurrent. Then play the rhythm as it's written against that ever-dependable pounding foot. It should sound: "Bom bom Bom chick-a chick-a chick-a Boom-chick-a." Last, damp the strings with your left hand whenever you see an **X** in the diagram:

Shakin' Up The Nation was composed by David Blake, a song writer who doubles as an Assistant Principal of a New York Junior High School. The song sounds fine when played on an electric guitar using fuzz and a wah wah, but also makes it nicely without them. It should get you into the Motown groove. Use one pattern unit for each measure of the verse. On the chorus, use two pattern units for each measure.

Other Song Possibilities

You Keep Me Hangin' On / The Word / High Heel Sneakers / Yes Indeed / Long Train Comin' / Midnight Hour / Eight Days A Week / Unchain My Heart / I've Got News For You / I Heard It Through The Grape Vine

(See song on page 146.)

fast bass soul $\frac{4}{4}$

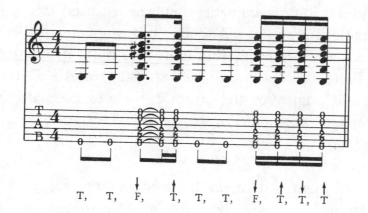

T,   T,   F,   T,   T,   T,   F,   T,   T,   T

This strum works best when used with bar chords. When you play this strum on your damped chords you'll get a muted rhythmic sound with a heavy, syncopated feeling.

There's A New World I Can See—We developed this song using the traditional gospel tune *Just A Closer Walk With Thee.* The rest of the music and the lyrics grew from our optimism, which we hope may be contagious. Use one pattern unit for each measure and play it fast and chunky.

Other Song Possibilities

I Heard It Through the Grape Vine / I Want To Take You Higher / On Broadway / For Once In My Life / I Want To Hold Your Hand / Hey Jude / Hazy Shade Of Winter / Last Time / Got My Mo-Jo Workin' / Taxman

(See song on page 155.)

Percussive Patterns

Percussive patterns are distinguished by their use of one or more *percussive motions*. This motion provides a jolting dramatic texture when used in conjunction with motions of the other pattern groupings. Although it is uniquely characteristic, the *percussive motion* never actually begins a strum unit. Generally, it functions as a distinctive substitute for the *Fingers-Down* hitting motion, but creates such a dominant texture, that it colors the whole quality of the strum. It has a toneless, driving sound and can make it seem as though some other instrument beyond your guitar is "jumping in" with a rhythmic effect.

Each of the accompaniment patterns in this grouping, regardless of their meter or the total number of motions used, will always be included somewhere in its basic unit: at least one *percussive motion*, and one or more motions from either of these groupings.

    1. the Fast Patterns (see p. 95 for details)

    2. the Fast Bass Patterns (see p. 106 for details)

The sequence depends on each of the following motions:

The *percussive motion* is a bit tricky at first, but once you've got it, you'll wonder why you didn't get it sooner. The four fingers of the right hand hit down across the strings and are immediately followed by the palm, which forcefully lands on those strings, muffling the sound just created by the fingers.

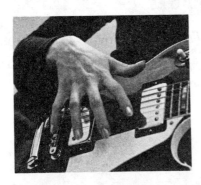 

When there are *bass strings* used in a *percussive pattern* and you want to alternate them, refer to the *alternate bass string* table given for *bass patterns*. If no *bass strings* are isolated, you only have to make sure that strings beyond the *root bass strings* of your chord are not sounded.

percussive fast $\frac{4}{4}$

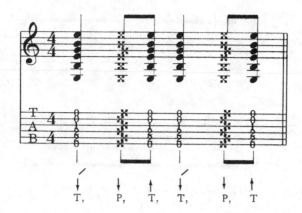

This is one strum where being heavy handed is actually helpful! Where the "P" symbol is indicated, come down forcefully with the right hand palm. This action dampens the strings, and gives the strum a chunky, "toneless" sound. The rhythm should sound "Bom chuck-a," and will give any song a nice gritty backing.

Joshua is a popular spiritual which serves as a perfect vehicle for learning this strum. Since the whole song only requires two chords, you'll have plenty of time to concentrate on developing the new percussive motion. Use two pattern units for each measure.

Other Song Possibilities

Aquarius / Mrs. Robinson / American Pie / I Should've Known Better / Mack the Knife / Black and White / Hard Days Night / People Got to Be Free / Joy to the World / If I Had a Hammer

(See song on page 168.)

percussive rock $\frac{4}{4}$

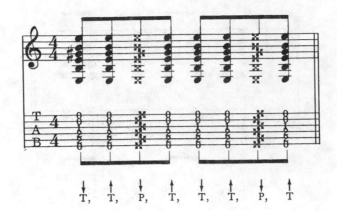

By using the *percussive motion* on the third beat of a Fast Rock $\frac{4}{4}$, we now have a strum that functions equally well as a rock or (believe or not) a cha cha strum! The song suggestions are somewhat schizophrenic but they all work very nicely.

Midnight Special—A Southern prison song which captures, in a very simple lyric, some of the experience and feeling of the man of the inside and his woman on the outside. The name of the song refers to the old superstition that if the light from a passing midnight train shines on a man through his cell bars, he'll soon go free. Use two pattern units for each measure.

Other Song Possibilities

Poco Pelo / Cherry Pink / Sway / Dancero / Por Favor / Proud Mary / The Letter / Commin Into Los Angeles / Satisfaction / Georgy Girl

(See song on page 157.)

percussive light rock $\frac{4}{4}$

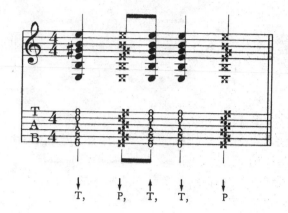

This strum is very suitable for light rock. Don't forget to muffle the second and fifth motions. The rhythm should sound: "Bom chick-a Bom chick."

When The Saints Go Marching In is one of the best known spirituals. Two marvelously different versions of *Saints* that made it to the "top of the charts" were done by The Weavers and by Lois Armstrong. Use one pattern unit for each measure. We've provided some extra chords (in parenthesis) for those who want to dress up the song a little. For measures with two chords, the second chord gets the last two motions.

Other Song Possibilities

Rag Doll / I Should Have Known Better / One Mint Julep / When I Was a Cowboy / This Magic Moment / Mellow Yellow / Baby You're a Rich Man / Under The Boardwalk / Dawn / Comin' Home Baby

(See song on page 155.)

percussive bass note rock $\frac{4}{4}$

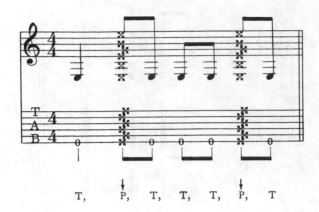

T,   P,   T,   T,   T,   P,   T

Use the *percussive motion* on the second and sixth beats of the unit. Because of all the bass notes that spice this pattern, the strum gives the impression that two people playing; you and a bass player. The rhythm should sound "Boom, chick bom, bom bom, chick bom."

I'm On My Way is one of those favorites you keep coming back to. It raises your spirits and determination to do whatever needs doing. Use one pattern unit for each measure. Also try this song with the Fast $\frac{4}{4}$ and some of the rock strums, for a different feeling.

Other Song Possibilities

Lean On Me / Walk On By / Nowhere Man / Sunday Will Never Be the Same / Diana / Eleanor Rigby / Dancing in the Streets / To Sir With Love / Sunny / Let the Sun Shine

(See song on page 154.)

percussive bass blues $\frac{4}{4}$

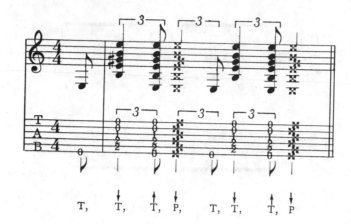

This strum has the unusual quality of beginning on the upbeat of the preceding measure. The pattern consists of two eighth note triplets for each units; but don't let that scare you: It sounds more difficult than it is. First, count out loud, 123, 123, over and over again. Then start the strum on the number 3. It should sound 312312. The rhythm should sound "A-Boom-A-Chick, A-Boom-A-Chick."

Gallows Pole—Odetta does this song in her grand, booming voice and the delivery can really shake you up! You actually feel relieved when the sweetheart comes through in the end and saves the singers life. Use two pattern units for each measure.

Other Song Possibilities

I Been Living With The Blues / St. Louis Blues / Darlin' / Alberta / Trouble In Mind / Sixteen Tons / Fools Paradise / Number Twelve Train / Been In The Pen So Long / Easy Rider

(See song on page 167.)

percussive pinch rock ⁴₄

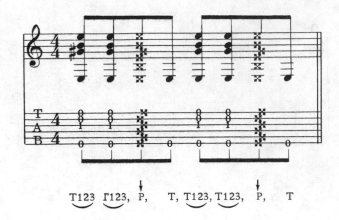

T123 Γ123, P,   T, T123, T123, P,   T

This pattern employs both *pinch* and *percussive motions* for their contrasting characteristics. It's a good strum for rock and blues tunes where the chords change frequently. The rhythm should sound: "Bom Bom Chuck Bom."

Long Chains was written by the Rev. F. D. Kirkpatrick. In an effort to bring people of varied backgrounds together he created the concept and the institution of the Hey Brother Coffee House. Hey Brother provides a truly open forum for musical and social exchange. This song is one example of the material Rev. Kirkpatrick uses. Use two pattern units for each measure.

Other Song Possibilities

That'll Be the Day / People Get Ready / Mr. Big Shot / Hound Dog / Dancing in the Streets / Cathy's Clown / Ya Ya / Turn, Turn, Turn / Whiter Shade of Pale / You're So Vain

(See song on page 146.)

percussive pinch blues $\frac{4}{4}$

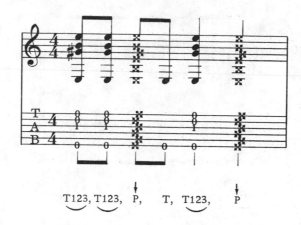

As with the *percussive pinch rock* pattern, the *pinch motion* is used in conjunction with the *percussive motion* to give this strum a unique flavor. It will sound good with many medium tempo blues and rock tunes. The rhythm will sound: "Bom bom, chick-bom, Bom chick."

Darlin' refers sarcastically in this song to the captain, or conversationally, to the worker's wife, or sweetheart. Use one pattern unit for each measure. Also try this with the Percussive Blues $\frac{4}{4}$ strum.

Other Song Possibilities

Comin' Home Baby / Fever / Ya Ya / Bag's Groove / Night in Tunisia / Sermonette / Out of This World / Our Day Will Come / How Deep Is the Ocean / Work Song

(See song on page 147.)

percussive tambor $\frac{3}{4}$

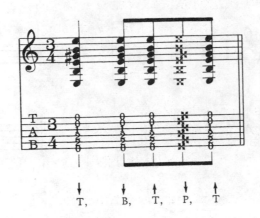

This is an impressive looking strum. To help you sound as good as you'll look, we describe this step by step.

Play a thumb down motion (thumb sweeps all the strings). Then, for the tambor (a drum-like motion), swing your right hand above the bridge and strike it with your second and third fingers. (You should hear a thump accompanied by a deep ringing sound resonating from the guitar.) Swing your hand in an arc and bring your thumb sweeping back up across the strings. Now, use an abrupt percussive motion with the palm followed by the thumb sweeping back across the strings again.

La Llorona is from the Tehuantepec region of the state of Oaxaca. *La Llorona* means "The Weeping One." Use one pattern unit for each measure. Also try this with the Rasqueado Huapanga $\frac{3}{4}$.

Other Song Possibilities

Malaguena Salerosa / Mi Caballo Blanco / Coplas / Los Cuatro Generales / Venga Jaleo / Noches De Luna / Los Contrabandistos de Ronda / Cielito Lindo / A La Una Naci Yo / Una Tarde Fresquita De Mayo

(See song on page 145.)

Rasgueado Patterns

The Rasgueado Patterns are distinguished by their use of a Spanish and Latin American guitar technique, creating a drum-roll like effect. It carries the sound of the strings' rippling tones, along with its percussive quality. Although it certainly has a marked Latin flavor, it can also be worked into Rock and Folk music very well.

Each of the accompaniment patterns in this grouping, regardless of their meter or the total number of motions used, will always include the following core of motions somewhere (the sequence depends on the particular pattern) in its basic unit:

1. at least one *rasgueado motion* combined with
2. at least one motion from any of the following groupings:
   the *fast patterns* (details on page 95),
   the *percussive patterns* (details on page 112),
   the *slow patterns* (details on page 42),
   the *pull patterns* (details on page 32).

A unit need not begin with any specific motion; and remember, the sequence of motions varies with each pattern. In standard notation and tablature a *rasqueado* is indicated by a wiggly-line ⸮ next to the chord, notes or tablature numbers. In the *pattern code,* it is indicated by an "R".

Note: The *rasgueado* is not the same perpendicular, simultaneous motion as the *fingers-down* (F) motion of the *fast patterns:* here, the fingers move separately, consecutively, down the strings, in a somewhat diagonal direction (toward the bridge end of instrument).

The *rasgueado motion* is executed in the following manner:
   Curl your fingers into a loose fist, and rest the thumb on the 6th string, comfy?

You're now in position to spray the fingers down across the strings.
   Now, leading with your fourth finger (and following with the third, second and first fingers), spray the fingers out from their closed position, evenly across the

strings. Only the outer-side part of the fingertip and nail will actually touch the strings as you sweep down.

Then follow through that staggered, finger spraying motion, by veering to the right, as you circle back to the starting position.

If your fingers get stuck in the strings, or the rhythm seems helplessly choppy, don't worry—it's par for the course with the first attempts. If you can get an even reasonably uniform roll, you're ahead of the game! An unbroken, balanced roll may take some time, but it will be well worth the effort.

If the use of *alternate bass strings* are desired, these are the recommended possibilities:

	A-B-C	D-F	E-G
Root Bass Strings	5	4	6
Standard Alternate			
a. Primary	5-4	4-5	6-5
b. Supplementary	5-6	4-5	6-4
Moving Bass Alternate			
a. Primary	5-4-4	4-5-5	6-5-5
b. Supplementary	5-4-6	4-6-5	6-5-4

rasgueado pull $\frac{3}{4}$

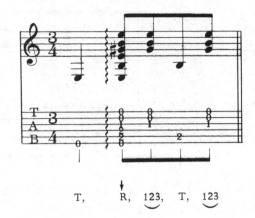

T,   R,   123,   T,   123

Rasgueado Pull $\frac{3}{4}$ is the first of the *rasgueado* Patterns, and shouldn't prove to be too difficult. Start by sounding the *bass string,* and then spray out the *rasgueado.* (Remember, one finger at a time!) Now, make a quick recovery by bringing your fingers back for that *pull motion.* That's the spot to watch out for; the rest should be smooth sailing. This strum is very active and has some really nice sound contrasts.

Los Quatro Generales, a Spanish Civil War song (to the tune of *Los Cuatro Muleros)* is about the four generals who betrayed Spain and the brave people who did not. Use one pattern unit for each measure. Also try the Fast $\frac{3}{4}$ on this if you want to underplay the song a bit.

Other Song Possibilities

Coplas (Spanish) / Chim Chim Cheree / Venga Jaleo (Spanish) / Dark As a Dungeon / Forbidden Games / Lady of Spain / A Million Tomorrows / Mangwainn Mpuleli (African) / Charade / South Coast

(See song on page 154.)

rasgueado moving bass pull $\frac{4}{4}$

T,   R,   123,   T,   123,   T,   123

Here you'll combine 3 features into one grand strum: The *rasgueado,* the pull motion and the moving bass strings. After your *bass string motion* and the *rasgueado,* bring your fingers back for the pull motion. The unit closes with simple enough motions, so the only thing to remember is that the bass strings alternate fiercely according to the bass string chart for *moving bass patterns.*

Love Alone is a lively Calypso commentary (much of Calypso singing is improvised and topical) written in the late 1930's and sung by Blind Blake. It concerns the abdication of King Edward III. Use one pattern unit for each measure. In the last measure, the B⁷ will get the first three pattern motions and the Em will get the last four pattern motions.

Other Song Possibilities

Guardian Beauty Contest / Will His Love Be Like His Rum / She Promised to Meet Me / Ob-La-Di / Maryanne / Last Train to San Fernando / The Big Bamboo / I Do Adore Her / Sloop John B / Money is King

(See song on page 164.)

rasgueado Mexican $\frac{3}{4}$

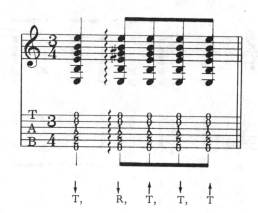

In this unit you'll substitute the Rasgueado for the second motion of the Fast $\frac{3}{4}$ strum. This Rasgueado, uses not only the four fingers of the right hand, but also a follow through with the thumb. Remember, it should sound like a smooth drum roll.

The rhythm for this strum should sound "Bom, Brrrm, bom bom bom."

Coplas is a "vaquero" (cowboy) song from Mexico. Cynthia Gooding has recorded it, as have the Triodelas Rancheros. Some of the acerbic verses are delicately suggestive. Use one pattern unit per measure.

Other Song Possibilities

Venga Jaleo / La Llorona / Subo / Los Quatro Generales / Mi Caballo Blanco / Forbidden Games / Echen Confites / Dos Puntos Tiene El Camino / El Pequeno / Cuando Yo Me Muera

(See song on page 171.)

rasgueado Spanish $\frac{4}{4}$

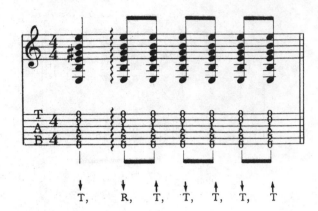

As in the Rasgueado Mexican $\frac{3}{4}$, here we're using the *rasgueado* motion with the fingers, and then following through with the thumb. Actually, two thumb motions are added, giving the pattern a fourth beat, and of course quite a different feeling. The new rhythm should sound "Boom, brrrm bom, bom, bom, bom, bom."

Viva La Quince Brigada is our adaptation of an inspired, powerful Spanish Civil War song, commemorating the effort of The International Brigade. We start in $\frac{3}{4}$ time, change to $\frac{4}{4}$ and then return to $\frac{3}{4}$. So, start with the Rasgueado $\frac{3}{4}$, then the new Rasgueado $\frac{4}{4}$ and then return to Rasgueado $\frac{3}{4}$. Use one pattern unit per measure.

Other Song Possibilities

Si Tu Quieros Escribir (Spanish) / Por Favor (Spanish) / Perfidia / Miami Beach Rhumba / Que Bonita Bandera (Spanish) / Carnival (Portugese) / Arriverderci Roma (Italian) / Kay Shoshana (Hebrew) / Besame Mucho (Spanish) / Love Alone

(See song on page 171.)

rasgueado rock $\frac{4}{4}$

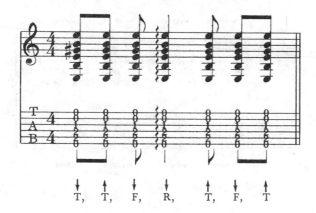

As you may have gathered, this strum combines two types of music: Rock and Flamenco. They can work quite well together, perhaps because both are highly rhythmic styles, and are most often used to accompany some form of dance. Drums and Rock are inseparable, and in using the Rasgueado, with its snare-like effect on the 4th motion, you are adding a very suitable percussive element. Note that the Rasgueado Motion is longer than the other strum motions. The rhythm should sound "Bom-a chick-Brrrm, a-chick-a."

Come and Go With Me To That Land is a Gospel tune that lends itself to group singing. You'll probably want to add your own verses. Use one pattern unit for each measure.

Other Song Possibilities

Put your Hand in the Hand / Baby Love / Spanish Flea / I'll Never Find Another You / Crockodile Rock / Do You Wanna Dance / All My Lovin' / Runaway / Save the Last Dance For Me / Goin' Out of My Head

(See song on page 179.)

rasgueado percussive rock $\frac{4}{4}$

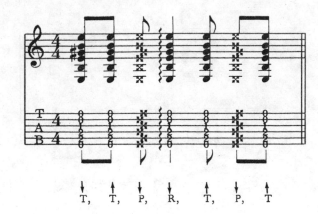

T,　T,　P,　R,　T,　P,　T

As with the regular Rasgueado Rock $\frac{4}{4}$, you are adding a *rasgueado* to the basic *fast rock* unit to create a drum-roll-like effect. But now, to carry the concept of percussion one step further, damp the strings with the percussive motion on the 3rd and 6th motions. The rhythm should sound "Bom Bom Chick Brrrm Bom Chick Bom."

Will the Circle Be Unbroken—There's sadness and dignity in this song. It was recorded in the 1920's by the Metropolitan Quartet, the Silver Leaf Quartet of Norfolk, and the Carter Family. Use one pattern unit for each measure. In measures with two chords, the second chord will get the last four motions. Also try the Fast Rock $\frac{4}{4}$ and some of the Pattern Picking strums with this song.

Other Song Possibilities

Evil Ways / Splish Splash / Doctor My Eyes / Historia De Un Amor (Spanish) / The Beat Goes On / Goody Goody / We'll Sing in the Sunshine / What Now My Love / Volare (Italian) / Stop! In the Name of Love

(See song on page 178.)

rasgueado tango $\frac{4}{4}$

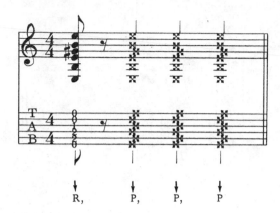

There aren't too many people tangoing around these days, but we've provided the *rasgueado tango* because we like to feel that this collection will prepare you for almost any musical event. In playing this pattern, remember to keep the motions short and clipped (except for the *rasgueado* motion).

Last Tango On Canal Street was written on the I.R.T. You can sing the melody on any syllable: "lai" or "loo" or "oye," depending on your mood and geographic location. Use one pattern unit for each measure.

Other Song Possibilities

La Comparsita / Caminito Tango / La Moma / Whatever Lola Wants / Blue Tango / Hernandos Hideaway / Masochistic Tango / Adios Muchachos (I Get Ideas) / Tango Della Gelosia / Kiss of Fire

(See song on page 161.)

rasgueado huapanga $\frac{3}{4}$

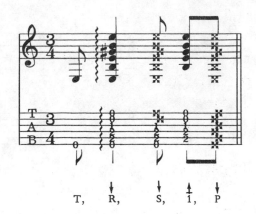

This is an authentic *mexican huapanga* strum which can also be played on songs from other Latin American countries. For the first motion, play the *bass string* with your thumb. Second, roll your fingers for the *rasgueado*. Third, slap the strings with your palm, so the fingers extend past the sound hole and can strike the guitar face. (This motion should give you a toneless, rasping sound from the strings, with a resonant thumb reverberating from the guitar.) Fourth, sweep your index finger back up the strings. Fifth, use the *percussive motion*. This is a one of a kind strum and creates a feeling that really must be heard to be believed.

Subo is an Argentian Indian song which has a beautiful, haunting quality. Subo means "I climb," and the song evokes images of a lone climber making his way up the high South American mountains. Use one pattern unit for each regular measure; when there are two chords in a measure, the second chord uses the last two motions.

Other Song Possibilities

La Llorona / Coplas / Venga Jaleo / Mi Caballo Blanco / Los Cuatro Generales / Con Las Abejas / Noches De La Luna / Cuando Yo Me Muerta / Vidalita / A La Una Naci Yo

(See song on page 169.)

Snap Back Patterns

These patterns are as much fun to play as they are to listen to. Although they are very distinctive, a particular touch or a certain tempo can change the mood of a *snap back* strum quite a bit. Apart from the obvious *country-folk* quality they usually convey, they can also be cutting and defiant, bright and energetic, twangy and sorrowful. It can even back sunshine rock! Mostly these patterns will give you the irresistible urge to smile broadly.

Each of the accompaniment patterns in this grouping, regardless of their meter or the total number of motions used, always includes in its basic unit three specific motions. Most of these motions, forming the core of *snap back* patterns, need not be played consecutively. Only the first motion listed must be played first.

1. Your thumb plays a single *bass string* to start each pattern. The string varies depending on the chord. (A *free stroke* is recommended for the light, flexible touch necessary for this grouping.)

The next two motions that follow may appear in any order.

2. Your 2nd finger (some people use the 2nd and 3rd together, as one finger) sharply flicks down across the top 3 strings.

3. That 2nd finger "snaps back" (pulls up), catching (and therefore sounding) only the 1st string.

The *alternate bass strings* recommended for *snap back patterns* are as follows:

	A-B-C	D-F	E-G
Standard Alternates			
1. Primary	5-4	4-5	6-5
2. Supplementary	5-6	4-5	6-4

snap back Carter style $\frac{4}{4}$

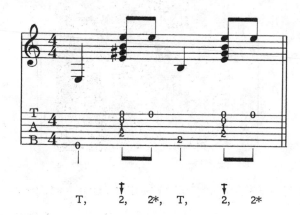

Here is the same rhythm as a Fast $\frac{4}{4}$ unit ("Bom chick-a"). Of course, the use of the *snap-back motion* provides this pattern with a totally unique effect. It's different from any previous pattern in $\frac{4}{4}$ time. Since you'll usually play two pattern units for each measure, the second bass string can be comfortably hammered-on for a saucier, more interesting Carter-style effect. You might also want to try using *runs*. (See the section on *special techniques*.)

Darling Corey is a well known favorite banjo tune from Kentucky. It's a perfect vehicle for Carter style picking. Use four pattern units for each measure.

Other Song Possibilities

Keep on the Sunnyside / Mr. Tambourine Man / I Ain't Got No Home in This World Anymore / Ruben James / 900 Miles / Wildwood Flower / Circle Game / Bury Me Beneath the Willow / Mountain Dew / Pal of Mine

(See song on page 172.)

snap back Carter style $\frac{3}{4}$

This pattern uses the same rhythm as the Fast $\frac{3}{4}$ ("Bom chick-a chick-a"), however the feeling is quite different. This pattern sounds especially good when you alternate the *bass strings*. As with the Snap-Back Carter $\frac{4}{4}$, you can try *hammer-ons* or *runs* when you are comfortable with the basic motions.

Who's Gonna Shoe Your Pretty Little Foot is a traditional American folk song from the singing of Woody Guthrie. Use one pattern unit for each measure. You might also want to try the Arpeggiated $\frac{3}{4}$ strum; both are equally effective here.

Other Song Possibilities

Little Moses / Stewball / Mockingbird Hill / Beautiful Brown Eyes / Tennessee Waltz / The Cyclone of Rye Cove / My Children Are Laughing Behind My Back / He'll Have To Go / I'm a Rambler, I'm a Gambler / Roll On, Columbia

(See song on page 180.)

snap back bluegrass style $\frac{4}{4}$

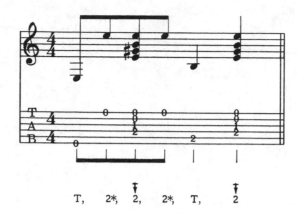

T, 2*, 2, 2*, T, 2

Even those who haven't heard much Blue Grass music are surprised how much playing this strum really turns them on! You can create a Blue-Grass sound more faithfully if you utilize this strum in conjunction with *runs* and *hammering*. (See the section on *special techniques.*) The rhythm should sound "Bida Bida Bom chick."

Wildwood Flower—According to Jack Baker of the Fretted Instruments School, Maybelle Carter (and the Carter Family) provide the definitive version of this sardonic, sadly defiant song. Maybelle plays all their lead work, both finger-style and flat-picking, and she is still going strong in her late sixties! We suggest you listen to their recording. Use one pattern unit for each measure.

Other Song Possibilities

Sugar in the Mornin' / Take a Whiff On Me / Long Time Man / Weary and a Lonesome Traveler / Cindy / Railroad Bill / Pastures of Plenty / Done Laid Around / Putting On the Style / Hard Ain't It Hard

(See song on page 179.)

snap back country style $\frac{4}{4}$

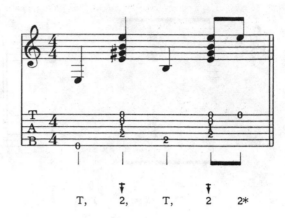

T,   2,   T,   2   2*

The rhythm for this pattern should sound "Bom chick, Bom Chick-a." Listen to records by Doc Watson and Lester Flatt and Earl Scruggs (among others) in order to get a good idea of this sound. The *hammering* technique also fits in well with this strum unit.

Silver Dagger—This American ballad is believed to have British roots. Joan Baez re-introduced it with the simple beautiful arrangement she did on her first album. Use two pattern units for each measure.

Other Song Possibilities

Country Roads / I am a Pilgrim / John Hardy / Jesse James / Wabash Cannonball / Gentle On My Mind / Hard Travellin' / Buffalo Skinners / Salty Dog / Old Joe Clark

(See song on page 180.)

snap back Nashville style $\frac{4}{4}$

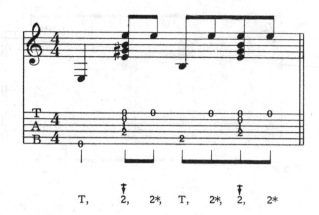

T,   2,   2*,   T,   2*,   2,   2*

The rhythm of this strum should sound "Bom chick-a Bumpa chick-a." This Nashville sound is basically a polished version of Southern and Country-Western music. One of the best known forums for listening and participating in this type of music is the Grand Ol' Opry. (This was a program originating in Tennessee. Since 1925 the Grand Ol' Opry has promoted many C & W performers and songs beyond local levels and into national prominence.)

Banks Of The Ohio is an American ballad with a beautiful melody and extremely depressing lyrics. It would appear that acts of hostility are not uncommon subjects for many American ballads. Use one pattern unit for each measure.

Other Song Possibilities

Help Me Make It Through the Night / Everything Is Beautiful / Blueberry Hill / The City of New Orleans / Your Cheating Heart / King of the Road / Me and Bobby McGhee / Look What They've Done to My Song / The Night They Drove Old Dixie Down / I Walk the Line

(See song on page 176.)

snap back slow $\frac{4}{4}$

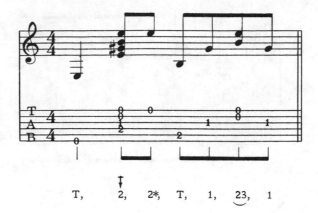

T,   2,   2*,   T,   1,   23,   1

This strum combines the Snap Back Carter $\frac{4}{4}$ with a Slow $\frac{4}{4}$ strum. It is a great example of how opposite textures can attract and work together successfully. The only tricky part is getting your right hand in position to do the Slow $\frac{4}{4}$ strum after having just completed the *snap back* motion, but it can be done! Just don't exaggerate the *snap back* motion, and keep your thumb and fingers ready to pounce on the strings. You can also alternate your *bass strings* for variety.

Follow The Drinkin' Gourd is a song of the Underground Railroad from pre-Civil War times. *The Drinkin' Gourd* was a code name for the Big Dipper which escaping slaves would use in order to get their bearing while fleeing up North. Use one pattern unit for each measure.

Other Song Possibilities

Look What They've Done to My Song / Playboys and Playgirls / You Won't See Me / Will the Circle Be Unbroken / Summertime and the Living Is Easy / I Rode My Bicycle Past Your Window / Beautiful Balloon / A Man of Constant Sorrow / Blowin in the Wind / Bill Bailey Won't You Please Come Home

(See song on page 164.)

snap back folk $\frac{4}{4}$

T,   2,   2*,   2*,   2,   2*

Here we utilize the same rhythm which was employed in the Fast Folk $\frac{4}{4}$, only the motions have been changed to create a spicy but more delicate feeling. The rhythm should sound: "Bom chick Boom-a, chicka."

This Little Light is one of the most loved gospel tunes around. It is sometimes sung with middle verses, but here we've used a more basic version, which should prove excellent as a sing-along. Use one pattern unit for each measure.

Other Song Possibilities

Chelsea Morning / Someday Soon / Colours / Go Tell It on the Mountain / Puff the Magic Dragon / Thirsty Boots / Autumn to May / Don't Think Twice / Midnight Special / I'm Goin' Down That Road Feeling Bad

(See song on page 179.)

snap back double bass 4/4

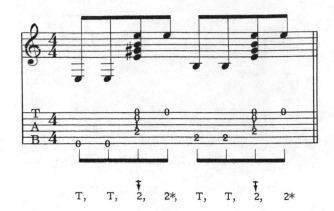

T,   T,   2,   2*,   T,   T,   2,   2*

The rhythm for this unit will sound "Bom Bom Chick-Chick." This strum functions very nicely as an accompaniment for soft Rock tunes and Folk and Country songs with a mild "oomph." You can alternate the *bass note strings* on the second pattern in each measure, if the spirit moves you.

Hey You Never Will Know Me—If you've ever felt shut out by someone you love, you should be able to identify with this song. Use two strum units for each measure. In measure six on the Bridge, where there are three chords, the A gets the first two *bass notes* of the strum while the C#, gets the two second finger motions. The F#m gets a full pattern unit.

Other Song Possibilities

I Can't Stop Lovin' You / Someday Soon / I'd Like To Teach the World To Sing / You're So Vain / Sweet Caroline / Monday, Monday / Green, Green Grass of Home / Anticipation / Danny's Song / Your Cheating Heart

(See song on page 161.)

snap back arpeggiated $\frac{4}{4}$

T,   1,   2,   1,   3,   1,   2   2*

As the name implies, we are combining an Arpeggiated unit with the old and fondly regarded *snap-back*. Begin your Arpeggiated $\frac{4}{4}$ pattern. For the last 2 motions of the unit, switch and flick out the *snap back* motion. The rhythm should sound: "Bom, bom, Bom bom, Bom, bom, Chick-a." This strum uses nice textural variety and achieves an unusual quality of restful motions.

East Virginia is an American ballad widely known in the Southern Mountains and widely loved just about everywhere. Joan Baez (among others) did a particularly lovely recording of this one. Use one strum unit for each measure.

Other Song Possibilities

Where Or When / I'm Old Fashioned / United Nations / Love Letters / Shenandoah / Somewhere Over The Rainbow / Out of Nowhere / Fare Thee Well / Green Leaves Of Summer / That Old Feeling

(See song on page 155.)

pull slow bass rock 4/4
Swing Low, Sweet Chariot

Swing low, sweet char-i-ot,___ com-in' for to car-ry me

home. Swing__ low, sweet char-i-ot___ com-in' for to car-ry me

home. I looked o-ver Jor-dan and what did I see,___

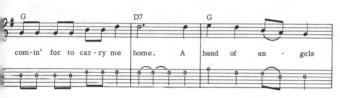

com-in' for to car-ry me home. A band of an - gels

com-in' af-ter me.___ Com-in' for to car-ry me home.

you get there before I do, etc.
all my friends I'm coming, too, etc.

sometimes up an' sometimes down, etc.
still my soul feels heavenly boun', etc.

I never went to Heaven, but I been told, etc.
The streets in Heaven am paved with gold, etc.

(See accompaniment pattern on page 34.)

fast 3/4
The Housewife's Lament

Verse:
One day I was walk-ing I heard a com-plain-ing, and

saw an old wom-an the pic-ture of gloom. She

gazed at the mud on her door-step ('twas rain-ing) and

this was her song as she wield-ed her broom.

Chorus:
Oh life is a toil___ and love is a trou-ble,___

beau-ty will fade___ and rich-es will flee.

Pleas-ures they dwin-dle and pric-es they dou-ble and

noth-ing is as I would wish it to be.

There's too much of worriment goes to a bonnet,
There's too much of ironing goes to a shirt.
There's nothing that pays for the time you waste on it,
There's nothing that lasts us but trouble and dirt.

In March it is mud, it is slush in December,
The midsummer breezes are loaded with dust.
In fall the leaves litter, in muddy September,
The wallpaper rots and the candlesticks rust.

There are worms on the cherries and slugs on the roses,
And ants in the sugar and mice in the pies.
The rubbish of spiders no mortal supposes,
And ravaging roaches and damaging flies.

It's sweeping at six and it's dusting at seven,
It's victuals at eight and it's dishes at nine.
It's potting and panning from ten to eleven,
We scarce break our fast till we plan how to dine.

With grease and with grime from corner to center,
Forever at war and forever alert.
No rest for a day lest the enemy enter,
I spend my whole life in struggle with dirt.

Last night in my dreams I was stationed forever
On a far little rock in the midst of the sea.
My one chance of life was a ceaseless endeavor,
To sweep off the waves as they swept over me.

Alas! Twas no dream; ahead I behold it,
I see I am helpless my fate to avert.
She lay down her broom her apron she folded,
She lay down and died and was buried in dirt.

(See accompaniment pattern on page 24.)

travis pattern picking 4/4
Freight Train

When I am dead and in my grave,
No more good times here I'll crave,
Place the stones at my head and feet,
And tell them all that I'm gone to sleep.

When I die, Lord, bury me deep,
Way down on old Chestnut Street,
So I can hear old Number Nine,
As she comes rolling by.

When I die, Lord, bury me deep,
Way down on old Chestnut Street,
Place the stones at my head and feet,
And tell them all that I'm gone to sleep.

(See accompaniment pattern on page 31.)

pull arpeggiated 4/4
Sakura

(See accompaniment pattern on page 36.)

fast rock 4/4
This Train

This This train don't carry no gamblers, this train,
This train don't carry no gamblers, this train.
This train don't carry no gamblers,
No hypocrites, no midnight ramblers,
This train is bound for glory, this train.

This train is built for speed now, etc.
Fastest train you ever did see,
This train is bound for glory, this train.

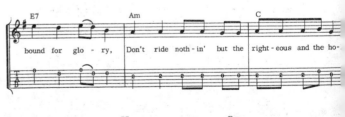

This train don't carry no liars, etc.
No hypocrites and no high flyers,
This train is bound for glory, this train.

This train you don't pay no transportation, etc.
No Jim Crow and no discrimination,
This train is bound for glory, this train.

This train don't carry no rustlers, etc.
Sidestreet walkers, two-bit hustlers,
This train is bound for glory, this train.

(See accompaniment pattern on page)

percussive tambor $\frac{3}{4}$
La Llorona

Chorus:

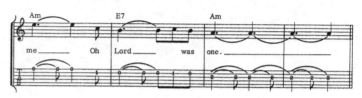

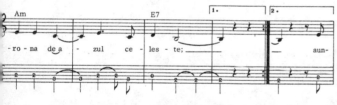

arpeggiated triplet $\frac{4}{4}$
House of the Rising Sun

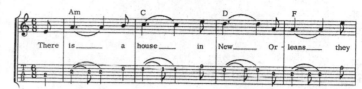

My mother is a tailor,
She sews those new blue jeans.
My sweetheart is a drunkard, Lord,
Drinks down in New Orleans.

The only thing a drunkard needs,
Is a suitcase and a trunk.
The only time he's satisfied,
Is when he's on a drunk.

Go tell my baby sister,
Never do like I have done.
To shun that house in New Orleans,
They call The Rising Sun.

It's one foot on the platform,
And the other one on the train.
I'm going back to New Orleans,
To wear the ball and chain.

I'm going back to New Orleans,
My race is almost run.
I'm going back to spend my life,
Beneath that Rising Sun.

If I had listened to what mama said,
I'd be at home today.
But being so young and foolish, poor girl,
Let a gambler lead me astray.

(See accompaniment pattern on page 18.)

If cielo subir pudiera llorona,
estrellas te bajara; } 2×
na a tus pies pusiera, llorona,
el sol te coronara. } 2×

de mí! llorona, } 2×
ona de azul celeste;
que la vida me cueste, llorona, } 2×
lejaré de quererte.

en que no tengo duelo, llorona, } 2×
que no me ven llorar.
muertos que no hacen ruido, llorona, } 2×
más grande su pena.

¡Ay de mí! llorona,
llorona de ayer y hoy; } 2×
ayer maravilla fui, llorona,
y ahora ni la sombra soy! } 2×

Salías del templo un día, llorona,
cuando al pasar yo te vi; } 2×
Hermoso huipil llevabas, llorona,
que la virgen te creí. } 2×

¡Ay de mí! llorona,
llorona llévame al mar; } 2×
A ver a los buceadores, llorona,
que perlas van a sacar. } 2×

If I could climb to the sky, llorona,
I'd bring down some stars for you,
The moon I'd put at your feet, llorona,
With the sun I'd crown you.

Dear oh me! llorona,
Llorona, of heavenly blue,
Even though it costs me my life, llorona,
I shan't stop loving you.

Everyone says I'm not in pain,
Because they don't see me cry;
There are corpses that make no noise, llorona,
And their pain is greater than mine!

Dear oh me! llorona,
Llorona of yesterday and today . . .
Yesterday I was the love of your life,
And today I'm not even a shadow!

You came out of the temple one day, llorona,
And I saw you while passing by;
You were wearing such a beautiful blouse, llorona,
That I thought you to be the Virgin!

Dear Oh me! llorona,
Llorona, take me down to the sea,
To see the pearl fisherman, llorona,
and what pearls they've found so far.

(See accompaniment pattern on page 120.)

percussive pinch rock $\frac{4}{4}$
Long Chains

It was late one evenin', clouds turnin' yellow,
The sun slowly goin' down,
Man came runnin' 'cross the cornfield,
In the distance we heard bloodhounds.

He ran into the little old country shack,
He didn't stay very long,
When the stranger left, I asked my mother,
Who's the man with the long chains on,
(Hum one verse tune thru)

She looked at me with her hung-down head,
Her eyes was very sad,
Said "Oh my son, that man was no stranger,
That man, he was your Dad."

It was later that evenin', we was eatin' dinner,
A knock rang upon the door,
The high sheriff said "Your nigger lie dead,
In the dust beside the county store."

My mother ran all the way downtown,
She fell upon the ground,
She pulled his bleedin' body up to hers,
Blood was all over her gown.

He says, "Matilda, I am dyin',
Still I never been free,
Please tell God, when I get home,
Take the long chains off me,
Take the long chains off me,
Take the long chains off me,
Oh Matilda, Lord, Matilda"

(See accompaniment pattern on page 118.)

fast bass Motown rock $\frac{4}{4}$
Shakin' Up The Nation

© Copyright 1972
Gothic Music Publishers
1225 Woodycrest Ave. Bronx, N.Y.

Words and music by David Blake.

The younger generation,
Is shakin' up the nation,
Fightin' for a fraction of the action,
What a pity and a shame,
Some think its just a game,
And won't give them,
A bit of satisfaction.

The poor population,
Is shakin' up the nation,
They want to live the same as you and I.
But we go on our way,
Getting fatter by the day,
Not caring whether they live or die.

(See accompaniment pattern on page 110.)

full complex pattern picking $\frac{4}{4}$
Miner's Life

Min - er's life_____ is like a sail - or's,_____ 'board a
rocks_____ they're fall - ing dai - ly,_____ care - less

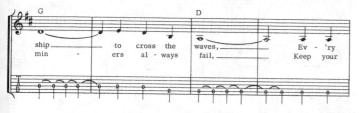

ship_____ to cross the waves,_____ Ev - 'ry
min - ers al - ways fail,_____ Keep your

day_____ his life's in dan - ger_____ still he
hand_____ up - on the dol - lar_____

ven - tures be - ing brave._____ Watch the

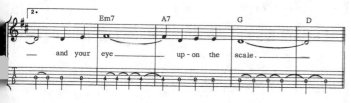

_____ and your eye_____ up - on the scale._____

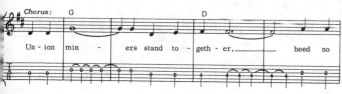

Chorus:
Un - ion min - ers stand to - geth - er,_____ heed no

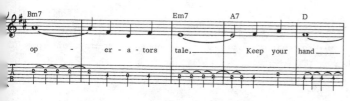

op - er - a - tors tale,_____ Keep your hand

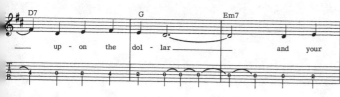

up - on the dol - lar_____ and your

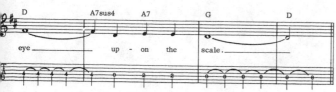

eye_____ up - on the scale.

percussive pinch blues $\frac{4}{4}$
Darlin'

If I'd a - known my cap - tain was blind, Dar - lin',

If I'd a - known my cap - tain was blind, Dar - lin',

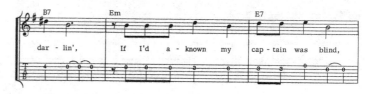

dar - lin', If I'd a - known my cap - tain was blind,

would - na gone to work 'til half - past nine,

Dar - lin', Dar - lin', Dar - lin'.

I asked my captain for the time of day, darlin', darlin',
I asked my captain for the time of day, darlin', darlin',
I asked my captain for the time of day,
He got so mad he threw his watch away, darlin', darlin'.

Fight my captain and I'll land in jail, darlin', darlin',
Fight my captain and I'll land in jail, darlin', darlin',
Fight my captain and I'll land in jail,
Nobody 'round to go my bail, darlin', darlin'.

Told my captain he don't know my mind, darlin', darlin',
Told my captain he don't know my mind, darlin', darlin',
Told my captain he don't know my mind,
I'm a-laughin' just to keep from cryin', darlin', darlin'.

(See accompaniment pattern on page 119.)

You've been docked and docked my boys,
You've been loading two to one,
What have you to show for working,
Since this mining has begun?

Overalls and cans for rockers,
In your shanties sleep on rails,
Keep your hand upon the dollar,
And your eyes upon the scale.

In conclusion, bear in memory,
Keep the password in your mind,
God provides for every nation,
When in union they combine.

Stand like men, and link together,
Victory for you'll prevail,
Keep your hands upon the dollar,
And your eyes upon the scale.

(See accompaniment pattern on page 92.)

full inflected pattern picking 4/4
Wabash Cannonball

From the great At - lan - tic O - cean, To the

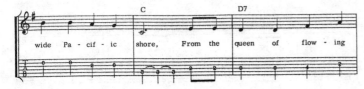

wide Pa - cif - ic shore, From the queen of flow - ing

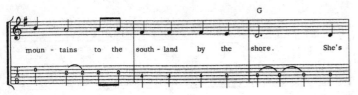

moun - tains to the south - land by the shore. She's

might - y tall and hand - some and quite well known by all,

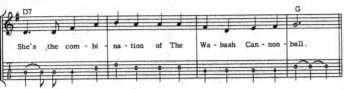

She's the com - bi - na - tion of The Wa - bash Can - non - ball.

Listen to the jingle, the rumble and the roar,
As she glides along the woodland, through the hills and by
the shore,
Hear the mighty rush of the engine, and the lonesome
hobo squall,
You're travlin' through the jungle, on the Wabash
Cannonball.

She come down from Birmingham, one cold December
day,
As she rolled into the station, you'd hear the people say,
There's a girl from Birmingham, she's long and she is tall,
She just came down from Birmingham, on the Wabash
Cannonball

Here's to Daddy Claxton, may his name forever stand,
And always be remembered, in the courts of our whole
land,
His earthly race is over, and the curtains round him fall,
We'll carry him home to victory, on the Wabash
Cannonball.

(See accompaniment pattern on page 91.)

fast rhythm and blues shuffle 4/4
Twelve Gates To The City

The sun shines down on the beautiful city, etc.
Peace will come to the beautiful city, etc.
Brothers and sisters together in the city, etc.

(See accompaniment pattern on page 101.)

pinch folk Israeli 4/4

Hava Na Gila

(See accompaniment pattern on page 59.)

pinch bossa nova 4/4

O Sole Mio

(See accompaniment pattern on page 61.)

inverted pattern picking 4/4
Good Boy

Music © Copyright 1973
Abe Mandelblatt. Words traditional.

I have led a good life full of peace and qui-et,
I have been a good boy wed to peace and stud-y,

I shall have an old age full of rum and ri-ot.
I shall have an old age rib-ald course and blood-y.

I have nev-er cut throats e-ven when I yearned to,

nev-er sa-ang dirt-y songs that my fan-cy turned to.

I have been a nice boy and done what was ex-pect-ed,

I shall be an old bum loved but un-re-spect-ed.

(See accompaniment pattern on page 81.)

full pinch pattern picking 4/4
Go Tell Aunt Rhody

Go tell Aunt Rho-dy, go tell Aunt Rho-dy,

Go tell Aunt Rho-dy that the old gray goose is dead.

2. The one she's been saving . . . to make a feather bed.
3. She died in the mill pond . . . a standing on her head.
4. The goslings are crying . . . because their mother's dead.
5. The old gander's weeping . . . because his wife is dead.

pinch samba 4/4
Nava

© Copyright 1972
Abe Mandelblatt (ASCAP)

(See accompaniment pattern on page 60.)

pull jazz ⁵⁄₄
Take Five

Music by Paul Desmond, Words by Iola Brubeck.

Won't you stop and take a lit-tle time out with me, Just____ take five. Just____ take five. Stop your bus-y day and take the time out to see I'm a-live, I'm a-live. Tho' I'm go-in' out of my way just so I can pass by each day, Not a sin-gle word do we say, it's a pan-to-mime and not a play. Still I know all eyes are for me, I feel tin-gles down to my feet when your smile gets much too dis-creet, Sends me on my way, would-n't it be bet-ter not to be so po-lite, you____ could of-fer____ a

light. Start a lit-tle con-ver-sa-tion now. It's all right, Just____ take five, Just____ take

Coda

five, Just____ take five.

(See accompaniment pattern on page 39.)

pull waltz ³⁄₄
Grand and Glorious Feeling

What a grand and glo-ri-ous fee-ee-ling, glo-ri-ous fee-ee-ling, When the bells of Peace are ri-ing-ing, peace are ri-ing-ing, peace on earth, peace on earth, peace on earth.

(See accompaniment pattern on page 12.)

151

pull jazz 3/4
Something Borrowed

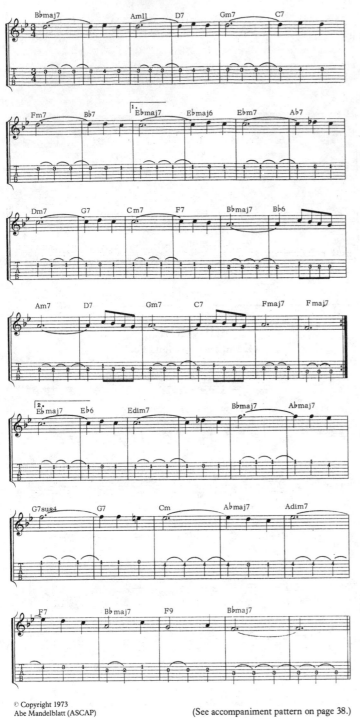

(See accompaniment pattern on page 38.)

fast merengue 4/4
Aviva's Merengue

Dad - dy, let's go to the zoo now. See the am - i - nals are
Dad - dy, have you seen the pea - cup? It's a nice day for a

eat - ing. Mom - my, see the spar - rot fly - ing.___ From
pick - nit. Mom - my, see the pink fla - min - goat.___ I

walk - ing I have blin - tzes on my feet.
want a chock - late pup - cake for my teef.

(See accompaniment pattern on page 105.)

fast rock 3/4
Mangwaini Mpulel

Mang - wa - ni impu - le - le, ki - nel - wa ki - tu - la (A Mang-wa-ni)

Mang - wa - ni impu - le - le ki - nel - wa ki - tu - la.

Fine

Le - hae - le mu - la, le hae - le mu - le

ki - nel - wa Ki - tu - la A Mang - wa - ni Le - la.

D.C. al Fine

(See accompaniment pattern on page 97.)

152

moving bass pinch $\frac{3}{4}$
Scarlet Ribbons

Evelyn Danzig & Jack Segal

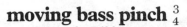

I peeked in to say good-night, And I
All the stores were dark and shut-tered, All the

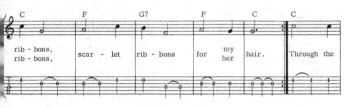

saw my child in prayer. And for me some scar-let
streets were dark and bare. In our town no scar-let

rib-bons, scar-let rib-bons for my hair. Through the
rib-bons, scar-let rib-bons for her hair.

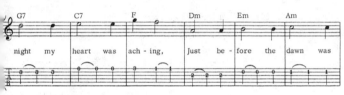

night my heart was ach-ing, Just be-fore the dawn was

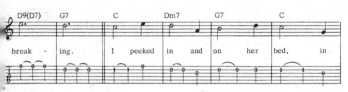

break-ing. I peeked in and on her bed, in

gay pro-fu-sion ly-ing there, I saw rib-bons,

scar-let rib-bons, scar-let rib-bons for her hair.

If I live to be one hun-dred I will nev-er

know from where came those love-ly scar-let

rib-bons, scar-let rib-bons for her hair.

(See accompaniment pattern on page 70.)

moving bass pinch ballad $\frac{4}{4}$
What Have They Done to the Rain?

Words and music by Malvina Reynolds

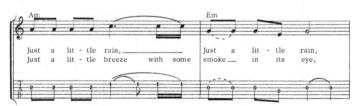

Just a lit-tle rain fall-ing all a-round, The
Just a lit-tle breeze out of the sky, The

grass lifts its head to the heav-en-ly sound,
leaves pat their hands as the breeze blows by,

Just a lit-tle rain, Just a lit-tle rain,
Just a lit-tle breeze with some smoke in its eye,

What have they done to the rain? Just a lit-tle boy
What have they done to the rain?

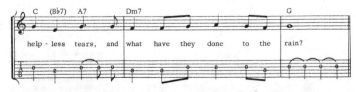

stand-ing in the rain, The gen-tle rain that falls for years. And the

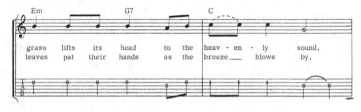

grass is gone. The boy dis-ap-pears, And the rain keeps fall-ing like

help-less tears, and what have they done to the rain?

(See accompaniment pattern on page 27.)

rasgueado pull $\frac{3}{4}$
Los Cuatro Generales

Madrid, que bien resistes...
Mamita mia,
Los bombardeos...

The four insurgent generals...
Mamita mia,
They tried to betray us...

Madrid, you wondrous city...
Mamita mia,
They wanted to take you...

But your courageous children...
Mamita mia,
They did not disgrace you...

(See accompaniment pattern on page 123.)

percussive bass note rock $\frac{4}{4}$
I'm On My Way

I asked my brother to come with me,
I asked my brother to come with me,
I asked my brother to come with me,
I'm on my way, great God, I'm on my way.

I asked my sister (mother, father, etc.) to come with me,
etc.

If they won't come, I'll go alone, etc.

I'm on my way, to freedom's land, etc.

I'm on my way and I won't turn back, etc.

(See accompaniment pattern on page 11⬦)

full extended complex picking $\frac{4}{4}$
Worried Man Blues

I went across the river, and I lay down to sleep,
When I woke up, there were shackles on my feet.

Twenty-nine links of chain around my leg,
And on each link, an initial of my name.

I asked the judge, what might be my fine,
"Twenty-one years on the R.C. Mountain Line.

The train arrived, sixteen coaches long,
The girl I love is on that train and gone.

I looked down that track as far as I could see,
And a little bitty hand was waving after me.

If anyone asks you who wrote this song,
Tell 'em it was me and I sing it all day long.

(See accompaniment pattern on page 9⬦)

percussive light rock $\frac{4}{4}$
When the Saints Go Marching In

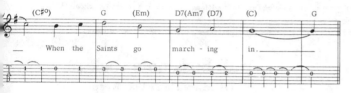

Oh, when the new world is revealed, etc.

And when the sun no more will shine, etc.

And when the moon has turned to blood, etc.

And on that hallelujah day, etc.

Oh, when the Saints go marching in, etc.

(See accompaniment pattern on page 115.)

fast bass soul $\frac{4}{4}$
There's a New World I Can See

Oh the hard times they are here,
Side by side, we will not fear.
Change does not come easily,
But there's a new world I can see.

Share the burden, make it less,
Leave behind the bitterness.
Change does not come easily,
But there's a new world I can see.

Tell the others so they'll know,
They can join us as we go.
Change does not come easily,
But there's a new world I can see.

(See accompaniment pattern on page 111.)

© Copyright 1973
Abe Mandelblatt and Malká Ackerman Mandelblatt
(ASCAP)

snap back arpeggiated $\frac{4}{4}$
East Virginia

Well, her hair was dark of color,
And her cheeks were rosy red;
On her breast she wore white lilies,
Where I longed to lay my head.

I'd rather be in some dark holler,
Where the sun refuses to shine;
Than for you to be another man's darling,
And to know you'll never be mine.

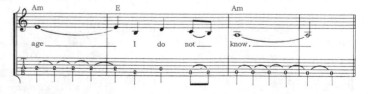

In my heart you are my darling,
At my door you're welcome in;
By my gate I'll always greet you,
For you're the girl I've tried to win.

I don't want your greenback dollar,
I don't want your silver chain;
All I want is your love, darling,
Won't you take me back again?

Repeat the first verse

(See accompaniment pattern on page 141.)

155

full pattern picking $\frac{4}{4}$
Please Don't Lay Your Trip On Me

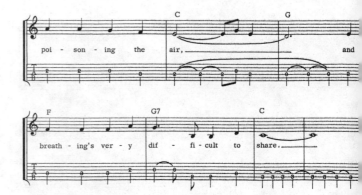

Please do not lay your trip on me, Mr. Hate and Fear,
I cannot turn my back on all the cries I seem to hear,
My hands can touch their loneliness, my arms can bring
  them near,
So please don't lay your trip on me, ol' Hate and Fear.
Bridge
Please do not lay your trip on me, Lady Guilt and Shame,
I'm sorry for the past, but let's do more than lay the
  blame,
My ears can hear our childrens tears, let's work so they
  may gain,
Oh please don't lay your trip on me, Guilt and Shame.

Please do not lay your trip on me, Mr. Hate and Fear,
There are no winners in a war, we all lose that's clear,
I know it seems that the dreams we dreamed, can never
  more be found,
But I think it's time we started looking 'round.
Bridge

(See accompaniment pattern on page 89.)

© Copyright 1972
Malká Ackerman Mandelblatt (ASCAP)

pull bass note rock $\frac{4}{4}$
Oh Mary Don't You Weep

Mary wore three links of chain,
Every link was Freedom's name.
Pharaoh's army got drownded,
Oh, Mary don't you weep.

One of these nights about twelve o'clock,
This old world is gonna reel and rock.
Pharaoh's army got drownded,
Oh, Mary don't you weep.

Moses stood on the Red Sea shore,
Smotin' the water with a two-by-four.
Pharaoh's army got drownded,
Oh, Mary don't you weep.

God gave Noah the rainbow sign,
No more water but fire next time.
Pharaoh's army got drownded,
Oh, Mary don't you weep.

The Lord told Moses what to do,
To lead those Hebrew children through.
Pharaoh's army got drownded,
Oh, Mary don't you weep.

(See accompaniment pattern on page 41.)

fast latin $\frac{4}{4}$
La Bamba

Bam-ba Bam-ba Bam-ba Bam-ba

Bam-ba, pa-ra bai - lar la bam-ba, pa-ra bai - lar la

bam-ba se ne ce - si - ta u-na po-ca de gra-cia u-na po-ca de

gra - cia yo - tra co - si ta. Ya-rri-ba ya-rri-ba

y a-rri-ba ya-rri-ba ya-rri-ba i ré, yo no soy ma-ri ne-ro

yo no soy ma-ri ne-ro, por ti se - ré, por ti se - ré, por ti se-ré!

a bailar la bamba, para bailar la bamba se necesita,
s pies ligeritos, unos pies ligeritos y otra cosita.

e canto la bamba, yo te canto la bamba sin pretensión,
que pongo delante, porque pongo delante mi corazón.

bonita es la bamba, qué bonita es la bamba en la
nadruga,
o todos la bailan, como todas la bailan bien zapateo.

que yo te pido, oye que yo te pido de compasión,
se acabe la bamba, que se acabe la bamba y venga otro
on.

dance La Bamba,
dance La Bamba,
must have nimble feet,
that are nimble,
then a little something else.

I'll sing you La Bamba,
I'll sing you La Bamba without any frills,
ause I put into it,
ause I put into it all my heart!

lovely is La Bamba,
lovely is La Bamba early in the morning,
veryone does it,
veryone does it, clicking their heels.

en now to my plea;
en now to my impassioned plea,
ind up La Bamba,
ind up La Bamba and play another Son.
us:

(See accompaniment pattern on page 19.)

percussive rock $\frac{4}{4}$
Midnight Special

Well, you wake up in the morn-ing, hear the big bell

ring, You go march-ing to the ta-ble,

see the same damn thing. Knife and fork are on the

ta-ble, ain't noth-ing in the pan,

And if you say an-y-thing a-bout it

you're in trou-ble with the man. Let the Mid-night

Spe-cial shine her light on me. Let the Mid-night

Spe-cial shine her ev-er-lov-in' light on me.

If you ever go to Houston, well ya better walk right,
You better not stagger, and you better not fight.
Cause the sheriff will arrest you, and he'll carry you down,
And if the jury finds you guilty, you're penitentiary
bound.

Yonder comes Miss Rosie, how in the world do you know,
Well I can tell by her apron, and the dress that she wore.
Umbrella on her shoulder, piece of paper in her hand,
She goes a marchin' to the Captain, she says I want my
man.

Well the man comes in the mornin', just a while before
day,
And he brought me the news, my wife has left and gone
away.
Oh that started me grievin' whoppin', hollerin' and cryin',
And it started me to thinkin', bout my great long time.

(See accompaniment pattern on page 114.)

157

fast twist $\frac{4}{4}$
Let's Twist Again

Kal Mann and David Appell.

Let's twist a-gain___ like we did last sum-mer.

Yeah, let's twist a-gain___ like we did last year.

Do you re-mem-ber when___ things were real-ly hum-min',

Yeah, let's twist a-gain___ twist-in' time is here,

a-round and a-round and on up and down we go a-

-gain. Oh ba-by, make me know you love me so a-

gain, Let's twist a-gain___ like we did last sum-mer.

Yeah, let's twist a-gain___ like we did last year.

(See accompaniment pattern on page 100.)

accented moving bass pinch $\frac{4}{4}$
When I Wake

Oh how I try to wake that sleep-ing spir-it in-

side of me, She's so a-fraid to o-pen up and

see If she_ is real, if she can

be, She may scare her-self and me.

Chorus:

When I wake I will find___ that I real-ly have a
think I can feel___ I won't break, oh I am

mind and I can sing the songs of the world in
real. Oh let us sing the songs of the world and

one part har-mo-ny. I can free.
set our sis-ters

When that spirit is born, of the sleeping women lost
 inside,
She'll drop her painted mask, she won't want to hide.
Her mouth will open to say, Her eyes will open to see,
She may shake society.

Every woman seems to have a sleeping spirit deep inside,
She's not just a teacher, a princess or a bride.
She's something much less sure, She's something much
 less pure,
She can drive as well as ride.

I know the truth can free her, if we're willing to let her go,
It may be hard to leave the world she may outgrow.
So her sisters must help her through, but there's just so
 much they can do,
She will need her brothers too.

(See accompaniment pattern on page 72.)

slow multiple bass $\frac{4}{4}$
Zog Nit Keinmol

full inverted pattern picking $\frac{4}{4}$
Silver's Really Grey

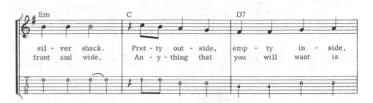

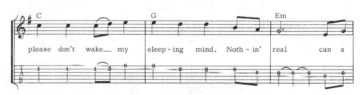

Never liked my mama's ways, I tried to make it on my
    own,
Thinkin' I could find some answers, with my head so
    grown,
So fully grown.
I tripped my way through love and friendship, until I
    found my way to God,
When I found him blind and deaf, it hit me pretty hard,
Hit me so very hard.

So I looked to lofty thinkers, livin' high ideals and such,
But politics moved very slowly, and health foods nothin'
    much,
No, it's not really much.
Every side that I have turned to, for a meaning or a way,
Has led me to a silver shack, is silver really grey,
Is it really grey?

Ever since I can remember, life has been a silver shack,
Pretty outside, empty inside, all the weeds growin' out,
    out in back,
I have found there are no answers; not in prophets, not in
    drink,
I'm sitting in my silver shack, and trying not to think,
Yes, Silver's Really Grey.

rom land of palm-tree to the far-off land of snow,
e shall be coming with our torment and our woe;
d everywhere our blood has sunk into the earth,
all our bravery, our vigor blossom forth.

e'll have the morning sun to set our day a-glow,
d all our yesterdays shall vanish with the foe;
en let this song go like a signal through the years.

his song was written with our blood and not with lead,
s not a song that summer birds sing overhead;
was a people among toppling barricades,
at sang this song of ours with pistols and grenades.

peat 1ˢᵗ Verse

Fun grinem palmen-land biz vaytn land fun shney,
Mir kumen on mit undzer payn, mit undzer vey;
Un vu gefaln iz a shprits fun undzer blut,
Shprotsn vet dort undzer g'vure, undzer mut.

S'vet di morgn-zun bagildn undz dem haynt,
Undzer nechtn vet farshvindn mitn faynt;
Nor oyb farzamen vet di zun un der kayor,
Vi a parol zol geyn dos lid fun dor tsu dor!

Dos lid geshribn iz mit blut un nit mit blay,
S'iz nit kayn lidi fun a foygl oyf der fray;
Dos hot a folk ts'vishn faldike vent,
Dos lid gezungen mit nagenes in di hent!

Repeat 1ˢᵗ Verse

(See accompaniment pattern on page 46.)

(See accompaniment pattern on page 90.)

slow bass pull ⁴⁄₄
All My Trials

Bridge:

Hush Hush little baby, don't you cry,
You know your daddy was born to die.
All my trials, Lord, etc.

I had a little book, 'twas given to me,
And every page spelled "Victory."
All my trials, Lord, etc.

(See accompaniment pattern on page 25.)

accented folk rock ⁴⁄₄
Study War No More

I'm gonna walk with the people of Peace,
down by the riverside,
down by the riverside,
down by the riverside,
I'm gonna walk with the people of Peace,
down by the riverside,
And study war no more.

Yes, I'm a'gonna shake hands around the world,
down by the riverside,
down by the riverside,
down by the riverside,
I'm gonna shake hands around the world,
down by the riverside,
And study war no more.

(See accompaniment pattern on page ?

snap back double bass 4/4
Hey, You Never Will Know Me

I be-long to my-self,___ Babe,___ I won't let you set me
I took all of my soft-ness to you,___ Gave you ev-'ry-thing I

free. It___ took time___ but I re- al-ize
had. But___ when you___ got it all

that you nev - er will know me.
Oh, the but - ter it turned bad.

Hey, you nev - er will know me.
Hey, you nev - er will know me.

Sweet - ness___ in my life gone___ sour, I cried___ hour

af - ter___ hour, Soft - ness___ in my heart gone rough,

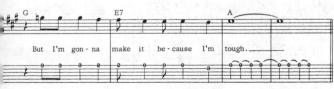

But I'm gon - na make it be - cause I'm tough.

u told me open up your mind,
d you didn't like to play,
en you would twist my every thought,
suit you anyway,
, you never will know me.

 I know that it ain't you my friend,
the way the world must be,
d though I, cannot trust you,
u you also can't trust me,
, you never will know me.

(See accompaniment pattern on page 140.)

dge

fast back beat rock 4/4
We Shall Not Be Moved

We shall not, we shall not be moved. We shall not,

we shall not be moved, Just like a tree that's stand - ing by the

wa - ter, We shall not be moved.

1. Workin' for a new world, etc.

2. With our brothers and our sisters, etc.

3. Black and white together, etc.

4. The Union is behind us, etc.

5. Young and old together, etc.

(See accompaniment pattern on page 99.)

rasgueado tango 4/4
Last Tango On Canal Street

D.C. al ⊕   Fine

(See accompaniment pattern on page 129.)

arpeggiated triplet 3/4
Suliram

Oh little child, small and soft and warm, so warm,
Let me hold and keep you while I may;
Oh how I'll try to spare you from life's fears and pains,
And hope my love may prepare you for dark days.

Life can be giving and life can be cruel, little child,
Some grow to serve, and some grow to rule, little child;
I care not if you follow or take lead,
If love goes with you, you'll never want or need.

(See accompaniment pattern on page 50.)

inflected pattern picking 4/4
Make Me a Pallet

I'd be more than satisfied,
If I could catch that train and ride,
If I reach Atlanta with no place to go,
Make me a pallet on your floor.

Gonna give everybody my regards,
Even if I have to ride the rods,
If I reach Atlanta with no place to go,
Make me a pallet on your floor.

(See accompaniment pattern on page 8)

complex pattern picking 4/4
Hobo's Lullaby

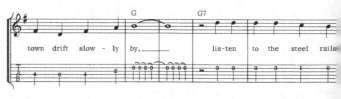

Do not think about tomorrow,
Let tomorrow come and go,
Tonight you have a nice warm boxcar,
Free from all the ice and snow.

I know the police cause you trouble,
They make trouble everywhere,
But when you die and go to heaven,
You won't find no police there.

Sometimes people they seem frightened,
Hobo's rags don't look so fine,
In the morning light lay sleeping,
Empty belly, troubled mind.

(See accompaniment pattern on page 85.)

arpeggiated $\frac{3}{4}$
River of My People

By Pete Seeger

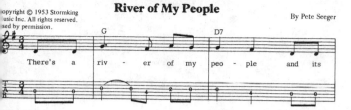

There's a riv-er of my peo-ple and its

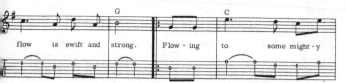

flow is swift and strong. Flow-ing to some might-y

o-cean, though its course is deep and long.

ny rocks and reefs and mountains,
k to bar its stormy way.
t relentlessly this river,
ks its brothers in the sea.
t relentlessly this river,
ks its brothers in the sea.

u will find me in the mainstream,
ering surely through the foam.
beyond the raging waters,
n see our certain home.
beyond the raging waters,
n see our certain home.

For I have mapped this river,
And I know its living force.
And the courage that this gives me,
Will hold me to my course.
And the courage that this gives me,
Will hold me to my course.

Oh, river of my people,
Together we must go.
Hasten onward to that meeting,
Where my brothers wait below.
Hasten onward to that meeting,
Where my brothers wait below.

(See accompaniment pattern on page 22.)

slow $\frac{4}{4}$
Kumbaya

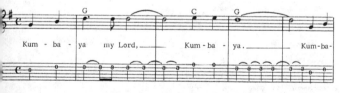

Kum-ba-ya my Lord,— Kum-ba-ya.— Kum-ba-

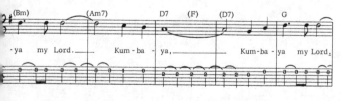

-ya my Lord.— Kum-ba-ya,— Kum-ba-ya my Lord.

Kum-ba-ya.— Oh Lord Kum-ba-ya.—

eone's singing my Lord, Kumbaya—etc.
eone's dancing my Lord, Kumbaya—etc.
eone's dying my Lord, Kumbaya—etc.

eone's living my Lord, Kumbaya—etc.
eone's crying my Lord, Kumbaya—etc.
eone's laughing my Lord, Kumbaya—etc.

(See accompaniment pattern on page 13.)

moving bass pull Spanish $\frac{4}{4}$
Que Bonita Bandera

Chorus:

Que bo-ni-ta ban-der-a, Que bo-ni-ta ban-

-der-a, Que bo-ni-ta ban-de-ra es la ban-

-der-a Puer-to-ri-que-ña. Verse: Az-ul blan-ca y co-lo-

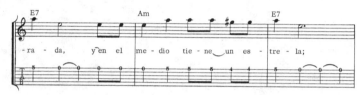

-ra-da, y'en el me-dio tie-ne un es-tre-la;

Bo-ni-ta se-ñor-es es la ban-de-ra Puer-to-ri-que-ña.

Todo bien Puertoriquena,
Es bueno que la defienda,
Bonita senores, es la bandera Puertoriquena.

Bonita senora es,
Que bonita es ella,
Que bonita senores es la bandera, Puertoriquena.

(See accompaniment pattern on page 63.)

snap back slow 4/4
Follow the Drinkin' Gourd

The river ends between two hills,
Follow the drinking gourd,
There's another river on the other side,
If you follow the drinking gourd.

The river bank will make a very good road,
The dead trees show you the way,
Left foot, peg foot, travellin' on,
Follow the drinkin' gourd.

(See accompaniment pattern on page 138.)

rasgueado moving bass pull 4/4
Love Alone

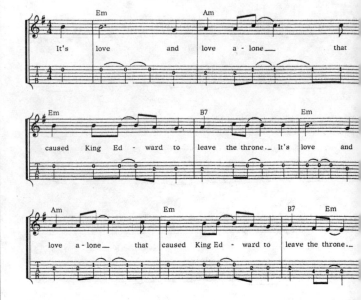

(See accompaniment pattern on page 12

I know King Edward was noble and great,
But it's love what caused him to abdicate.
It's love and love alone,
That caused King Edward to leave the throne.

I know my mama she gonna grieve,
He said, "I cannot help but I am bound to leave."
It's love. . . .

And he got the money and he got the talk,
And the fancy walk just to suit New York.

You can take me throne, you can take me crown,
But leave me Miss Simpson to renown.

Come a reel come a roll upon my mind,
I cannot leave Miss Simpson behind.

If a plane and a ship don't carry me free,
I'll walk with Miss Simpson across the sea.

On the 10th of December you heard the talk,
When he give the throne to the Duke of York.

Then Baldwin want to break down his stand,
He said, "I'm giving up with my government."

Now he's the victim of circumstance,
Now they live in the south of France.

If you see Mrs. Simpson across the street,
You can guarantee she is a busy bee.

Let the organ roll, let the church bell ring,
He said, "Good luck" to our second bachelor King.

moving bass displaced $\frac{4}{4}$
Far Far Away

I've gone far, far a-way, Giv-en up

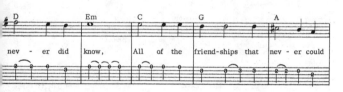

mon-ey and clothes as they say, Left all the peo-ple I

nev-er did know, All of the friend-ships that nev-er could

Chorus:

grow. I think why did I go?

Fine

Was I a-fraid to let them know,

that part of me, so lost and free?

D.C. al Fine

(See accompaniment pattern on page 67.)

a different song,
at to my mind could never sound wrong,
g for the outside from inside of me,
nded so full without harmony.

ning here, one high thought is clear,
things are harder to face when you're near,
aded the strangness of my city home,
new empty strangness, I live all alone.

ome from far far away,
up money and clothes as they say,
with the people I never will know,
with the friendships that never can grow.

---

pinch slow $\frac{4}{4}$
Rose

Rose, Rose, Rose, Rose, will I ev-er see thee wed?

I will mar-ry at thy will, sire, at thy will.

Love, Love, Love, Love,
Love makes all things new again.
Cleanses like the morning dew,
Love lights the way.

(See accompaniment pattern on page 21.)

---

fast $\frac{6}{4}$
Asikatali

A-si-ka-ta-li no-ma-siya bozh', si-zi-mi-se-lin ku-lu-le

ko ub-zu-na kim-twa-lo, u-fu-na ma-do da.

(See accompaniment pattern on page 102.)

Tina bantwan baseh Afrik',
(Basses: Afrika)
Sizimiseli nkululeko.
Tina bantwan baseh Afrik',
(Basses: Afrika)
Sizimiseli nkululeko,
Unzima lomtwalo,
Ufuna madoda.
Unzima lomtwalo,
Ufuna madoda.

Singable English Translation
Oh we don't care if we go to jail,
It is for freedom that we gladly go.
Oh we don't care if we go to jail,
It is for freedom that we gladly go.
A heavy load, a heavy load!
And it will need some real men.
A heavy load, a heavy load!
And it will need some real men.

Come help us sing for a better world,
And as we sing, we will work.   } 2×
For peace on earth, for peace on earth,
And brotherhood for all men.   } 2×

If all the nations could lift their eyes,
And see the pain of their fellow man. } 2×
The world would grow, the world would grow,
And we would rise to a new day.   } 2×

fast bass hard rock $\frac{4}{4}$
Can't Beat That Roach

Can't beat that roach, can't beat that roach,

Old New York roach. Can't beat that roach.

You sprayed it, you raid it, Can't beat that roach.

(See accompaniment pattern on page 107.)

slow syncopated $\frac{4}{4}$
I Know Where I'm Going

I know where I'm go - in' And I know who's goin' with me.

I know who I love, ___ But the dev - il knows who I'll mar - ry.

I know where I'm going and I know who's going with me;
I know who I love, and my dear knows who I'll marry.

Feather beds are soft and painted rooms are bonnie;
But I would trade them all for my handsome winsome
    Johnie.

I have stockings of silk and shoes of bright green leather;
Combs to buckle my hair and a ring for every finger.

(See accompaniment pattern on page

moving bass arpeggiated calypso $\frac{4}{4}$
Sloop John B

Verse:

We came on the Sloop John B., my grand-fa-ther and me,

Round Nas-sau town we_ did roam. Drink-in' all night we got in-

fight, I feel so break - up I wan-ta go home.

Chorus:
So, hoist up the John B sails,
See how the main sail sets,
Send for the Captain ashore, let me go home,
Let me go home, let me go home,
I feel so break up. I want to go home.

The poor cook got the fits,
Threw away all of the grits,
then he took and ate up all of my corn.
Sherrif John Stone,
Please leave me alone,
I feel so breakup, I want to go home.

(See accompaniment pattern on pag

pull folk Chasidic 4/4
Zum Gali Gali

Zum ga-li, ga-li, ga-li, Zum ga-li, ga-li.

Solo:

He - cha - lutz le'-man _____ a - vo - dah, A - vo -

da le' - man _____ he - cha - lutz. He - cha - lutz.

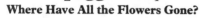

cha-lutz le'man ha-b'tulah;
b'tulah le'man he'cha-lutz.

sha-lom le'man ha'a'min;
a-min le'man ha-sha-lom.

(See accompaniment pattern on page 37.)

percussive bass blues 4/4
Gallows Pole

Hang - man, hang - man, slack your rope, slack it for a while.

Think I see my fa - ther com - in', ___ rid - in' man - y a mile.

Papa, did you bring me silver?	Hangman, . . . etc.
Papa, did you bring me gold?	Think I see my sweetheart comin', . . . etc.
Did you come to see me hangin',	
By the gallows pole?	Honey, did you bring me silver? . . . etc.
Well, I couldn't bring no silver,	I brought you a little silver,
I didn't bring no gold.	Brought you a little gold,
I come to see you hangin',	Didn't come to see you hangin',
By the gallows pole.	By the gallows pole.
Hangman, . . . etc.	
Think I see my mother comin', . . . etc.	
Mother, did you bring me silver? . . . etc.	
Well, I couldn't bring no silver, . . . etc.	

(See accompaniment pattern on page 117.)

arpeggiated 4/4
Where Have All the Flowers Gone?

Where have all the flow - ers gone? Long time pass - ing,

Where have all the flow - ers gone? Long time a - go,

Where have all the flow - ers gone? Young girls picked them

Chorus:

ev - 'ry one, When will they ev - er learn,

When will they ev - er learn. _____

Where have all the young girls gone,
Long time passing.
Where have all the young girls gone,
Long time ago.
Where have all the young girls gone,
Gone for husbands, everyone.

Where have all the husbands gone,
Long time passing.
Where have all the young men gone,
Long time ago.
Where have all these young men gone,
Gone for soldiers everyone.

Where have all the soldiers gone,
Long time passing.
Where have all the soldiers gone,
Long time ago.
Where have all the soldiers gone,
Gone to graveyards, everyone.

Where have all the graveyeards gone,
Long time passing.
Where have all the graveyards gone,
Long time ago.
Where have all the graveyards gone,
Gone to flowers, everyone.

(See accompaniment pattern on page 20.)

Words and Music by Pete Seeger
Copyright 1961 Fall River Music Inc.

moving bass pull (folk) Greek 7/8
Yerakina

Kiepese mesto pigadi,	And she fell into the well,
Kievgale foni megali.	And gave a loud cry.
Kietrekse o kosmos olos,	All the people ran,
Kietreksa kego o kaimenos,	And I, poor soul, also ran.
Yerakhina tha se vgalo,	Yerakina, I will rescue you,
Ke yineka tha se paro,	And take you for my wife.

(See accompaniment pattern on page 64.)

percussive fast 4/4
Joshua

Fine

pull 4/4
He's Got the Whole World

He's got the little bitty baby in His hands, (3x)	He's got you and me sister, in His hands (3x)
He's got the whole world in His hands.	He's got the whole world in His hands.
He's got you and me, brother, in His hands, (3x)	He's got everybody here, in His hands (3x)
He's got the whole world in His hands.	He's got the whole world in His hands.

(See accompaniment pattern on page 11.)

Up to the walls of Jericho,	There's no man like Joshua,
He marched with spear in hand,	No man like Saul.
"Go blow those ram-horns," Joshua cried,	No man like Joshua,
"Cause the battle is in my hands."	At the battle of Jericho.
Then the lamb ram sheephorns began to blow,	
The trumpets began to sound.	
Joshua commanded the children to shout,	
And the walls come a tumbling down.	

(See accompaniment pattern on page 11.)

arpeggiated pull $\frac{4}{4}$
Michael

Mi-chael, row the boat a - shore, Hal - le -
- lu - u-u - ya. Mi-chael, row the boat a -
- shore, Hal - le - lu_____ u-u - ya.

er help to trim the sail, Halleluya. (2×)

lan's River is deep and wide, Halleluya,
t my mother on the other side, Halleluya.

an's River is chilly and cold, Halleluya,
ls the body but not the soul, Halleluya.

hael's boat is a music boat, Halleluya. (2×)

(See accompaniment pattern on page 53.)

rasgueado huapanga $\frac{3}{4}$
Subo

Me voy a los ce - rros al - tos,___ a llo - rar a

so - las, le - jos.___ A - ver si se a

pu - na el do - lor, Su - bo, su - bo.

I'm going to the high mountains,
To cry alone, far away...

Perhaps there I shall be rid of my sorrow,
I climb, I climb...

The flute sadly trills,
And it cries, as it speaks to me of you.

The farms are lost in the distance,
The clouds are very close now.

Me voy a los cerros altos,
a llorar a solas, lejos...

A ver si se apuna el dolor,
Subo, subo...

La quena muy triste tocó
y me habla llorando de vos.

Los ranchos quedaron atrás,
las nubes muy cerca están ya.

(See accompaniment pattern on page 130.)

fast calypso $\frac{4}{4}$
Jamaica Farewell

Verse:

Words and Music by Lord Burgess

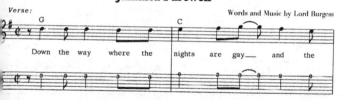

Down the way where the nights are gay___ and the

sun shines dai - ly on the moun-tain top,___ I took a trip on a

sail - ing ship___ and when I reached Ja-mai - ca I made a stop. But I'm

Chorus:

sad to say, I'm on my way;___ Won't be back for

man - y a day.___ My heart is down,___ my head is

turn - ing a-round___ I had to leave a lit - tle girl in King - ston Town.___

Down at the market you can hear,
Ladies cry out while on their heads they bear,
Acki rice, salt fish are nice,
And the rum tastes fine any time of year.

Sounds of laughter everywhere,
As the dancing girls swing to and fro,
I must declare that my heart is there,
Though I've been from Maine to Mexico.

(See accompaniment pattern on page 26.)

slow bass pull $\frac{3}{4}$
The Lass from the Low Country

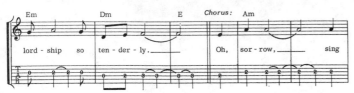

So if you be a lass from the low country,
Don't love of no Lord of high degree.
For they ain't got no heart or sympathy,
Oh, sorrow, sing sorrow, etc.

One day when the snow was on the mead,
He passed her by on a milk-white steed.
She spoke to him low but he paid no heed,
Oh, sorrow, sing sorrow, etc.

(See accompaniment pattern on page 47.)

fast r & b Bo Diddly $\frac{4}{4}$
We Are Crossing Jordan's River

When I get to heaven I'm gonna sit down and I'm gonna
crow, (2x) etc.

We are climbing Jacob's ladder, one by one, one by one,
(2x) etc.

All you sinners get together and follow me, follow me,
(2x) etc.

(See accompaniment pattern on page 103.)

pinch slow $\frac{3}{4}$
Down in the Valley

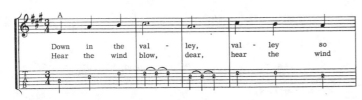

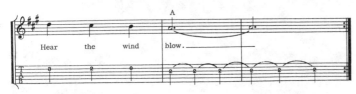

Roses love sunshine, violets love dew,
Angels in heaven, know I love you,
Know I love you dear, know I love you,
Angels in heaven, know I love you.

Build me a castle forty feet high,
So I can see him as he rides by,
As he rides by love, as he rides by,
So I can see him as he rides by.

Write me a letter, send it by mail,
Send it in care of Birmingham jail,
Birmingham jail love, Birmingham jail,
Send it in care of Birmingham jail.

Repeat 1st Verse

(See accompaniment pattern on page 56.)

170

extended complex pattern picking $\frac{4}{4}$
Hard Ain't It Hard

It's hard, ain't it hard, ain't it hard_____ to love one who nev-er did love you_____ It's hard, ain't it hard, ain't it hard, great God, To love one who nev-er will be true._____

(See accompaniment pattern on page 86.)

...e is a place in this old town,
...hat's where my true love lays around.
...e takes other women down on his knee,
...o tell them what he never does tell me.

...go there a drinking and a gambling,
...go there your sorrows for to drown.
...hard likker place is a low-down disgrace,
...e meanest damn' place in this town.

...rst time I saw my true love,
...as standing in the door.
...he last time I saw his false-hearted face,
...as dead on the barroom floor.

rasgueado Spanish $\frac{4}{4}$
Viva La Quince Brigada

Lai lai lai, Lai lai lai, Lai lai lai, Lai___ Lai.

Verse:

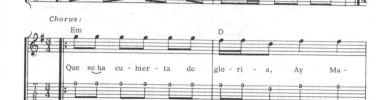

Vi - va la Quin - ce Bri - ga - da Rhum - ba - la rhum - ba rhum - ba - la.

Chorus:

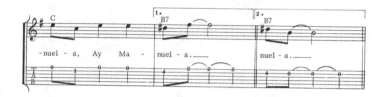

Que se ha cu - bier - ta de glo - ri - a, Ay Ma -nuel - a, Ay Ma - nuel - a. nuel - a.

Verse
Luchamos contra los Morros…(etc.)
Chorus
Mercenarios y fascistas…(etc.)

Verse
Soloex nuestro deseo…(etc.)
Chorus
Acabar con el fascismo…(etc.)

Interlude
Verse
En el frente de Jarama…(etc.)
Chorus
No tenemos ni aviones, ni canones, Ay Manuela. (Repeat)

Verse
Ya salimos de Espana…(etc.)
Chorus
Por Luchar en otras frentes…(etc.)

(See accompaniment pattern on page 126.)

rasgueado Mexican $\frac{3}{4}$
Coplas

Chi - le ver - de me per - dis - te Chi - le ver - de te da - re.

Va - mo - nos pa - ra la huer - ta Que a - lla te lo cor - ta - re.

Chorus:

Ay lai, lai lai, Ay lai, lai lai, Ay lai, lai lai lai, lai lai.

Dicen que los de tu casa,
Ninguno me puede ver,
Diles que no batan l'agua,
Que al cabo lo han de beber.

La mujer que quiere a dos,
Los quiere como hermanitos,
Al uno le pone cuernos,
Y al otro lo pitoncitos.

La mula que yo monte,
La monta hoy mi compadre,
Eso a mi no me importa,
Pues yo la monte primero.

La noche que me casa,
No pude dormirme un rato,
Por estrar toda la noche,
Corriendo detra de un gato.

Me dijiste que fue un gato,
El que entro por tu balcon,
Yo no he visto gato prieto,
Con sombrero y pantalon.

They say your family,
Can't stand to see me,
Tell them not to muddy the water;
In the end they'll have to drink it.

The woman who loves two men,
Loves them like brothers,
She puts big horns on one,
And budding horns on the other.

The mule I used to ride,
Is now ridden by my friend,
I don't care,
Because I broke her in.

The night I got married,
I couldn't sleep all night,
I spent the whole night,
Chasing a black cat.

You said it was a black cat,
That came in through your balcony,
I've never seen a black cat before,
Wearing a hat and trousers.

(See accompaniment pattern on page 125.)

snap back Carter style $\frac{4}{4}$
Darling Corey

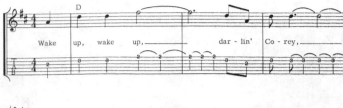

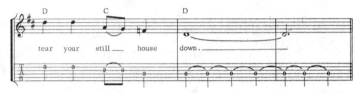

The first time I saw darlin' Corey,	Go 'way from me darlin' Corey,
She was standin' on the banks of the sea,	Quit hangin' around my bed,
She had two pistols strapped around her body,	Pretty women run me distracted,
And a banjo on her knee.	Corn liquor's killed me dead.
The last time I saw darlin' Corey,	Go and dig me a hole in the meadow,
She had a drawn glass in her hand,	Dig a hole in the cold, cold ground,
She was drinkin' away her troubles,	Go and dig me a hole in the meadow,
With a low-down sorry man.	Just to lay darlin' Corey down.

(See accompaniment pattern on page 133.)

inverted pattern picking $\frac{3}{4}$
Un Canadien Errant

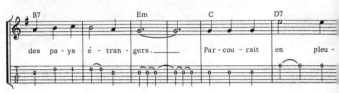

Un jour triste et pensif,	Once a Canadian man,
Assis au bord des flots, (2×)	Was banished from his own home,
Au courant fugitif,	With long lonely years ahead,
Il adressa ces moto. (2×)	To a traveling friend he once said.
Si tu voir mon pays,	If by some chance you should see,
Mon pays malheureux, (2×)	My poor unhappy land,
Va, dis a mes amis,	Tell my friends for me,
Que je me souviens d'eux. (2×)	I miss and remember them.

(See accompaniment pattern on page 80.)

accented pinch blues triplet $\frac{4}{4}$
Come Back Baby

I love you baby, tell the world I do,
I don't love nobody else but you, etc.

Long long train, mean engineer,
Took my baby left me standin' here, etc.

If I could holler like a mountain jack,
I'd climb this mountain, call my baby back, etc.

(See accompaniment pattern on page 75.)

Erev Shel Shoshanim

By Moshe Dor and J. Hadar

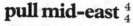

Er-ev shel sho-sha-nim, ne-tze-na el ha-bu-stan.

Mor be-sa-mim u-le-va-nah, Le-ra-gleich mif-tan.

Lay-la yo-red le-at-veh ru-ach sho-shan nosh vah.

Ha-va el-chash-lach shir ba-lat, Ze-mer shel a-ha-vah.

...hacha oma yona,
...oshech malay t'laleem.
...eech el ha boker shoshannah,
...ck te feh nu lee.

(See accompaniment pattern on page 35.)

slow $\frac{3}{4}$

Scarborough Fair

Are you go-in' to Scar-bor-ough Fair? Pars-ley,

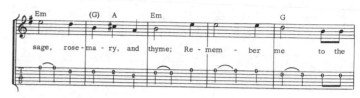

sage, rose-ma-ry, and thyme; Re-mem-ber me to the

one who lives there,___ She once was a true love of mine.

Tell her to make me a cambric shirt,
Parsley, sage, rosemary and thyme;
Without any seam or fine needlework,
And then she'll be a true love of mine.

Tell her to wash it in yonder dry well,
Parsley, sage, rosemary and thyme;
Where water he'er sprung, nor drop of rain fell,
And then she'll be a true love of mine.

Tell her to dry it on yonder thorn,
Parsley, sage, rosemary and thyme;
Which never bore blossom since Adam was born,
And then she'll be a true love of mine.

Oh, will you find me an acre of land,
Parsley, sage, rosemary and thyme;
Between the sea foam and the sea sand,
Or never be a true lover of mine.

Oh, will you plough it with a lamb's horn,
Parsley, sage, rosemary and thyme;
And sow it all over with one peppercorn,
Or never be a true lover of mine.

Oh, will you reap it with a sickle of leather,
Parsley, sage, rosemary and thyme;
And tie it all up with a peacock's feather,
Or never be a true lover of mine.

And when you have done and finished your work,
Parsley, sage, rosemary and thyme;
Then come to me for your cambric shirt,
And you shall be a true love of mine.

(See accompaniment pattern on page 14.)

accented pinch bossa nova $\frac{4}{4}$

Night Boat

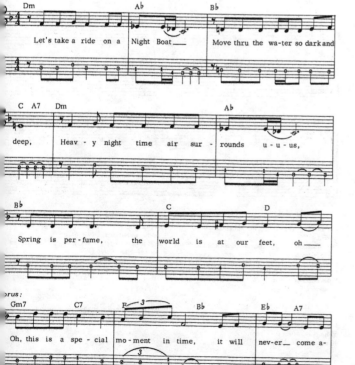

Let's take a ride on a Night Boat.___ Move thru the wa-ter so dark and

deep, Heav-y night time air sur-rounds u-u-us,

Spring is per-fume, the world is at our feet, oh___

...rus:

Oh, this is a spe-cial mo-ment in time, it will nev-er___ come a-

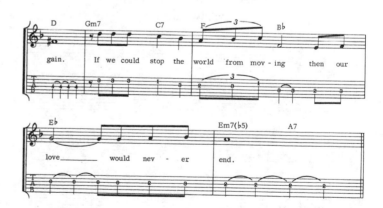

gain. If we could stop the world from mov-ing then our

love___ would nev-er end.

I feel your breath in the night time,
I want to hold you, touch you lips;
My mind is spinning, senses growing inside,
Our knees are touching as we sit, in the dark, feeling

Night boats are a place for lovers like us,
Your touch can make my mouth run dry;
I look at you and want to know you inside,
You look at me and want to cry, so do I, because

(See accompaniment pattern on page 77.)

pinch extended slow 4/4
Man of Constant Sorrow

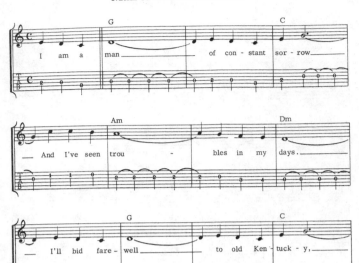

I am a man of con-stant sor-row

And I've seen trou-bles in my days.

I'll bid fare-well to old Ken-tuck-y,

The state where I was born and raised.

For six long years I've been in trouble,
No pleasure here on earth I found;
For in this world I'm bound to ramble,
I have no friends to help me now.

It's fare you well, my own true lover,
I never expect to see you again;
For I'm bound to ride that northern railroad,
Perhaps I'll die upon this train.

You may bury me in some deep valley,
For many years where I may lay;
Then you may learn to love another
While I am sleeping in my grave.

Maybe your friends think I'm just a stranger,
My face you never will see no more;
But there is one promise that is given,
I'll meet you on God's golden shore.

(See accompaniment pattern on page 23.)

fast folk 4/4
Everybody Loves Saturday Night

Ev-'ry-bod-y loves Sat-ur-day night,

Ev-'ry-bod-y loves Sat-ur-day night,

Ev-'ry-bod-y, ev-'ry-bod-y, ev-'ry-bod-y, ev-'ry-bod-y,

Ev-'ry-bod-y loves Sat-ur-day night.

Japanese: Da re demo do yo bi gasuki.
Czech: Kazhdi ma rad sabotu vietcher.
Hebrew: Kulam Ohavim Motzeh Shabat.
Spanish: A todos les gusta la noche del sabado.

Nigerian: Bobo waro fero Sato deh.
French: Tout le monde aime Samedi soir.
Yiddish: Yeder eyne hot lieb Shabas ba nacht.
Chinese: Ren ren si huan li pai lu.
Russian: Vsiem nravitsa subbota vietcheram.

(See accompaniment pattern on page 28.)

pinch slow bass 4/4
Two Brothers

By Irving Gordon

Two broth-ers on their way, two broth-ers on their way,

two broth-ers on their way. One wore blue and one wore grey,

One wore blue and one wore grey as they marched a-

-long their way. The fife and drum be-

-gan to play all on a beau-ti-ful morn-ing.

One was gentle, one was kind, one was gentle, one was kind.
One came home, one stayed behind, a cannon ball don't pay no mind.
A cannon ball don't pay no mind, if you're gentle or if you're kind,
It don't think of the folks behind, all on a beautiful morning.

Two girls waiting by the railroad track, two girls waiting by the railroad track,
Two girls waiting by the railroad track, one wore blue and one wore black.
One wore blue and one wore black, waiting by the railroad track,
For their darlins to come back, all on a beautiful morning.

(See accompaniment pattern on page 57.)

slow bass note $\frac{3}{4}$
Greensleeves

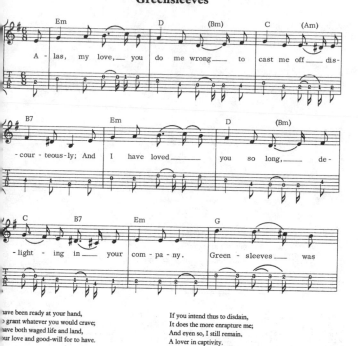

have been ready at your hand,
grant whatever you would crave;
have both waged life and land,
our love and good-will for to have.

If you intend thus to disdain,
It does the more enrapture me;
And even so, I still remain,
A lover in captivity.

My men were clothed all in green,
And they did ever wait on thee;
All this was gallant to be seen;
And yet thou wouldst not love me.

Thou couldst desire no earthly thing,
But still thou hadst it readily;
Thy music still to play and sing,
And yet thou wouldst not love me.

(See accompaniment pattern on page 45.)

fast bass rock $\frac{4}{4}$
Woke Up This Mornin'

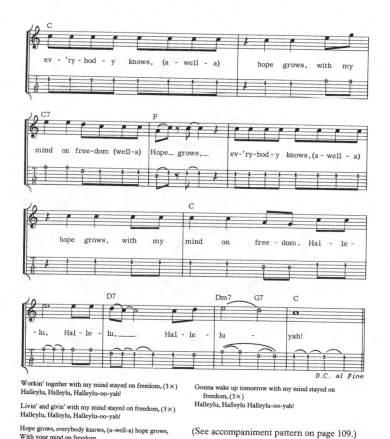

D.C. al Fine

Workin' together with my mind stayed on freedom, (3×)
Halleylu, Halleylu, Halleylu-oo-yah!

Livin' and givin' with my mind stayed on freedom, (3×)
Halleylu, Halleylu, Halleylu-oo-yah!

Hope grows, everybody knows, (a-well-a) hope grows,
With your mind on freedom,
Hope grows, everybody knows, (a-well-a) hope grows,
With your mind on freedom,
Halleylu, Halleylu, Halley-loo-oo yah!

Can't be afraid to keep your mind stayed on freedom, (3×)
Halleylu, Halleylu, Halleylu-oo-yah!

Gonna wake up tomorrow with my mind stayed on
freedom, (3×)
Halleylu, Halleylu Halleylu-oo-yah!

(See accompaniment pattern on page 109.)

accented bass note rock $\frac{4}{4}$
Easy Rider

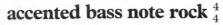

If you catch me stealing please don't tell on me, (2×)
I'm stealing back to my old times used to be.

If I was a catfish swimming in the deep blue sea, (2×)
I would set all you women diving after me.

(See accompaniment pattern on page 73.)

slow bass note $\frac{4}{4}$
The Cruel War

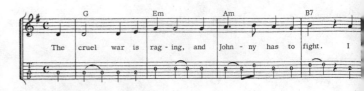

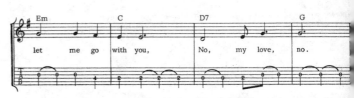

Tomorrow is Sunday and Monday is the day,
That your captain will call you and you must obey;
Your captain will call you it grieves my heart so,
Won't you let me go with you?—no, my love, no.

Your waist is too slender, your fingers are too small,
Your cheeks are too rosy to face the cannon ball;
Your cheeks are too rosy, it grieves my heart so,
Won't you let me go with you?—no, my love, no.

I'll tie back my hair, men's clothing I'll put on,
I'll pass as your comrade as we march along;
I'll pass as your comrade, no one will ever know,
Won't you let me go with you?—no, my love, no.

Johnny, oh Johnny, I think you are unkind,
I love you far better than all of mankind;
I love you far better than words can e'er express,
Won't you let me go with you?—yes, my love, yes.

(See accompaniment pattern on page 16.)

snap back Nashville style $\frac{4}{4}$
Banks of the Ohio

Chorus
Then only say that you'll be mine,
In no other arms entwined;
Down beside where the waters flow,
On the banks of the Ohio.

Verses
I asked your mother for you, dear,
And she said you were too young;
Only say that you'll be mine,
Happiness in my home you'll find.

I held a knife against her breast,
And gently in my arms she pressed;
Crying: Willie, oh Willie, don't murder me,
For I'm unprepared for eternity.

I took her by her lily white hand,
Led her down where the waters stand;
I picked her up and I pitched her in,
Watched her as she floated down.

I started back home twixt twelve and one,
Crying, My God, what have I done?
I've murdered the only woman I love,
Because she would not be my bride.

(See accompaniment pattern on page 137.)

fast $\frac{4}{4}$
Sinner Man

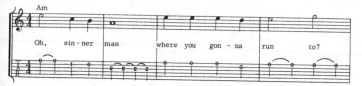

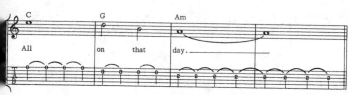

Run to the rock,
The rock was a-melting, (3x)
All on that day.

Run to the sea,
The sea was a-boiling, (3x)
All on that day.

Run to the Lord,
Lord won't you hide me? (3x)
All on that day.

Run to the Devil,
Devil was a-waiting, (3x)
All on that day.

Oh sinner man,
You oughta been a-praying, (3x)
All on that day.

(See accompaniment pattern on page 15.)

arpeggiated bass $\frac{4}{4}$
They Looked a Lot Like We

Woman:

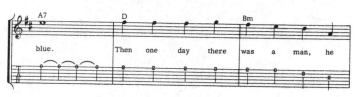

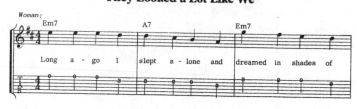

Woman:
I met him in Van Cortlandt Park,
His eyes were light and soft,
He seemed to sense my emptiness,
He took me to his loft, we both went to his loft.

We got there late, I made some tea,
I looked around and saw,
An old guitar, some home made chairs,
A mural on the door. His mattress on the floor.

Man:
Long ago my days were cold,
And sadness was not new,
Then one day there was a girl,
She looked a lot like you. She looked a lot like you.

I heard her singing in the park,
Her voice was sad and soft,
I spoke to her of dreams in blue,
We both went to my loft. We both went to my loft.

She brewed some tea, I changed the sheets,
It was a chilly day,
When we made love I felt so good,
I almost ran away, I was afraid to stay.

Woman:
And here we are together still,
I hope that you can see,
There was a girl whose life he changed,
You looked a lot like he, I looked a lot like she, they
    looked a lot like We.

(See accompaniment pattern on page 52.)

moving bass slow $\frac{4}{4}$
Delia

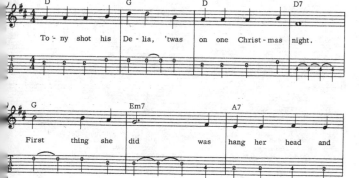

Delia, oh Delia,
Where you been so long?
Everybody's talkin' about
Poor Delia's dead and gone.

Sent for the doctor,
The doctor come too late,
Sent for the minister
To lay out Delia straight.

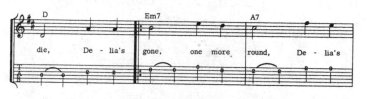

(See accompaniment pattern on page 66.)

rasgueado percussive rock $\frac{4}{4}$
Will the Circle Be Unbroken

I was stand-ing by the win-dow on one cold and cloud-y

day; and I saw the hearse come roll-ing for to

Chorus:

car-ry my ma-ma a-way. Will the cir-cle be un-

-bro-ken by-and-by, oh, by-and-by. There's a

bet-ter home a-wait-ing in the sky, oh,— in the sky.

Traditional

So I told the undertaker,
Undertaker please drive slow,
For this body you are hauling,
Well, I hate to see her go.

I followed close behind her,
tried to hold up and be brave,
But I could not hide my sorrow,
When they laid her in the grave.

Went back home and,
My home was lonesome,
Since my mother, she was gone,
All my brothers, sisters crying,
What a home so sad and lone.

(See accompaniment pattern on page 128.)

arpeggiated double bass triplet $\frac{4}{4}$
Every Night When the Sun Goes Down

Ev-'ry night when the sun goes in,
True love don't weep — true love don't mourn,—

— True love don't weep, when the sun goes in,
— Ev-'ry night true love don't mourn,—

— Ev-'ry night when the sun goes in
— True love don't weep or mourn for me,

I hang down my head and mourn-ful cry.
I'm go-ing a-way to Mar-ble town.

I wish to the Lord that train would come, (3×)
To take me back to where I come from.

It's once my apron hung down low, (3×)
He'd follow me through sleet and snow.

It's now my apron's to my chin, (3×)
He'll face my door and won't come in.

I wish to the Lord my babe was born,
A-sitting upon his papa's knee,
And me, poor girl, was dead and gone,
And the green grass growing over me.

(See accompaniment pattern on page 51.)

pinch blues triplet $\frac{4}{4}$
Sportin' Life

Well, I'm tired of run-nin' 'round, Think I will

mar-ry — and set-tle down. This old night life, this old

sport-in' life is kill-in' me.—

Got a letter from my home,
All of my friends are dead and gone,
This old night life, this old sportin' life is killin' me.

My mother used to say to me,
So young and foolish that I can't see,
Hey Son. Hey there Son why don't you change your ways.

I been a liar and a cheater too,
Spent all my money on booze and you,
This old night life, this old sportin' life is killin' me.

My mother used to say to me,
So young and foolish that I can't see,
Ain't got no mother, my sister and brother don't talk to me.

(See accompaniment pattern on page 58.)

178

snap back bluegrass style $\frac{4}{4}$
Wildwood Flower

he promised to love me,
promised to love,
cherish me always,
others above.
woke from my dream,
d my idol was clay,
y passion for loving,
d vanished away.

he taught me to love him,
called me his flower,
lossom to cheer him,
rough life's weary hour.
now he has gone,
d left me alone,
e wild flowers to weep,
d the wild birds to moan.

I'll dance and I'll sing,
And my life shall be gay,
I'll charm every heart,
In the crowd I survey.
Though my heart now is breaking,
He never shall know,
How his name makes me tremble,
My pale cheeks to glow.

I'll dance and I'll sing,
And my heart will be gay,
I'll banish this weeping,
Drive troubles away.
I'll live yet to see him,
Regret this dark hour,
When he won and neglected,
This frail wildwood flower.

(See accompaniment pattern on page 135.)

rasgueado rock $\frac{4}{4}$
Come and Go With Me To That Land

There ain't no moanin' in that land....
There ain't no bowin' in that land....
There ain't no kneelin' in that land....
There ain't no Jim Crow in that land....
There'll be singin' in that land....
There'll be lovin' in that land....
There'll be laughin' in that land....

(See accompaniment pattern on page 127.)

snap back folk $\frac{4}{4}$
This Little Light

I've got the light of Freedom—etc.

All over the people of Peace—etc.

All over the whole wide world—etc.

(See accompaniment pattern on page 139.)

snap back Carter style 3/4
Who's Gonna Shoe Your Pretty Little Foot

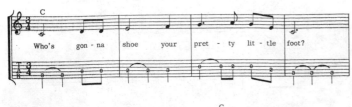

Who's gonna be your man?
Who's gonna be your man?
Who's gonna kiss your red ruby lips?
Who's gonna be your man?

Papa's gonna shoe my pretty little foot,
Mama's gonna glove my hand.
Sister's gonna kiss my red ruby lips,
I don't need no man.
I don't need no man,
I don't need no man,
Sister's gonna kiss my red ruby lips,
I don't need no man.

The longest train I ever did see
Was a hundred coaches long.
The only woman I ever did love
Was on that train and gone.
Was on that train and gone,
Was on that train and gone,
The only woman I ever did love
Was on that train and gone.

(See accompaniment pattern on page 134.)

moving bass pinch 4/4
The Water Is Wide

(See accompaniment pattern on page 69.)

A ship there is and she sails the sea,
She's loaded deep as deep can be.
But not so deep as the love I'm in,
And I know not how I sink or swim.

I leaned my back up against some young oak,
Thinking he was a trusty tree.
But first he bended, and then he broke,
And thus did my false love to me.

I put my hand into some soft bush,
Thinking the sweetest flower to find.
I pricked my finger to the bone,
And left the sweetest flower alone.

Oh, love is handsome and love is fine,
Gay as a jewel when first it is new.
But love grows old, and waxes cold,
And fades away like summer dew.

snap back Country style 4/4
Silver Dagger

All men are false, says my mother,
They'll tell you wicked, lovely lies,
And the very next evening, court another,
Leaving you alone to pine and sigh.

My father is a handsome devil,
He's got a chain that's five miles long,
And every link a heart does dangle,
Of some poor maid he's loved and wronged.

Wish that I was some little sparrow,
Yes, one of those that flies so high,
I'd fly away to my false true lover,
And when he'd speak I would deny.

On his breast, I'd light and flutter,
With my little tender wings,
I'd ask him who he meant to flatter,
Or who he meant to deceive.

Go court some other tender lady,
And I hope that she will be your wife,
'Cause I've been warned and I've decided,
To sleep alone all of my life.

(See accompaniment pattern on page 136.)

moving bass inverted pinch $\frac{4}{4}$

Could You Ever

Could you ev-er cry, ___ could you ev-er feel, Have you al-ways tread-ed

just out-side what's real-ly real? Is your laugh so dry ___ that you feel no pain,

Are you al-ways smart e-nough to spot the cloud with rain? ___

Chorus:

Are you strange-ly strong and ver-y deep in-side or is it

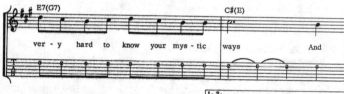

numb-ness and a fear of love your wall has grown to hide? It's

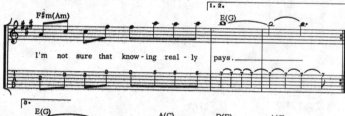

ver-y hard to know your mys-tic ways   And

I'm not sure that know-ing real-ly pays.

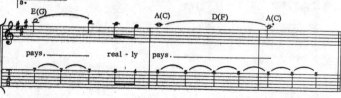

pays, ___   real-ly pays.

Could you always hide,
What was on your mind?
Did you always have a clever line to hide behind?
Did you ever care,
Did you ever give,
Did you ever think that there's a fuller way to live?

Could you always know,
When love came too near?
Did you always deal the same way with your private fear?
Will you open up,
Shall I try once more?
Please don't close off life as you have always done before.

(See accompaniment pattern on page 65.)

Chords

Every key has 3 basic chords with which you can play thousands of songs. The following 7 keys use chords that can all be played in the first 3 frets! You can use these chord groupings to figure out songs, and for practicing new accompaniment patterns.

Here's the information you'll need to decipher the chord diagrams in this, and most other books.

1. The vertical lines represent the 6 strings. Number 1 (far right) represents the highest pitched string.
2. The horizontal lines mark off the frets.
3. The large numbered circles indicate where the strings should be fretted (pressed).
4. The white numbers inside the circles show which left hand fingers should fret the indicated string.
5. The wiggly vertical line indicates the Root Bass String of the chord (The string from which the chord should be played).
6. An **X** over a string means that the string should not be sounded at all, or that it should be muffled.

So, in order to play the G chord of this diagram, you would
- a. Press (fret) your first finger on the 5th string, 2nd fret
- b. Press your second finger on the 6th string, 3rd fret, and
- c. Press your third finger on the 1st string, 3rd fret.
  then
  You'd play the chord from the 6th string, sounding all strings.

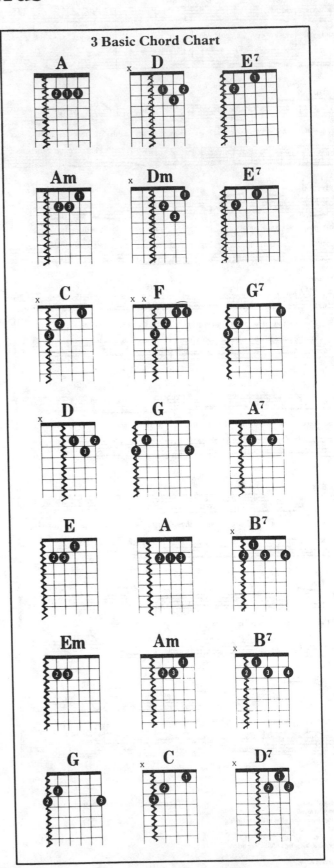

182

Bar Chords

The term *bar chord* (from the French, barré), means to cover two or more strings with one finger. Usually, for a *full bar chord*, 5 or 6 strings are covered by one finger (often the index), as the remaining fingers fret any additional notes needed. For a Half Bar Chord, two to four strings are covered by one finger, as the remaining fingers fret additional notes. And sometimes the term "Bar Chord" simply describes any movable chord form (i.e. a C⁷ chord).

The *bar chords* here are listed in 2 groups. *First form bar chords*, with their root on the 6th string, and *second form bar chords* with their Root on the 5th string.

A. First Form Bar Chords: The name of the note you fret on *the 6th string gives you the chord name* for first form chords. For example, when you bar a first form major chord in the first fret, your covered (fretted) 6th string becomes an F note, therefore, your chord is an F chord. If you move the same fingering up to the 3rd fret, your covered 6th string becomes G, and therefore your chord is G. This principle applies to the minor chord, and the dominant 7th fingerings as well.

B. Second Form Bar Chords: Similarly, for this form, the name of the note you fret on the *5th string tells you the name of the chord.* When you play a Second Form *minor* chord in the 1st fret, your 5th string is A♯ (or B♭) so, the name of your chord is A♯ (or B♭m). Moving that fingering to the 3rd fret, the 5th string covered is C so the chord will be Cm; in the 5th fret Dm, etc.

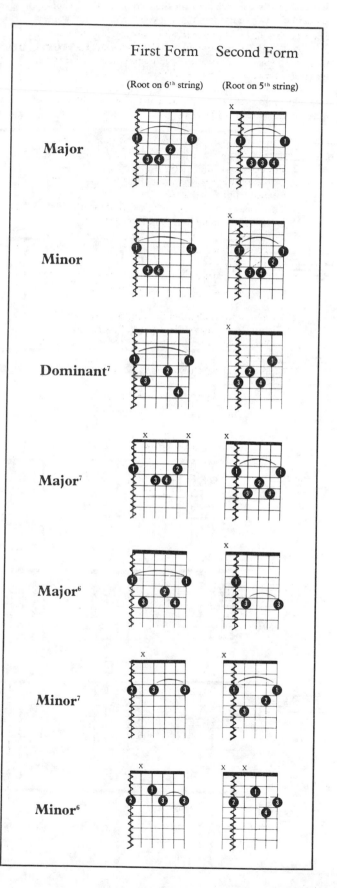

	First Form	Second Form
	(Root on 6ᵗʰ string)	(Root on 5ᵗʰ string)
Major		
Minor		
Dominant⁷		
Major⁷		
Major⁶		
Minor⁷		
Minor⁶		

The Master Chord Chart includes the 3 Basic Chords from each major and relative minor key. Also included are 6 supplementary chords, which add some really interesting and unconventional chords to your repetoire. These provide unusual but very useful colors that can greatly enhance your music. Certain of these chords can give even the most commonplace song a fairly hip sound. If the standard chords you use aren't giving you the sound you want, you're bound to find that sound somewhere in here.

Master Chord Chart

3 Basic Chords • Major   3 Basic Chords • Relative Minor

Supplementary Chords

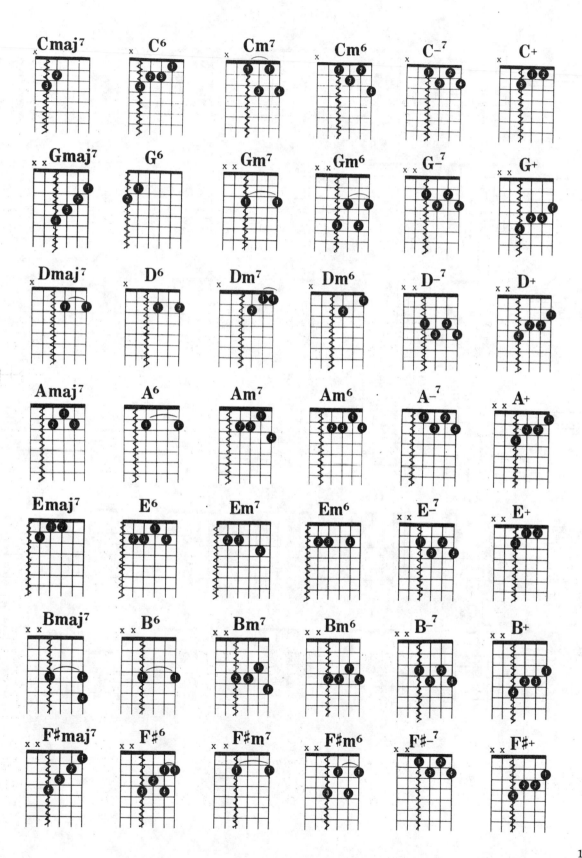

Master Chord Chart

3 Basic Chords • Major

3 Basic Chords • Relative Minor

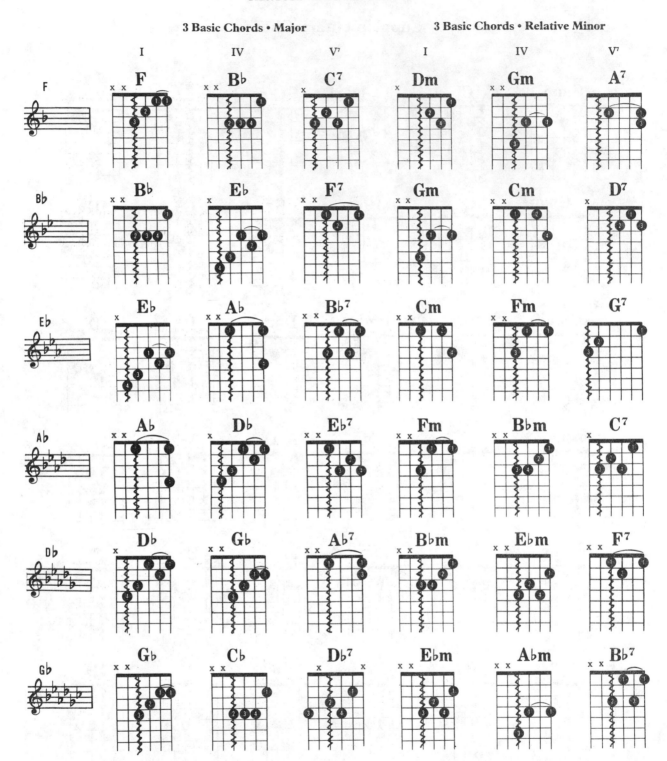

Supplementary Chords

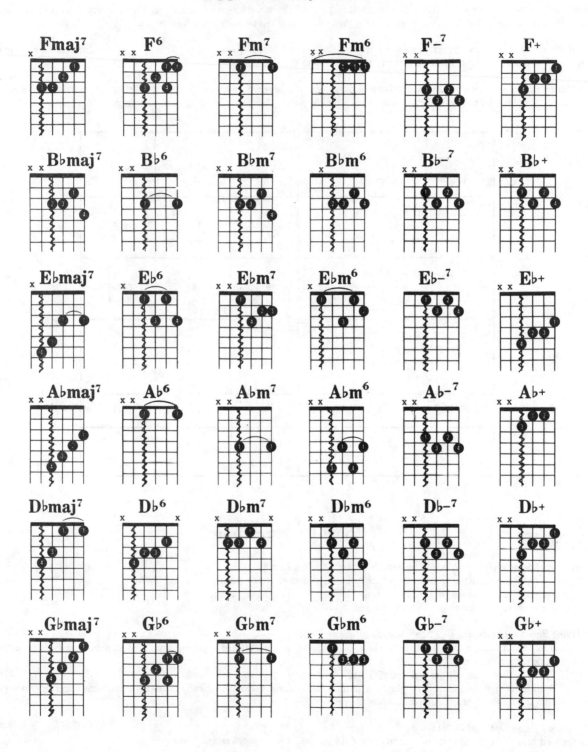

Now that you have a good idea of all the chord possibilities, we'll take you back a bit, and fill you in on how you can vary your chords still further. Until now, you have been playing your chords from their *root bass string*, but now for the "seasoning" to flavor your style: *alternating bass strings.*

Alternate Bass Strings

When you're first learning the 3 Basic chords chart, play them all from their *root bass strings*. Then, as you learn different *accompaniment patterns,* you'll find that by changing *bass strings,* your sound can be made more interesting.

As will be noted, certain pattern groupings require specific *bass* and *alternate bass strings*. This book uses 6 different *bass string* categories. Within these groupings there are Alternate sub-groupings provided.

What follows is a summary of all the *bass string* groupings. Specific information concerning pattern groupings and their recommended Bass String groupings are presented throughout the book in the *pattern key* page preceding each pattern grouping.

	A-B-C 5	D-F 4	E-G 6
1. Root Bass Strings			

2. Standard Alternates
  a. Primary*
  b. Supplementary*
	5-4
	5-6
		4-5
		4-5
			6-5
			6-4

3. Moving Bass Alternates
  a. Primary
  b. Supplementary**
	5-4-4
	5-4-6
		4-5-5
		4-6-5
			6-5-5
			6-5-4

4. Pattern Picking Alternates
  a. Primary
  b. Supplementary
  c. Optional***
	5-3
	5-4
	5-3-4-3
		4-3
		4-3
		4-3-5-3
			6-3
			6-4
			6-3-5-3

5. Full Pattern Picking Alternates	5-4	4-5	6-4
6. Hammering Alternates	5-4	4-3	6-5

Chart Clarifications

Primary and Supplementary Bass Strings require certain fingering alterations:
1. For the B chord, move your 2nd finger across to the 2nd fret on the 6th string.
2. For the C chord, move your 3rd finger across to the 3rd fret, on the 6th string.
3. For F chord, you move your 3rd finger across to the 3rd fret on the 5th string.

**Moving Bass Supplementary Bass Strings* require these alterations:
1. Both B and C type chords utilize the same 6 string bass as the standard supplementary bass strings. The F chord however, must be played as a bar F.
2. The D or D⁷ chords require that you play an F on the bass string with the thumb.
3. D minor cannot comfortably be played with these bass strings without drastically changing its present fingering. So we must exempt it and when the occasion arises, play the *primary bass strings.*

***Pattern Picking Optional Bass Line*
The F chord bass string changes strings exactly as it did with the *standard supplementary bass strings.*

Alternate Bass Strings for "Bar" Chords
All bar chords with their *root note* on the 6th string will follow all rules applicable to an E chord. All *bar* chords with their *root note* on the 5th string will follow the rules applicable to an A chord.

This has been a fairly broad introduction to chords. The rest is up to you.

Appendix
Special Techniques

The common approaches to plucking the strings that we refer to occasionally, are the *rest stroke* and the *free stroke*.

1. Finger-Strokes:

Free Stroke: The fingers curl and lift up. They don't touch any other strings. This stroke gives a medium to light sound. It's the finger motion most frequently used. The lower finger tip and underside of its nail are the parts of the finger that touch the string to pluck it.

Rest-Stroke: As the name implies, the finger presses onto the string and then *rests* on the adjacent string. The fingers *do not* curl, but are held straight out from the second joint, as they play. The inner finger pad and underside of its nail are used to sound a string. This is a supported stroke, so you have more leverage and can provide greater volume. It's often used to bring out a melody.

2. Thumb Strokes:

Free Stroke: The thumb moves in a circular motion, first moving down to pluck the string and then up and around, back towards the starting position. Here, you circle your thumb around and *away* from the guitar.

Rest Stroke: The thumb strikes the string and continues its downward sweep until it rests ("lands") on the next highest sounding string. As with the *fingers rest-stroke*, this is a firm, strong stroke for bringing out a melody or bass line.

Now that you've undoubtedly mastered at least 90 or 95 of the strums, if you still have any energy left, you might like to dress up your accompaniment with some "special techniques." The techniques covered in this chapter can be used in conjunction with most of the patterns you've just learned.

A. THE HAMMER-ON: The *hammer-on* is an ascending slur that abruptly raises the pitch of a single tone or chord. As the pitch is raised, you can hear the original tone scoop up to the new tone. Only the first of the 2 tones heard is actually sounded by the right hand.

Most notes are played by fretting a note (tone) and *then* playing the string. But with *hammering,* You reverse the procedure. First you play the open string, and *then* fret the tone. Or you can play a fretted string, and then hammer down with your 2$^{nd.}$ 3$^{rd.}$ or 4th finger, onto an adjacent higher fret.

The *hammer-on* is indicated in music notation or tablature with the curved slur line ⌒ , connecting two different notes. The second note of the two, will be the one hammered-on.

B. THE PULL-OFF: The *pull-off* is a descending slur, which is the reverse of the *hammer-on.* Instead of raising the pitch of a chord or tone, the *pull-off* causes a tone to be abruptly lowered.

After sounding a fretted (pressed) string, *forcefully* pull your left hand finger down and off the string. This will cause it to sound a second time, but with a twangy quality.

The *pull-off* is indicated in music with a curved, slur line that connects 2 notes (see example). The second note of the two is the one that is pulled off the string. You'll know the difference between the *hammer-on* and the *pull-off* by the direction of the notes: In a *pull-off* the note goes down, in a *hammer-on,* it goes up.

C. BENDING: As with *hammering, bending* a note causes an ascending slur. But this technique causes a gradual raise in pitch, rather than the abrupt jump of the *hammer-on.* Another difference is that in *bending,* you start with a fretted string and you press that string against the fretboard, pushing it either up or down, to obtain the whining effect.

The further you push or pull that fretted string, the more exaggerated the change in its pitch will be. This can also be done with a fretted chord. Be careful not to release the strings after you've pushed or pulled them. . . . just let the finger return with the string to the original note position.

D. DAMPING: This technique involves stopping a string or strings from vibrating once they have been sounded. This creates a percussive or drum-like quality. Here are two methods of effecting this quality.

1. Right-Hand Damping: Place the palm of your right hand over the ringing strings after the chord has been sounded. This type of damping characterizes all the *percussive accompaniment patterns* in this book, and are discussed in detail in the "Key to Percussive Patterns," page 112.

To use this method with *pattern-picking* (for a Nashville sound), place the right hand palm on the guitar bridge. The fleshy part of the palm should muffle the 3 bass strings, permitting the treble strings to ring out clearly. It can create the feeling of two instruments playing.

2. Left-Hand Damping: As you fret a bar chord, play it as usual, and then release the pressure of the fretting hand on the strings. The chord will stop ringing abruptly.

E. THE SLIDE: The slide, as might be expected, utilizes a sliding motion on a single string or a group of strings. The slide will raise or lower the pitch of the original note (or chord), depending on which direction the fretting fingers travel. As with the hammer-on and pull-off, only the first tone (or tones) is actually played by the right hand. The *slide* should make the transition from one tone to the next very gently. It's usually produced, by sliding your finger over the frets along the same string from the starting note to the next desired note. In standard notation a *slide* usually is indicated by a slur marking a small curved line which bears a striking resemblence to a tie. As a matter of fact, the resemblence is so striking, that the only way you can tell them apart is that a "slur" marking *connects* two different notes, while a tie connects two of the same notes.

ascending   descending

F. THE VIBRATO: This technique enables the guitarist to sustain a note beyond its normal duration and to give it a quivering vibrating intensity.

a. The *classical vibrato* is produced by fretting a tone and moving your finger from side to side as you press the string against the fingerboard.

b. The *rock vibrato* is produced by fretting a tone and moving your finger up and down as you press the string against the fingerboard.

BASS RUNS:

The technique of using bass runs together with *accompaniment patterns* can add great variety and interest to your style.

Bass runs are short single-note passages played on the bass strings. They're used to link one chord to another. Generally, they fall into two categories:

1. *Diatonic runs*—these are passages that use notes from a major or a minor scale. They are usually used to link two chords that are three or four steps apart.

2. *Chromatic runs*—are those passages that use every note in the path of one chord to another. They proceed in half steps and are used to bridge 2 chords with a small distance between them.

Try the runs in this chart with a Pull $\frac{4}{4}$ pattern first. Each bass run will take the place of one *accompaniment pattern* with two beats. Use three pattern units and one run for each chord. When you're comfortable, begin alternating your bass strings. When you're really feeling good, try these runs using some of the *snap-back* patterns.

The following charts, illustrate the *runs* linking the 3 basic chords in 7 keys.

1. The first chart (A) gives only *diatonic runs*. They are used to connect the 3 basic chords when you return to the "I" chord after each new chord you play.

2. The second chart (B) gives both *diatonic* and *chromatic* runs. They are used to connect the 3 basic chords when played consecutively.

The arrow underneath the "run" indicates the direction in which your *bass notes* are moving.

For some chords, special *bass notes* are given because the character of the run dictates that; the bass notes move into these new areas. They appear in a rectangle above the chord.

The string number is listed next to the note name. In other words, G³ means that the first bass note G is played on the 3ʳᵈ string (open).

Connecting Bass Runs

191

Parts of the Guitar
A. The Acoustic Guitar

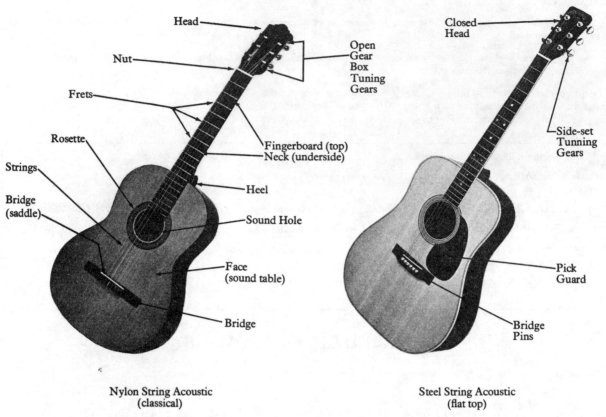

Head

Nut

Frets

Rosette

Strings

Bridge
(saddle)

Open
Gear
Box
Tuning
Gears

Fingerboard (top)
Neck (underside)

Heel

Sound Hole

Face
(sound table)

Bridge

Closed
Head

Side-set
Tunning
Gears

Pick
Guard

Bridge
Pins

Nylon String Acoustic
(classical)

Steel String Acoustic
(flat top)

All the major parts of an acoustic guitar have been noted in the illustration of the classical model on the left. The steel string guitar has many different features, but only the clearly visible feature differences have been pointed out.

B. The Solid Body Electric Guitar

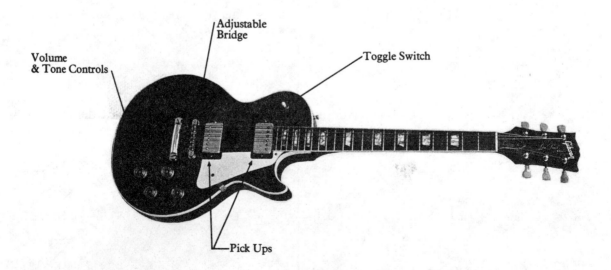

Adjustable
Bridge

Toggle Switch

Volume
& Tone Controls

Pick Ups

The electric guitar is obviously, quite different from any acoustic guitar. Although again, we've only noted the features that are not found on acoustic instruments.   These diagrams are intended to give you an idea of what the basic parts of the guitar are and where they can be found on three fairly typical models.

Tuning the Guitar

Tuning the Guitar All the enthusiasm in the world won't help you sound good if you're playing a guitar that's out of tune. So, unless you live near a music shop, or you have a neighbor who almost plays mandolin, or some such convenient arrangement you'll really have to master this skill.

Tuning is the method by which you adjust an instrument to some standard of pitch, absolute or relative, either you adjust the instrument so it is brought into agreement with a standard tuning device, or with another instrument, or, at least, so it is in agreement with itself. When you tune, you judge whether or not the strings are set at the correct intervals to each other. You'll play and listen to the tone of one string, and then compare it to a "constant" or "standard."

In order to make the necessary adjustments, you should know the mechanics of how to alter the tension in the strings:

This is done by turning the tuning gears that are mounted on the head of the guitar, at the side of the gear box.

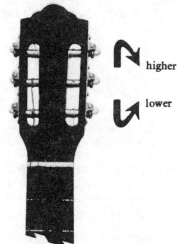

When you want to raise the pitch of a string, make it sound higher, tighten its tension by turning its tuning gear clockwise.

When you want to lower the pitch or make it sound lower, loosen the strings tension by turning its gear counter-clockwise.

Method #1. Desert Island Tuning; The guitar will be "in tune" with itself. This procedure requires no special devices to use for sound comparisons. The idea is to set your 6ᵗʰ string (the lowest pitched string), as close to the sound of "E" as your memory (or your good luck) can approximate. Then you'll tune the rest of the strings using the 6ᵗʰ string as your "standard." This is how you begin:

First, gradually raise the pitch of the slackened 6ᵗʰ string until it no longer buzzes against the frets. Now we optimistically proceed on the assumption that you 6ᵗʰ string is "in tune."

Press the 6ᵗʰ string at the fifth fret. Then pluck it alternately, several times, with the 5ᵗʰ string, and compare the sounds. Turn the appropriate tuning gear and adjust the 5ᵗʰ string so that (open) it sounds like the 6ᵗʰ string when it is pressed at the fifth fret.

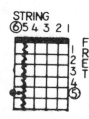

Press the 5ᵗʰ string at its fifth fret. Pluck it alternately with the 4ᵗʰ string, as you compare the sounds. Now, adjust the 4ᵗʰ string so that it sounds like the 5ᵗʰ string when it is pressed at the fifth fret.

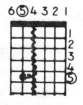

Press the 4ᵗʰ string at its fifth fret. Compare. Adjust the 3ʳᵈ string so it sounds like the 4ᵗʰ string pressed at the fifth fret.

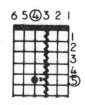

Press the 3rd string at its *fourth* fret. Compare. Adjust the 2nd string so it sounds like the 3rd string at the *fourth* fret.

Lastly, press the 2nd string at the fifth fret and compare the sounds. Adjust the 1st string so that it sounds like the 2nd string when it is pressed at the fifth fret.

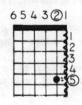

If all went well, you should now be in tune with yourself. You may not be in tune with a record, or your neighbors mandolin, but you can at least play by yourself successfully. And that's a nice beginning.

Notice that your 1st string and your 6th string are the same tones, but in different registers (two octaves apart).

Method #2, Pitch Pipe Tuning: This system is almost as portable as your memory, and much more reliable.

There are two pitch pipes you can choose from: One is the standard guitar model, made of 6 metal and plastic tubes that are joined together. The other is the chromatic pipe, which is round, and is also made of metal and plastic. The chromatic model is thought to be the more accurate, but having 12 tones, it does leave you to locate the 6 guitar tones all by your lonesome.

In any case, pick your poison, and we can proceed as follows:

Take your pitch pipe, and blow gently (so you won't distort its tone), into the low "E". Adjust the corresponding 6th string, (your low "E"), until you feel you've matched the sound. And that's it! You just continue matching the tones of the pipe to the rest of the strings.

Keep in mind, that the timbre of the pipe (the quality of its sound), is different from that of the guitar. Your ear will have to take this into account.

Method #3, Tuning Fork Tuning: The tuning fork is the most accurate sound gauge available. Its a somewhat Y shaped metal device that commonly comes in two frequencies (tones), A and B♭. The A is most often used for guitars.

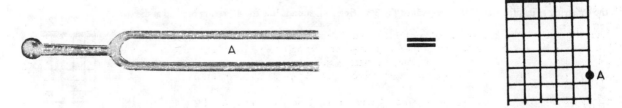

Here, you'll tune one string to the perfect pitch of the fork. Like Desert Island Tuning, adjust the other strings to your one tuned string.

Pinch the fork prongs, and spring a release. As the tone sounds, place the leg of the fork on the guitar, or on any piece of wood that will help to amplify the tone. Then, adjust your 1ˢᵗ string pressed at the fifth fret, until you match that tone. Pressed at the fifth fret, the 1ˢᵗ string now produces an "A" tone; release your finger from that fret, and the open 1ˢᵗ string is an "E".

Although this is the most accurate method, some feel that it's the most difficult. If you're not that agile, you may find you need a third arm.

Method #4, Guitar to Piano Tuning: Although it is rather expensive to purchase a piano as a tuning device for a guitar, if you already have one, you're in luck! This is a dandy method, simple and painless.

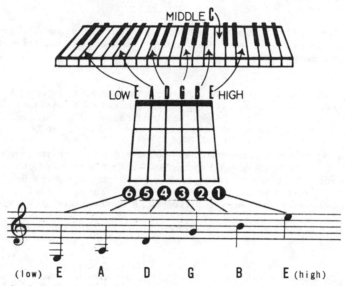

Following the diagram above, simply strike the piano key that corresponds to the open guitar string that you want to tune. As with all the preceding methods, listen to the tone of your "constant" (the piano), and adjust the string to match the sound. Using a piano, you may find the difference in instrument timbre less distracting. This has something to do with the fact that beyond the imposing exterior of every piano, lays a heart made of strings. And those strings ultimately produce the tones you hear. Therefore, the tone qualities of both instruments have more in common than the other devices discussed before. Pick the method you're most comfortable with, and work on it until you really develop the skill. This is an ability that will serve you well.

The Capo

Basically the *capo* is a mechanical device used for changing keys. Whichever model you choose, each of them performs the same function. When it is fixed onto the fingerboard, it exerts enough pressure on all 6 strings to raise the pitch of the instrument by ½ step degrees. The keys are changed simply by shifting the position of the capo on the fingerboard.

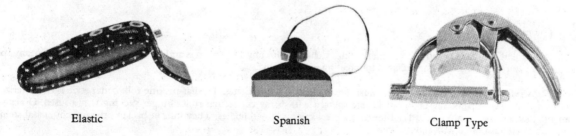

Elastic   Spanish   Clamp Type

We strongly recommend the elastic model over the clamp style or the spanish style. The elastic one will never scratch the neck or damage the guitar in any way.

The clamp-like wonder can often save the day musically, but shouldn't be a substitute for learning a full range of chords. But if you have to change keys, but want to retain the original fingering (and voicing) of your chords, this may be your answer. If a song is too low, simply place the capo behind the fret that brings the pitch of the guitar up to the pitch best suited to your vocal range. If the song is too high, use the capo several frets above, and then sing an octave under the new, higher key.

Remember, make sure the *capo* is adjusted just behind the fret you've chosen, so there won't be any string buzz.

Glossary

ACCIDENTALS: These are the group of symbols used in music notations to indicate when a sound alteration of a single note must be made. An accidental is only applicable within the measure it appears. These are some common symbols and the directions they indicate.

♯	(sharp)	raises the note a half step (tone)
♭	(flat)	lowers the note a half step
♮	(natural)	cancels the effect of a previous alteration
✕	(double sharp)	raises the note one whole step
♭♭	(double flat)	lowers the note one whole step

ACCOMPANIMENT PATTERNS: (Strums) These refer to the huge variety of rhythmic patterns that can be played by the right hand, on a stringed instrument. They can, in conjunction with chords played by the left hand, create the supportive music for a vocalist, or the background and rhythmic music for other melody instruments. Because accompaniment patterns are created for a supportive role, the variety of techniques that can be utilized is all but limitless. They are generally devised to compliment a musical piece, and can be incredibly adaptable.

ACID-ROCK: (Head music) A branch of rock music that developed around the same time as the American drug culture was taking form. The sound is characterized by intensely high volumes, and a rather frenzied quality. Strains of oriental influence could be heard. Use of distortion devices and controlled feedback marked their techniques: The music itself was improvisationally structured and often quite lengthy.

ACTION: The term used to describe the ease (or difficulty) of playing on the fingerboard of a guitar. Conditions that effect the action are: (1) the distance between the strings and the frets of the fingerboard, (2) the size and shape of the neck, and (3) the width and curve of the actual fingerboard. The closer the strings are to the frets, the better the action will be; this quality, oddly enough, is called "low action," and it is generally preferred to "high action," except in the case where the strings are so low that they buzz against the frets.

AMPLIFIERS: An amplifier is the electronic unit that enables an instrument (or microphone) to increase its' volume to various levels suitable to the musicians needs. These levels, and certain qualities of the sound produced, are adjusted through its control panel. This unit enables you to spread your talents to the far corners of any room, or disperse large crowds at will.

ARPEGGIO: A series of tones in a chord, played consecutively (as opposed to simultaneously) in an ascending or descending order.

AXE (slang): When someone asks you what kind of axe you use, don't look around for the lumber jack you think he's talking to.... He just wants to know the type of guitar you play. Yes, for reasons that elude most of us, an axe is a musical instrument (in our case, a guitar).

BACK BEAT: It's the 2nd and 4th beats in a measure that are heavily accented in order to give a rock or percussive feeling to the music.

BACK-UP BAND: A standing group, or, an ad-hoc group, put together to accompany a singer or to "fill out" the music for a group. This is done at live performances as well as for recording sessions.

BACK-UP MUSIC: Music structured to support and augment a vocalist or a lead melody instrument. It doesn't stand on its own.

BAR (BARRÉ): The procedure of fingering chords, which differs from normal first position fingering. Instead of each finger individually fretting one tone, now one finger presses down, fretting from two to six strings. The 2nd, 3rd and 4th fingers are still able to individually fret other tones that form a particular chord. When you bar all 6 strings at a fret, you raise the pitch of the whole guitar. This can be done mechanically with a capo. (See Capo.)

BITE: Although this may sound like orthodontist jargon, it is actually a guitar slang word used to describe the quality of a sharp attack in a musical sound. It can also refer to the tone quality that a certain guitar or amp can obtain, or the sound a guitarist can get in his technique.

BLOW: To improvise.

BLUES: A folk and jazz style or music form that's usually characterized by 12 Bar songs and the use of the blues scale. Many special techniques like slurs, slides, & bending are used for creating a blues sound.

BLUE-GRASS: Bluegrass is a White-country-music of the South-Eastern States. The flat-picking folk guitar style is characterized by simple, recurrent down-up motion of the pick, interspersed with many connecting runs. Finger picking is also used. Other string instruments that are commonly played for Blue Grass are banjo, bass and fiddles. They join in backing the punchy, nasal sounding singing, associated most often with country musics.

BLUES SCALE: Imposes a minor scale over a major scale. The 3rd, 5th and 7th notes of the scale are flatted ½ a step. It gives blues its characteristic mornful quality.

CALYPSO: A regional (West Indian) ballad music characterized by lyrics of political, social or sexual content, and has a highly strident, syncopated rhythm.

CAPO: The clamp-like device used to change keys mechanically on a stringed instrument.

COOKING: This is actually a jazz idiom, meaning that the music or the musician is really moving, tight and/or in a good groove. It can also mean the music has reached a high level of excitement.

COUNTRY SOUND: In its most basic form, it can be produced on the guitar when the player uses his pick to hit a single Bass String, and then brushes the pick down, across the top 3 or 4 strings and pulls the pick back across those same strings, on his way to the next bass string.

COUNTRY-WESTERN: One of the styles of folk music that is characterized by simple major and minor chords, sweet and uncomplex harmonies, and uses mainly stringed instruments. The voices are often nasal and the stringed instruments make use of various "twanging" techniques.

CROSS PICKING: Using 3 strings, the player picks various patterns with a flat pick. It's kind of Scruggs-banjo style, with rapid eighth note passages spicing its syncopated rhythm.

ECHO (1) A subdued repetition of a riff or musical phrase. (2) Electronically, an electric unit that causes a fractional delay of an instrumental (or vocal) sound. This unit can add body and fullness to that sound or create interesting effects. It is used in performances and in recording.

ELECTRONIC MUSIC: Originally, music created *solely* by electronic means, rather than music produced by recording *already* existing acoustic sounds. Now, these methods are so inter-related, they're all viewed as being part of the same grouping. So electronic music would be defined as any music produced, reproduced, amplified, modified or recorded by any electronic devices or electro-acoustical means.

FEEDBACK: The uncontrolled, high pitched screetching that comes from electric amplifying units. It's caused by the sound from the speaker being picked up by the guitar pickup (or mike), which is feeding it back again into the amp's speaker. This vicious cycle is frustrating to the musician and to anyone within a two mile radius of him or her! But feedback can not only be adjusted, but can be controlled and used for intentional distortion effects.

FILL: This is the term used to describe both musical or rhythmic phrases (riffs) which fill out a pause in the music. Can also refer to a riff that bridges two musical thoughts.

FINGERPICKING: A country folk style of guitar characterized by an alternating bass string technique interspersed with various treble patterns.

FLAT PICK: A useful coin-sized device for strumming & picking on stringed instruments.

FLAT PICKING: A (steel-string) folk style utilizing the flat pick.

FOLK-ROCK: In some ways, this was a synthesis of the lyric social-consciousness of folk music and the rhythmic and electric qualities of rock. Depending on whether the music has more of one or the other, the characteristics will vary.

FREE STROKE: The weaker, unsupported thumb or finger stroke. Helpful·when speed is desired. Necessary when the thumb is used simultaneously with another finger. Accompaniment patterns use free strokes for the fingers. In classical music the fingers as well as the thumb may use rest strokes.

FRET: (1) The metal strips (fret wires) that are set into the fingerboard to divide the tone intervals on the guitar. (2) To press a string directly behind the fret wire (metal strip) on the fingerboard, in order to obtain a certain tone.

FUNKY: As a descriptive term for music, Funky means "low down" bluesy feeling. (Not a pejorative.) Outside of its music connotation it's sometimes used to mean low-down, dirty etc. So it can be a compliment or a put-down depending on the circumstances.

FUZZ: Electronic distortion device, used for electric guitar. Creates a buzzing effect and greatly adds to the sustain of the tone.

HEAVY: A broad term generally used to describe meaningful, serious, or emotional music or style. Can also refer to a performers virtuosity.

HIP: This can refer to a piece of music or one's musicianship; usually meaning sophisticated, inovative, or independent of general (popular) trends. A hip piece is ... very difficult to define.

INTERLUDE: In modern music it can be a vocal or instrumental passage connecting one theme or verse to another theme or verse. It can also be inserted between a verse and chorus and the next verse.

JAZZ: Various styles constituting a period of modern American music which is characterized by improvised melodies and complex rhythmic structures.

KEY: Tonal center of gravity. All notes (tones) chords etc. should revolve compatibly around the note C in the Key of C, etc.

KEY SIGNATURE: The symbol used in standard notation used to prescribe the key that the music will be written in, on a staff.

LAYING-OUT: Not playing; a musician may "lay out" so another musician can take a solo, or he may lay out because he's unfamiliar with a particular section of the music. Rather than taking a chance, and hurting the group sound, he will "lay out" so as not to make unnecessary enemies.

LEAD GUITAR: The lead guitar player is responsible for playing the melodies and solos. Generally, its expected that such a player's musicianship is solid enough to enable him to expand creatively into improvisational soloing etc.

MIXER: In electronic music, a mixer is a device used to control the balance of tone and volume when a number of instruments are plugged into one amplification system. It generally will have 4 or 5 imputs with separate controls for each one. These controls can be adjusted to achieve a proper balance.

MODULATE: To (intentionally) change the key of a song, within that song, for harmonic variety. To be effective, a transitional segment (cadence) should lead into each modulation.

MOTOWN: (Detroit Sound) Originally Motown was the name of a Black owned record company based in Detroit. But because their records had such a distinctive sound, any songs now having those distinctive qualities, are thought of as having the "Motown Sound." The sound is built around a very heavy bass line, often played by a Fender Bass, with intricate, off-beat rhythms provided by guitars, electric pianos, distortion devices, etc.

MUFFLED BASS NOTES: This is a technique often associated with a Nashville sound. The bass strings are dampened with the right hand palm while the top 3 strings are picked "unmuffled" (clean).

NASHVILLE SOUND: This is a commercial, polished country-western sound characterized by pedal steel and regular electric guitars, banjos, and mandolins. They often utilize pure, simple vocal harmonies as a base. It's called "Nashville" because that's where most of the musicians and recording studios that work with this type of music are located.

OPEN NOTE (TONE): Tone produced by playing a string *without* fretting it (pressing your finger on string, at a fret). On wind instruments it means the "natural" tones that instrument produces without the use of its keys or valves.

OVERTONES: The secondary tones that form the components of every "individual" musical tone. Although tone is perceived by the human ear to be a single musical sound, it's actually made up of dominant and subordinate vibrations.

PEDAL POINT (PEDAL TONE): Is a sustained (or repeated) tone, usually in the bass register, which continues to sound throughout changing harmonies.

PATTERN PICKING: A Folk or accompaniment style of guitar playing.

PICK GUARD: (Sometimes called tap-plate.) Made of thin plastic, fiberglass (or other such material); it is put on the face of a guitar, usually near the soundhole, to protect the wood finish from the guitarists' enthusiasm.

PICKUP: This is the device used to convert an acoustic-sound-production system (of an instrument) to an electric-sound-production system. It is called an electromechanical transducor. Basically the unit converts the vibrations of magnetic strings into electronic signals.

PICKUP CABLE: The wire or chord that connects the guitar to an amp, or amp to a foot switch, or a foot switch to an amp, etc.

PICKUP SELECTOR: This is the switch that is used to direct which pickup will be powered, and how much. Usually, a toggle-type switch, it actually selects the power arrangement. Either it activates the pickup that effects the treble strings, or the pickup that effects the bass strings. It can also have a position that activates them both simultaneously.

PITCH: The height or depth of a tone determined by its number and rate of vibrations. A tone's place by the musical register.

PLECTRUMS: (picks) A small hand-held or worn device used to strum or pick a stringed instrument. Some flat, thin coin sized types are held between the thumb and 2nd finger. Others are shaped to fit either a finger or thumb and are made of metal or plastic.

POP MUSIC: Generally thought of as widely known current music performed in a somewhat synthesized variety of styles. Usually shares a common quality, of commercial palatable content and form.

POT: Short Term used for the potentiometer, which is the tone, volume or master control knobs of an amp.

RASGUEADO: A strum form that involves a staggered, spray-like motion of the fingers, across the strings. It produces a rapid arpeggio which is heard as a single "wall of sound" effect, rather than broken sounds.

RESONANCE: The sound reinforcing system that aids in the production of the musics' volume and quality. A resonating system may be acoustical, electrical, or physical (as in the resonating cavities of the chest, nose or mouth of the body). A non-electric resonator would have to be attached to, or in close proximity with, the source of sound, in order to best reverberate the original tone.

REST STROKE: A strong, supported thumb or finger stroke used in guitar playing. The thumb or finger presses down on one string, and "rests" (lands) on the adjacent string. It's helpful in bringing out volume.

REVERB: The built in or auxiliary unit of an amp that creates the effect of playing (or singing) in a large room with terrific acoustics. It can be a synthetic, over "echoey" sound, but in certain circumstances, it can be very helpful.

RHYTHM & BLUES: Pop music styles characterized by a synthesis of Black blues, jazz and gospel music.

198

RHYTHM GUITAR: Provides the backup chords that support the melody instruments or vocals. The rhythm guitarist should be strong enough to hold the group together rhythmically, but sensitive enough to compliment the melody, without being overpowering.

RIF: (1) A short melodic phase or segment (often repeated) that is played by one or more members of a group, behind their soloist (2) It is also used to establish a brief interlude between larger melodic themes.

ROCK: A broad term used to describe a music that developed in the 1950's and continues to grow today. It draws heavily from R & B, C & W, gospel, blues, and jazz. Originally, its wide spread appeal was its heavy back beat and dancable quality. Now, it also has a "listening" form as well. By and large, it uses mainly electric guitars, bass guitars, pianos, organs, drums and brass instruments.

ROUND: (Cannon) A musical piece, which, when sung by different people, each beginning at different points in the melody, harmonizes with itself. A round can often be divided into 2, 3, or 4 parts.

RUNS: Runs are the short, single note passages played in between two chords. The key signature of the musical piece will indicate which notes are available to use.

SCAT SINGING: The technique of singing, usually improvised, using comfortable vocal syllables (bop, ba ba, da da, etc.), rather than words. This has been utilized most often by Jazz vocalists, and is now becoming increasingly popular with Rock musicians.

SUSPENSION: A technique for creating a harmonic tension by taking a chord, and adding non-chord (tone) of its scale to it. The most common tone used is the suspended 4th.

SUSTAIN: The ability of a tone to continue sounding after it has physically been played. The lack of sustain can be a problem on a guitar where the tones can fade rather quickly. But now, through electronics, there are devices to control and increase the sustain of the tones for much greater lengths of time. Also, electric solid body guitars tend to sustain longer acoustic guitars even without extra electronic devices.

TIMBRE: (Pronounced *timber*). The quality or color of a tone. A tone may be the same pitch when a trumpet or a guitar produces it, but the quality is different: the trumpet may be biting or "brassy," the guitar, hopefully should be mellow and "woody."

TRAVIS PICKING: The 2 finger style picking techniques of Southern Black folk music that Merle Travis popularized. In his method, Travis rests the fingertips of his 2nd, 3rd, 4th finger on the guitar face and the thumb and index finger do all the picking.

TREMOLO: Physically, this is the rapid reiteration of a note, or the rapid alternation of 2 notes. (2) In connection with the electric guitar, it's the device that fluctuates the tone.

TRUSS ROD: The metal bar that is inserted into the guitar neck, extending its whole length. It is used to provide additional strength and also is available as an adjustable device to correct minor warping or bowing. Found mainly in steel string guitars.

WHA WHA PEDAL: A distortion device used for electric guitar. Creates a whining sound and increases sustain.

Song Title Index

This index includes over a thousand Folk, Rock, Jazz and Pop songs. For each song, 2 accompaniment patterns are suggested. The first pattern provided will generally be taken from the book's 20-Pattern Sampling. The second one will either be a more sophisticated variation of the first pattern, or, a different style strum that really gives the song a new feeling.

Some of these songs have already appeared on the lists of Song Possibilities throughout the book. Those songs have been relisted, but in many cases, present totally different alternative strums. Many other songs are completely new, offering an even broader selection of material.

A DARK BEAUTY (Greek) Moving Bass Pull Folk Greek $\frac{7}{8}$
A DAY IN THE LIFE Slow Bass $\frac{4}{4}$ / Pull Slow Bass Rock $\frac{4}{4}$
A DREAM IS A WISH YOUR HEART MAKES Slow $\frac{4}{4}$ / Pinch Slow $\frac{4}{4}$
A FELICIDADE (Brazil) Slow Bass Pull $\frac{4}{4}$ / Pinch Samba $\frac{4}{4}$
A FOGGY DAY Fast $\frac{4}{4}$ / Pinch Bossa Nova $\frac{4}{4}$
A HUNDRED POUNDS OF CLAY Fast Rock $\frac{4}{4}$ / Fast Bass Rock $\frac{4}{4}$
A LA UNA NACI YO (Spanish) Rasgueado Mexican $\frac{4}{4}$ / Rasgueado Huapanga $\frac{3}{4}$
A LITTLE HELP FROM MY FRIENDS Fast $\frac{4}{4}$ / Slow Syncopated $\frac{4}{4}$
A MILLION TO ONE Arpeggiated Triplet $\frac{4}{4}$ / Arpeggiated Double Bass Triplet $\frac{4}{4}$
A MILLION TOMORROWS Slow $\frac{3}{4}$ / Arpeggiated $\frac{3}{4}$
A TASTE OF HONEY Slow $\frac{3}{4}$ and Slow Bass $\frac{4}{4}$
ADIOS MUCHACHOS (I GET IDEAS) (Spanish) Fast Latin $\frac{4}{4}$ / Rasgueado Tango $\frac{4}{4}$
AFRICAN WALTZ Fast $\frac{3}{4}$ / Pull Jazz $\frac{3}{4}$
AFTER YOU'VE GONE Fast $\frac{4}{4}$ / Slow Syncopated $\frac{4}{4}$
AIN'T THAT A SHAME Fast Rock $\frac{4}{4}$ / Fast Rhythm And Blues Shuffle
AL COMPOS DEL MERANGUE (Spanish) Fast Latin $\frac{4}{4}$ / Fast Merangue $\frac{4}{4}$
AL DI LA (Italian) Arpeggiated Triplet $\frac{4}{4}$ / Arpeggiated Double Bass Triplet $\frac{4}{4}$
ALBERTA Arpeggiated Triplet $\frac{4}{4}$ / Pinch Blues Triplet $\frac{4}{4}$
ALICE'S RESTAURANT Travis Pattern Picking $\frac{4}{4}$ / Inflected Pattern Picking $\frac{4}{4}$
ALL I EVER NEED IS YOU Fast $\frac{4}{4}$ / Travis Pattern Picking $\frac{4}{4}$
ALL MY LOVIN' Fast $\frac{4}{4}$ / Fast Folk $\frac{4}{4}$
ALL MY TRIALS Slow $\frac{4}{4}$ / Moving Bass Ballad $\frac{4}{4}$
ALL OF ME Fast $\frac{4}{4}$ / Fast Folk $\frac{4}{4}$
ALL OF YOU Slow Bass $\frac{4}{4}$ / Accented Pinch Bossa Nova $\frac{4}{4}$
ALL THE THINGS YOU ARE Slow Bass Pull $\frac{4}{4}$ / Accented Pinch Bossa Nova $\frac{4}{4}$
ALL YOU NEED IS LOVE Fast $\frac{4}{4}$ / Slow Syncopated $\frac{4}{4}$
THE ALLEY CAT Fast $\frac{4}{4}$ / Slow Syncopated $\frac{4}{4}$
ALONE AGAIN Fast $\frac{4}{4}$ / Travis Pattern Picking $\frac{4}{4}$
ALWAYS Pull Waltz $\frac{3}{4}$ / Slow Bass Pull $\frac{3}{4}$
AMEN Fast $\frac{4}{4}$ / Percussive Rock $\frac{4}{4}$
AMERICAN PIE Slow $\frac{4}{4}$ / Fast Rock $\frac{4}{4}$
AND I LOVE HER Slow $\frac{4}{4}$ / Arpeggiated $\frac{4}{4}$
AND THE ANGELS SING Fast $\frac{4}{4}$ / Fast Folk $\frac{4}{4}$
ANGEL EYES Slow Bass $\frac{4}{4}$ / Arpeggiated Triplet $\frac{4}{4}$
ANNE BOLEYN Slow Syncopated $\frac{4}{4}$ / Fast Latin $\frac{4}{4}$
ANNEMARICKE (Dutch) Pull Waltz $\frac{3}{4}$ / Fast $\frac{3}{4}$
ANTICIPATION Fast $\frac{4}{4}$ / Slow Bass $\frac{4}{4}$
AQUARIUS Fast $\frac{4}{4}$ / Fast Folk $\frac{4}{4}$
AROUND THE WORLD Pull Waltz $\frac{3}{4}$ / Arpeggiated $\frac{3}{4}$
ARRIVERDERCI ROMA (Italian) Moving Bass Arpeggiated Calypso $\frac{4}{4}$ / Moving Bass Pull Spanish $\frac{4}{4}$
ARUANDO (Brazil) Slow Bass Pull $\frac{4}{4}$ / Pinch Samba $\frac{4}{4}$
AS TEARS GO BY Slow $\frac{4}{4}$ / Arpeggiated $\frac{4}{4}$
ASIKATALI (Swahili) Fast $\frac{3}{4}$ / Fast $\frac{6}{4}$
AU PRIVAVE Fast $\frac{4}{4}$ / Fast Folk $\frac{4}{4}$
AUNT RHODY Pull $\frac{4}{4}$ / Inflected Pattern Picking $\frac{4}{4}$
AUTUMN LEAVES Slow Bass $\frac{4}{4}$ / Accented Pinch Bossa Nova $\frac{4}{4}$
AUTUMN TO MAY Slow $\frac{4}{4}$ / Travis Pattern Picking $\frac{4}{4}$
AVALON Fast $\frac{4}{4}$ / Fast Folk $\frac{4}{4}$
AVIVA'S MERANGUE Fast Latin $\frac{4}{4}$ / Fast Merangue $\frac{4}{4}$
AZ DER REBEH TANZT (Yiddish) Slow $\frac{4}{4}$ / Slow Bass $\frac{4}{4}$
BA SHANA HABA'AH (Hebrew) Fast $\frac{4}{4}$ / Snap Back Carter Style $\frac{4}{4}$
BABY LOVE Slow Syncopated $\frac{4}{4}$ / Fast Latin $\frac{4}{4}$
BABY YOU'RE A RICH MAN Fast Rock $\frac{4}{4}$ / Percussive Rock $\frac{4}{4}$
BAGS GROVE Fast $\frac{4}{4}$ / Pull Slow Bass Rock $\frac{4}{4}$
BAILE DE PANDERO (Spanish) Pull Jazz $\frac{5}{4}$
THE BALLAD OF ADDIE CAROL Fast $\frac{3}{4}$ / Snap Back Carter Style $\frac{3}{4}$
BAMBOO Moving Bass Arpeggiated Calypso $\frac{4}{4}$ / Fast Calypso $\frac{4}{4}$
BANDERA ROSA (Italian) Fast $\frac{4}{4}$ / Slow Syncopated $\frac{4}{4}$
BANKS OF THE OHIO Fast $\frac{4}{4}$ / Snap Back Carter Style $\frac{4}{4}$
BARBARA ANN Fast Rock $\frac{4}{4}$ / Percussive Rock $\frac{4}{4}$

BASS REFLEX Pull Jazz $\frac{5}{4}$
BAUBLES, BANGLES AND BEADS Pull Waltz $\frac{3}{4}$ / Pull Jazz $\frac{3}{4}$
BE PREPARED Pull $\frac{4}{4}$ / Fast $\frac{4}{4}$
BEANS IN MY EARS Pull Waltz $\frac{3}{4}$ / Fast $\frac{3}{4}$
THE BEAT GOES ON Fast Rock $\frac{4}{4}$ / Percussive Rock $\frac{4}{4}$
BEAUTIFUL BALLOON Fast Folk $\frac{4}{4}$ / Slow Bass Pull $\frac{4}{4}$
BEAUTIFUL BROWN EYES Pull Waltz $\frac{3}{4}$ / Slow $\frac{3}{4}$
BEEN IN THE PEN SO LONG Slow Syncopated $\frac{4}{4}$ / Percussive Bass Blues $\frac{4}{4}$
BEER BARREL POLKA Pull $\frac{4}{4}$ / Snap Back Country Style $\frac{4}{4}$
BELTZ (Yiddish) Slow $\frac{4}{4}$ / Slow Bass Pull $\frac{4}{4}$
BERNIE'S TUNE Fast $\frac{4}{4}$ / Fast Folk $\frac{4}{4}$
BESSAME MUCHO Moving Bass Pull Spanish $\frac{4}{4}$ / Percussive Rock $\frac{4}{4}$
(THE) BEST THING FOR YOU WOULD BE ME Fast $\frac{4}{4}$ / Travis Pattern Picking $\frac{4}{4}$
BEWARE OF DARKNESS Slow Bass $\frac{4}{4}$ / Pull Slow Bass Rock $\frac{4}{4}$
(THE) BIG BAMBOO Moving Bass Arpeggiated Calypso $\frac{4}{4}$ / Fast Calypso $\frac{4}{4}$
BILL BAILEY WON'T YOU PLEASE COME HOME Fast $\frac{4}{4}$ / Fast Folk $\frac{4}{4}$
BILLIE'S BOUNCE Fast $\frac{4}{4}$ / Fast Folk $\frac{4}{4}$
BIM BOM Slow Bass Pull $\frac{4}{4}$ / Pinch Bossa Nova $\frac{4}{4}$
BIRMINGHAM SUNDAY Slow $\frac{3}{4}$ / Arpeggiated $\frac{3}{4}$
BLACK AND WHITE Fast Rock $\frac{4}{4}$ / Slow Syncopated $\frac{4}{4}$
BLOWIN' IN THE WIND Slow $\frac{4}{4}$ / Travis Pattern Picking $\frac{4}{4}$
BLUE TANGO Fast Latin $\frac{4}{4}$ / Percussive Tango $\frac{4}{4}$
BLUEBERRY HILL Fast Rock $\frac{4}{4}$ / Fast Rhythm And Blues Shuffle $\frac{4}{4}$
BLUESETTE Pull Waltz $\frac{3}{4}$ / Pull Jazz $\frac{3}{4}$
BO DIDDLEY Fast Rock $\frac{4}{4}$ / Fast Rhythm And Blues Bo Diddley $\frac{4}{4}$
BODY AND SOUL Slow $\frac{4}{4}$ / Slow Bass Pull $\frac{4}{4}$
BONSOIRE DAME Moving Bass Arpeggiated Calypso $\frac{4}{4}$ / Moving Bass Pinch Ballad $\frac{4}{4}$
BORN FREE Slow $\frac{4}{4}$ / Moving Bass Ballad $\frac{4}{4}$
BOTH SIDES NOW Slow $\frac{4}{4}$ / Moving Bass Pinch Ballad $\frac{4}{4}$
BOTTLE OF WINE Fast $\frac{4}{4}$ / Snap Back Folk $\frac{4}{4}$
BRANDY LEAVE ME ALONE Pull Waltz $\frac{3}{4}$ / Slow $\frac{3}{4}$
BREAKING UP IS HARD TO DO Fast Rock $\frac{4}{4}$ / Moving Bass Arpeggiated Calypso $\frac{4}{4}$
BRAZIL Moving Bass Pull Spanish $\frac{4}{4}$ / Rasgueado Moving Bass Pull $\frac{4}{4}$
BRIDGE OVER TROUBLED WATERS Slow $\frac{4}{4}$ / Slow Bass $\frac{4}{4}$
BRING FLOWERS Pull Waltz $\frac{3}{4}$ / Snap Back Carter Style $\frac{3}{4}$
BROKEN HEARTED MELODY Moving Bass Arpeggiated Calypso $\frac{4}{4}$ / Moving Bass Pinch Ballad $\frac{4}{4}$
BROTHER CAN YOU SPARE A DIME Fast $\frac{4}{4}$ / Slow $\frac{4}{4}$
BROTHERS AND SISTERS Fast Rock $\frac{4}{4}$ / Percussive Rock $\frac{4}{4}$
BROWN SKIN GIRL Moving Bass Arpeggiated Calypso $\frac{4}{4}$ / Fast Calypso $\frac{4}{4}$
BUFFALO SKINNERS Fast $\frac{4}{4}$ / Snap Back Carter Style $\frac{4}{4}$
BURY ME BENEATH THE WILLOW Fast $\frac{4}{4}$ / Full Pattern Picking $\frac{4}{4}$
BY THE TIME I GET TO PHOENIX Slow Bass $\frac{4}{4}$ / Pinch Bossa Nova $\frac{4}{4}$
BYE BYE BLACKBIRD Fast $\frac{4}{4}$ / Slow Bass Pull $\frac{4}{4}$
BYE BYE LOVE Fast $\frac{4}{4}$ / Snap Back Folk $\frac{4}{4}$
CABARET Pull $\frac{4}{4}$ / Fast $\frac{4}{4}$
CALIFORNIA DREAMIN' Slow Bass $\frac{4}{4}$ / Pinch Bossa Nova $\frac{4}{4}$
CALL ME Fast Folk $\frac{4}{4}$ / Moving Bass Pull Spanish $\frac{4}{4}$
CANDY MAN Fast $\frac{4}{4}$ / Complex Pattern Picking $\frac{4}{4}$
CAN'T BEAT THAT ROACH Fast Rock $\frac{4}{4}$ / Fast Bass Hard Rock $\frac{4}{4}$
CAN'T TAKE MY EYES OFF OF YOU Slow Bass $\frac{4}{4}$ / Moving Bass Pinch Ballad $\frac{4}{4}$
CARELESS LOVE Slow Bass $\frac{4}{4}$ / Percussive Bass Blues $\frac{4}{4}$
CARNIVAL Moving Bass Pull Spanish $\frac{4}{4}$ / Accented Pinch Bossa Nova $\frac{4}{4}$
CARRY IT ON Fast $\frac{4}{4}$ / Travis Pattern Picking $\frac{4}{4}$
CASTILLEAN DRUMS Pull Jazz $\frac{5}{4}$
CATCH THE WIND Arpeggiated Triplet $\frac{4}{4}$ / Arpeggiated Double Bass Triplet $\frac{4}{4}$
CATHY'S CLOWN Fast $\frac{4}{4}$ / Snap Back Nashville Style $\frac{4}{4}$
CELITO LINDO (Spanish) Pull Waltz $\frac{3}{4}$ / Slow $\frac{3}{4}$
CHANGES Arpeggiated $\frac{4}{4}$ / Travis Pattern Picking $\frac{4}{4}$

CHANTILLY LACE Fast Rock $^4_4$ / Percussive Rock $^4_4$
CHANUKAH OH CHANUKAH (Yiddish) Pull $^4_4$ / Fast $^4_4$
CHAPEL OF LOVE Fast $^4_4$ / Full Pattern Picking $^4_4$
CHARADE Pull Waltz $^3_4$ / Pull Jazz $^3_4$
CHARLIE BROWN Fast Rock $^4_4$ / Snap Back Double Bass $^4_4$
CHARLESTON Fast $^4_4$ / Fast Folk $^4_4$
CHELSEA MORNING Fast Folk $^4_4$ / Snap Back Folk $^4_4$
CHERRY PINK Moving Bass Pull Spanish $^4_4$ / Percussive Rock $^4_4$
CHICAGO Fast $^4_4$ / Fast Folk $^4_4$
CHIM CHIM CHEREE Pull Waltz $^3_4$ / Slow Bass Pull $^3_4$
CIAO CIAO BAMBINA (Italian) Slow Bass $^4_4$ / Moving Bass Pull Spanish $^4_4$
CINDY Fast $^4_4$ / Snap Back Carter $^4_4$
(THE) CIRCLE GAME Arpeggiated $^4_4$ / Travis Pattern Picking $^4_4$
(THE) CITY OF NEW ORLEANS Fast Folk $^4_4$ / Inflected Pattern Picking $^4_4$
CLEMENTINE Pull Waltz $^3_4$ / Slow $^3_4$
CLIMB EVERY MOUNTAIN Slow Bass $^4_4$ / Arpeggiated Triplet $^4_4$
CLOSE TO YOU Slow Bass $^4_4$ / Slow Syncopated $^4_4$
COLOURS Fast $^4_4$ / Travis Pattern Picking $^4_4$
COMBINATION OF THE TWO Fast Rock $^4_4$ / Fast Twist $^4_4$
COME AND GO WITH ME Slow Syncopated $^4_4$ / Fast Folk $^4_4$
COME AND GO WITH ME TO THAT LAND Fast $^4_4$ / Snap Back Carter Style $^4_4$
COME AWAY MELINDA Slow $^4_4$ / Slow Bass $^4_4$
COME BACK BABY Arpeggiated Triplet $^4_4$ / Pinch Blues Triplet $^4_4$
COME BACK LIZA Moving Bass Pinch Ballad $^4_4$ / Moving Bass Arpeggiated Calypso $^4_4$
COME SOFTLY TO ME Moving Bass Pinch Ballad $^4_4$ / Snap Back Arpeggiated $^4_4$
COMIN' HOME BABY Fast Latin $^4_4$ / Percussive Rock $^4_4$
COMIN' INTO LOS ANGELES Fast Rock $^4_4$ / Percussive Rock $^4_4$
(THE) COMIN' OF THE ROADS Arpeggiated $^4_4$ / Travis Pattern Picking $^4_4$
COMIN' THROUGH THE RYE Slow $^4_4$ / Slow Syncopated $^4_4$
COMPADRE PEDRO JUAN Moving Bass Spanish $^4_4$ / Fast Merangue $^4_4$
CON ALMA Slow Bass $^4_4$ / Slow Bass Pull $^4_4$
CON LOS ABEJAS Rasgueado Mexican $^3_4$ / Rasgueado Huapanga $^3_4$
COOL Fast $^4_4$ / Fast Folk $^4_4$
COPLAS Rasgueado Pull $^3_4$ / Rasgueado Mexican $^3_4$
COPPER KETTLE Fast $^3_4$ / Snap Back Carter $^3_4$
CORINNA Fast $^4_4$ / Accented Pinch Blues Triplet $^4_4$
COTTON FIELDS Fast $^4_4$ / Snap Back Country Style $^4_4$
COULD YOU EVER Slow $^4_4$ / Pinch Extended Slow $^4_4$
COUNTRY ROADS Fast $^4_4$ / Snap Back Folk $^4_4$
(THE) CRAWDAD SONG Fast $^4_4$ / Snap Back Carter Style $^4_4$
CROCODILE ROCK Fast Rock $^4_4$ / Fast Twist $^4_4$
(THE) CROW ON THE CRADLE Slow $^3_4$ / Slow Bass $^3_4$
CRUEL WAR Slow $^4_4$ / Arpeggiated $^4_4$
CRY ME A RIVER Slow Bass $^4_4$ / Slow Bass Pull $^4_4$
CUANDO CALIENTE EL SOL (Spanish) Arpeggiated Triplet $^4_4$ / Arpeggiated Double Bass Triplet $^4_4$
CUANDO YO ME MUERA (Spanish) Rasgueado Mexican $^3_4$ / Rasgueado Huapanga $^3_4$
(THE) CYCLONE OF RYE COVE Fast $^3_4$ / Snap Back Carter Style $^3_4$
DABAER ALI BE FRACHIM (Hebrew) Arpeggiated Triplet $^4_4$ / Arpeggiated Double Bass Triplet $^4_4$
DADDY'S HOME Arpeggiated Triplet $^4_4$ / Arpeggiated Double Bass Triplet $^4_4$
DANCE FROM ISAKONIA (Greek) Pull Jazz $^3_4$
DANCE OF ZOLONGA (Greek) Pull Greek $^7_8$
DANCE WITH ME HENRY Fast Rhythm And Blues Shuffle $^4_4$ / Percussive Bass Blues $^4_4$
DANCERO Moving Bass Pull Spanish $^4_4$ / Percussive Rock $^4_4$
DANCING IN THE DARK Slow Bass $^4_4$ / Slow Bass Pull $^4_4$
DANCING IN THE STREETS Slow Bass $^4_4$ / Pull Slow Bass Rock $^4_4$
DANNY BOY Slow $^4_4$ / Slow Bass $^4_4$
DANNY'S SONG Slow Bass $^4_4$ / Pull Slow Bass Rock $^4_4$
DARK AS A DUNGEON Pull Waltz $^3_4$ / Slow $^3_4$
DARLIN' Percussive Bass Blues $^4_4$ / Percussive Pinch Rock $^4_4$
DARLIN' CORY Fast $^4_4$ / Snap Back Carter Style $^4_4$
DARN THAT DREAM Slow $^4_4$ / Slow Bass Pull $^4_4$
DAWN Fast Rock $^4_4$ / Moving Bass Arpeggiated Calypso $^4_4$
DAY BY DAY Fast Latin $^4_4$ / Slow Bass Pull $^4_4$
DAY DREAM Slow Syncopated $^4_4$ / Fast Latin $^4_4$
DAYO Moving Bass Arpeggiated Calypso $^4_4$ / Fast Latin $^4_4$
(THE) DAYS OF WINE AND ROSES Slow Bass Pull $^4_4$ / Moving Bass Pull Spanish $^4_4$
DEAR HEART Pull Waltz $^3_4$ / Slow $^3_4$
DEEP BLUE SEA Fast $^4_4$ / Snap Back Carter Style $^4_4$
DEEP IN THE HEART OF TEXAS Fast $^4_4$ / Snap Back Carter Style $^4_4$
DEEP PURPLE Slow $^4_4$ / Slow Bass Pull $^4_4$
DEEP RIVER BLUES Travis Pattern Picking $^4_4$ / Full Inverted Pattern Picking $^4_4$
DELIA Moving Bass Pinch Ballad $^4_4$ / Moving Bass Arpeggiated Calypso $^4_4$
DELTA DAWN Fast Folk $^4_4$ / Pull Slow Bass Rock $^4_4$
DESAFINADO Slow Bass Pull $^4_4$ / Accented Pinch Bossa Nova $^4_4$
(THE) DESPERADO Fast $^4_4$ / Snap Back Carter Style $^4_4$
DIANA Moving Bass Pinch Ballad $^4_4$ / Moving Bass Arpeggiated Calypso $^4_4$
DID YOUR MOTHER COME FROM IRELAND Slow Syncopated $^4_4$ / Pinch Slow Bass $^4_4$
DIE GEDANKEN SIND FREI (German) Pull Waltz $^3_4$ / Slow $^3_4$
DIMME QUANDO (Italian) Moving Bass Pull Spanish $^4_4$ / Moving Bass Pull Arpeggiated $^4_4$
DIZZY Fast Rock $^4_4$ / Fast Latin $^4_4$
DO RE MI Pull $^4_4$ / Fast $^4_4$
DO YOU WANT TO DANCE Fast Rock $^4_4$ / Slow Bass $^4_4$
DO YOU WANT TO KNOW A SECRET Slow $^4_4$ / Moving Bass Arpeggiated Calypso $^4_4$
DOCK OF THE BAY Slow Bass $^4_4$ / Pull Bass Note Rock $^4_4$
DOCTOR MY EYES Fast Rock $^4_4$ / Percussive Rock $^4_4$
DONE LAID AROUND Fast $^4_4$ / Fast Folk $^4_4$
DON'T BE CRUEL Fast Rock $^4_4$ / Snap Back Nashville Style $^4_4$
DON'T BLAME ME Slow $^4_4$ / Slow Bass $^4_4$
DON'T BOTHER ME Fast Rock $^4_4$ / Percussive Rock $^4_4$
DON'T SLEEP IN THE SUBWAY Slow Bass $^4_4$ / Fast Latin $^4_4$
DON'T TAKE YOUR LOVE FROM ME Slow $^4_4$ / Arpeggiated $^4_4$
DON'T THINK TWICE Travis Pattern Picking $^4_4$ / Snap Back Carter Style $^4_4$
DONA, DONA Slow $^4_4$ / Slow Bass $^4_4$
DONNA Arpeggiated Triplet $^4_4$ / Arpeggiated Double Bass $^4_4$
DONNA NOBIS PACHIM (Latin) Slow $^3_4$ / Arpeggiated $^3_4$
DOODLIN' Fast $^4_4$ / Slow Syncopated $^4_4$
DOS PUNTOS TIENE EL CAMINO (Spanish) Rasgueado Mexican $^3_4$ / Rasgueado Huapanga $^3_4$
DOWN AND OUT BLUES Fast Rhythm And Blues Shuffle $^4_4$ / Percussive Bass Blues $^4_4$
DOWN BY THE LAZY RIVER Fast Rock $^4_4$ / Fast Folk $^4_4$
DOWN BY THE RIVERSIDE Fast $^4_4$ / Snap Back Nashville Style $^4_4$
DOWN IN THE VALLEY Pull Waltz $^3_4$ / Slow $^3_4$
DOWN TOWN Fast Rock $^4_4$ / Slow Bass Pull $^4_4$
DOXY Fast $^4_4$ / Slow Syncopated $^4_4$
DRAFT DODGER RAG Fast $^4_4$ / Travis Pattern Picking $^4_4$
DREAM Slow $^4_4$ / Slow Bass $^4_4$
DREAM LOVER Moving Bass Arpeggiated Calypso $^4_4$ / Moving Bass Pinch Ballad $^4_4$
DRILL YE TARRIERS DRILL Pull $^4_4$ / Snap Back Carter Style $^4_4$
DROWNIN' IN MY OWN TEARS Slow Bass $^4_4$
EARLY IN THE MORNING Fast $^4_4$ / Fast Folk $^4_4$
EARLY MORNING RAIN Travis Pattern Picking $^4_4$ / Snap Back Nashville Style $^4_4$
EAST VIRGINIA Fast $^4_4$ / Snap Back Carter Style $^4_4$
EASY LIVING Slow $^4_4$ / Slow Bass $^4_4$
EASY RIDER Fast Rhythm And Blues Shuffle $^4_4$ / Accented Pinch Blues Triplet $^4_4$
EASY TO LOVE Fast $^4_4$ / Fast Latin $^4_4$
EBB TIDE Slow $^4_4$ / Arpeggiated $^4_4$
ECHEN CONFITES Rasgueado Mexican $^3_4$ / Rasgueado Huapanga $^3_4$
EDDIE MY LOVE Arpeggiated Triplet $^4_4$ / Arpeggiated Double Bass Triplet $^4_4$
EIGHT DAYS A WEEK Fast Rock $^4_4$ / Fast Folk $^4_4$
EL CONDOR PASA Pull $^4_4$ / Slow Bass $^4_4$
EL PASO Pull Waltz $^3_4$ / Snap Back Carter Style $^3_4$
EL PEQUENO (Spanish) Rasgueado Mexican $^3_4$ / Rasgueado Huapanga $^3_4$
ELEANOR RIGBY Fast Rock $^4_4$ / Percussive Rock $^4_4$
EMBRACEABLE YOU Slow $^4_4$ / Slow Bass $^4_4$
ERETZ ZAVAT CHALAV (Hebrew) Fast $^4_4$ / Percussive Fast $^4_4$
EREV BA (Hebrew) Pull Mid-East $^4_4$ / Slow Bass Pull $^4_4$
EREV SHEL SHOSHANIM (Hebrew) Pull Mid-East $^4_4$ / Slow Bass Pull $^4_4$
EVERY DAY I HAVE THE BLUES Fast $^4_4$ / Arpeggiated Double Bass Triplet $^4_4$
EVERY TIME WE SAY GOODBYE Slow $^4_4$ / Slow Bass $^4_4$
EVERYBODY LOVES A LOVER Fast $^4_4$ / Snap Back Carter Style $^4_4$
EVERYBODY LOVES SATURDAY NIGHT Fast $^4_4$ / Fast Folk $^4_4$
EVERYBODY'S TALKIN' Moving Bass Pinch Ballad $^4_4$ / Pinch Bossa Nova $^4_4$
EVERYTHING IS BEAUTIFUL Slow Syncopated $^4_4$ / Fast Rhythm And Blues Shuffle $^4_4$
EVIL WAYS Fast Latin $^4_4$ / Percussive Rock $^4_4$
EXERCISE Fast Rock $^4_4$ / Percussive Rock $^4_4$
EXODUS Slow $^4_4$ / Arpeggiated $^4_4$
EXPATRIOT INCOMPATIBLE MARRIAGE Arpeggiated $^4_4$ / Moving Bass Pinch Ballad $^4_4$
FAR FAR AWAY Travis Pattern Picking $^4_4$ / Full Inflected Pattern Picking $^4_4$
FARE THEE WELL Fast $^4_4$ / Snap Back Carter Style $^4_4$
FARTHER ALONG Pull Waltz $^3_4$ / Snap Back Carter Style $^3_4$
FASCINATION Pull Waltz $^3_4$ / Slow $^3_4$
FEED THE BIRDS Pull Waltz $^3_4$ / Slow $^3_4$
FEELIN' GROOVY Fast $^4_4$ / Slow Syncopated $^4_4$
FEVER Slow Bass $^4_4$ / Fast Latin $^4_4$
FIDDLER ON THE ROOF Pull $^4_4$ / Pull Folk Chasidic $^4_4$
FIFTEEN Slow $^3_4$ / Arpeggiated $^3_4$
FIRE Fast Rock $^4_4$ / Percussive Rock $^4_4$
(THE) FIRST GIRL I LOVED Arpeggiated $^4_4$ / Full Inverted Pattern Picking $^4_4$
(THE) FIRST TIME EVER Arpeggiated $^4_4$ / Slow Bass $^4_4$
FIVE FOOT TWO Fast $^4_4$ / Fast Folk $^4_4$
FIVE HUNDRED MILES Slow $^4_4$ / Arpeggiated $^4_4$
FLUTE DIDDLEY Fast Rock $^4_4$ / Fast Rhythm And Blues Bo Diddley $^4_4$
FLY ME TO THE MOON Slow Bass Pull $^4_4$ / Pinch Bossa Nova $^4_4$
FOLLOW THE DRINKIN' GOURD Fast $^4_4$ / Snap Back Folk $^4_4$
FOLLOW THE FELLOW WHO FOLLOWS THE DREAM Pull Waltz $^3_4$ / Slow $^3_4$
(THE) FOOL ON THE HILL Arpeggiated $^4_4$ / Slow Bass $^4_4$
FOOLS PARADISE Arpeggiated Triplet $^4_4$ / Pinch Blues Triplet $^4_4$
FOOLS RUSH IN Slow Bass Pull $^4_4$ / Accented Pinch Bossa Nova $^4_4$
FOR LOVIN' ME Travis Pattern Picking $^4_4$ / Snap Back Carter Style $^4_4$
FOR NO ONE Arpeggiated $^4_4$ / Arpeggiated Bass $^4_4$
FOR ONCE IN MY LIFE Fast $^4_4$ / Fast Folk $^4_4$
FORBIDDEN GAMES Arpeggiated $^3_4$ / Rasgueado Pull $^3_4$
FOUR Fast $^4_4$ / Fast Folk $^4_4$
FOUR STRONG WINDS Slow Bass $^4_4$ / Arpeggiated $^4_4$
(THE) FOX Fast $^4_4$ / Snap Back Carter Style $^4_4$
FOXY LADY Fast Rock $^4_4$ / Fast Bass Hard Rock $^4_4$

FREEDOM TRAIN Fast Rock 4/4 / Percussive Rock 4/4
FREIGHT TRAIN Fast 4/4 / Travis Pattern Picking 4/4
FREIHIET Slow Syncopated 4/4 / Snap Back Double Bass 4/4
FRENCH GIRL Slow 4/4 / Slow Bass 4/4
FUN TIME Pull Jazz 5/4
GALLOWS POLE Percussive Bass Blues 4/4 / Percussive Pinch Rock 4/4
GDEYETA GDEVITCHKA Pull Waltz 3/4 / Slow 3/4
GENTLE ON MY MIND Fast 4/4 / Travis Pattern Picking 4/4
GEORGIA Slow 4/4 / Slow Bass 4/4
GEORGY GIRL Fast Rock 4/4 / Fast Folk 4/4
GET A JOB Fast Rock 4/4 / Percussive Rock 4/4
GET BACK Fast Rock 4/4 / Fast Latin 4/4
GET ME TO THE CHURCH ON TIME Pull 4/4 / Fast 4/4
GET TOGETHER Fast Rock 4/4 / Fast Latin 4/4
GHOST RIDERS IN THE SKY Fast 4/4 / Snap Back Carter Style 4/4
GILGARRY MOUNTAIN Fast 4/4 / Snap Back Country Style 4/4
GIRL Slow Bass 4/4 / Slow Syncopated 4/4
(THE) GIRL FROM IPANIMA Slow Bass Pull 4/4 / Accented Pinch Bossa Nova 4/4
(THE) GIRL THAT I MARRY Pull Waltz 3/4 / Slow 3/4
GIVE PEACE A CHANCE Fast 3/4 / Snap Back Carter 3/4
GO DOWN YOU MURDERERS Slow 4/4 / Slow Bass 4/4
GO TELL IT ON THE MOUNTAIN Fast 4/4 / Fast Folk 4/4
GOD BLESS THE CHILD Slow 4/4 / Slow Bass 4/4
GOIN' DOWN THAT ROAD FEELIN' BLUE Fast 4/4 / Snap Back Carter Style 4/4
GOIN' OUT OF MY HEAD Fast Latin 4/4 / Moving Bass Pull Spanish 4/4
GOLDEN EARRINGS Slow 4/4 / Slow Bass 4/4
(THE) GOOD BOY Slow 4/4 / Pinch Slow 4/4
GOOD DAY SUNSHINE Slow Syncopated 4/4 / Snap Back Double Bass 4/4
GOOD MORNING STARSHINE Fast 4/4 / Slow Bass 4/4
GOOD NEWS, CHARIOTS COMIN' Fast 4/4 / Fast Folk 4/4
(THE) GOOD SHIP LOLLIPOP Pull 4/4 / Fast 4/4
GOODNIGHT SWEETHEART Arpeggiated Triplet 4/4 / Slow Syncopated 4/4
GOODY GOODY Fast 4/4 / Fast Folk 4/4
GOT MY MO JO WORKIN' Fast Rock 4/4 / Percussive Rock 4/4
GOTTA TRAVEL ON Fast 4/4 / Snap Back Carter Style 4/4
GRAVEY WALTZ Pull Waltz 3/4 / Pull Jazz 3/4
GREAT BALLS OF FIRE Fast Rock 4/4 / Percussive Rock 4/4
(THE) GREAT PRETENDER Arpeggiated Triplet 4/4 / Arpeggiated Double Bass Triplet 4/4
GREEN DOLPHIN STREET Fast Folk 4/4 / Slow Bass Pull 4/4
GREEN FIELDS Arpeggiated Triplet 4/4 / Arpeggiated Double Bass Triplet 4/4
(THE) GREEN, GREEN GRASS OF HOME Arpeggiated 4/4 / Slow Bass 4/4
GREEN LEAVES OF SUMMER Arpeggiated Triplet 4/4 / Arpeggiated Double Bass Triplet 4/4
GREENSLEEVES Slow 3/4 / Arpeggiated 3/4
GROOVIN' Slow Syncopated 4/4 / Fast Latin 4/4
GUARDIAN BEAUTY CONTEST Moving Bass Arpeggiated Calypso 4/4 / Fast Calypso 4/4
HA TOV (Hebrew) Fast Folk 4/4 / Pinch Folk Israeli 4/4
HALF MOON Fast Back Beat Rock 4/4 / Fast Bass Rock 4/4
HANA'VA BABANOT (Hebrew) Pull Mid-East 4/4 / Slow Bass 4/4
HANDSOME JOHNNY Fast 4/4 / Fast Folk 4/4
HANG ON SLOOPY Fast Rock 4/4 / Fast Latin 4/4
HAPPY BIRTHDAY Pull Waltz 3/4 / Slow 3/4
HAPPY HAPPY BIRTHDAY BABY Arpeggiated Triplet 4/4 / Arpeggiated Double Bass Triplet 4/4
HAPPY TOGETHER Slow Syncopated 4/4 / Percussive Bass Blues 4/4
HARALAMBIS (Greek) Moving Bass Pull Folk Greek 7/8
HARD AIN'T IT HARD Fast 4/4 / Snap Back Carter Style 4/4
HARD DAYS NIGHT Fast Rock 4/4 / Fast Latin 4/4
HARD TRAVELIN' Fast 4/4 / Snap Back Carter Style 4/4
HAVA NA SHIRA (Hebrew) Slow 4/4 / Slow Bass 4/4
HAVA NAGILA (Hebrew) Pull 4/4 / Pinch Folk Israeli 4/4
HAVANU SHALOM ALEICHEM (Hebrew) Pull 4/4 / Fast 4/4
HAVE YOU MET MISS JONES Fast 4/4 / Slow Bass Pull 4/4
HAZY SHADE OF WINTER Fast 4/4 / Fast Rock 4/4
HE Arpeggiated Triplet 4/4 / Arpeggiated Triplet Double Bass 4/4
HE'S GOT THE WHOLE WORLD IN HIS HANDS Fast 4/4 / Slow Syncopated 4/4
HE'S NOT HEAVY, HE'S MY BROTHER Slow Bass 4/4 / Pull Slow Bass Rock 4/4
HEART AND SOUL Slow Syncopated 4/4 / Snap Back Double Bass 4/4
HEATING CONDITIONS Pull Waltz 3/4 / Arpeggiated 3/4
HE'LL HAVE TO GO Slow 3/4 / Snap Back Carter Style 3/4
HELLO DOLLY Fast 4/4 / Fast Folk 4/4
HELLO GOODBYE Fast Rock 4/4 / Fast Latin 4/4
HELLO YOUNG LOVERS Pull Waltz 3/4 / Slow 3/4
HELP Fast Rock 4/4 / Fast Folk 4/4
HELP ME MAKE IT THROUGH THE NIGHT Slow 4/4 / Slow Bass 4/4
HELPLESSLY HOPING Travis Pattern Picking 4/4 / Snap Back Carter 4/4
HENRY THE EIGHT Fast Rock 4/4 / Percussive Rock 4/4
HERE THERE AND EVERYWHERE Slow 4/4 / Slow Bass 4/4
HERE'S THAT RAINY DAY Slow Bass 4/4 / Slow Bass Pull 4/4
HERNANDO'S HIDEAWAY Fast Latin 4/4 / Rasgueado Tango 4/4
HEY BO DIDDLEY Fast Rhythm And Blues Bo Diddley 4/4
HEY JUDE Slow 4/4 / Pull Slow Bass Rock 4/4
HEY NELLIE NELLIE Fast 4/4 / Fast Folk 4/4
HEY THAT'S NO WAY TO SAY GOODBYE Arpeggiated 4/4 / Moving Bass Pinch Ballad 4/4
HEY THERE Slow Syncopated 4/4 / Fast 4/4
HEY WHAT ABOUT ME Slow Bass 4/4 / Fast Folk 4/4
HEY YOU NEVER WILL KNOW ME Fast Latin 4/4 / Slow Bass 4/4
HIGH HEEL SNEAKERS Pull Slow Bass Rock 4/4 / Fast Bass Hard Rock 4/4

HINE MA TOV (Hebrew) Pull Waltz 3/4 / Slow 3/4
HIROSHIMA Slow 3/4 / Arpeggiated 3/4
HISTORIA DE UN AMOR (Spanish) Slow 4/4 / Slow Bass 4/4
HOBO'S LULLABYE Travis Pattern Picking 4/4 / Snap Back Folk 4/4
HOME IN THAT ROCK Fast 4/4 / Snap Back Carter Style 4/4
HOUND DOG Fast 4/4 / Fast Folk 4/4
(THE) HOUSE OF THE RISING SUN Arpeggiated Triplet 4/4 / Arpeggiated Double Bass Triplet 4/4
HOUSEWIFE'S LAMENT Pull 3/4 / Snap Back Carter 3/4
HOW ARE THINGS IN GLOCCAMORA Slow 4/4 / Slow Bass 4/4
HOW CAN WE HANG ON TO A DREAM Slow 3/4 / Arpeggiated 3/4
HOW DEEP IS THE OCEAN Slow Bass 4/4 / Pinch Bossa Nova 4/4
HOW HIGH THE MOON Fast 4/4 / Fast Folk 4/4
HOW INSENSITIVE (Brazil) Slow Bass Pull 4/4 / Pinch Bossa Nova 4/4
HUSHA BYE Slow 4/4 / Slow Bass 4/4
I AIN'T GOT NO HOME Fast 4/4 / Snap Back Folk 4/4
I AM A PILGRIM Travis Pattern Picking 4/4 / Snap Back Carter Style 4/4
I AM WOMAN Slow 4/4 / Slow Bass 4/4
I BEEN LIVING WITH THE BLUES Fast Folk 4/4 / Percussive Bass Blues 4/4
I BELIEVE Slow 4/4 / Arpeggiated 4/4
I BELIEVE IN YOU Fast 4/4 / Fast Folk 4/4
I CAN SEE CLEARLY NOW Fast Latin 4/4 / Percussive Rock 4/4
I CAN'T HELP FALLING IN LOVE WITH YOU Arpeggiated Triplet 4/4 / Arpeggiated Double Bass Triplet 4/4
I CAN'T LIVE Slow Bass 4/4 / Arpeggiated 4/4
I CAN'T STOP LOVING YOU Slow 4/4 / Slow Bass 4/4
I COULD HAVE DANCED ALL NIGHT Pull 4/4 / Moving Bass Arpeggiated Calypso 4/4
I COULD WRITE A BOOK Fast 4/4 / Fast Folk 4/4
I DIDN'T KNOW WHAT TIME IT WAS Fast 4/4 / Slow Bass Pull 4/4
I DIG ROCK AND ROLL MUSIC Fast Rock 4/4 / Pull Slow Bass Rock 4/4
I DO ADORE HER Moving Bass Arpeggiated Calypso 4/4 / Fast Calypso 4/4
I DON'T KNOW HOW TO LOVE HIM Slow 4/4 / Slow Bass 4/4
I FEEL FINE Fast Rock 4/4 / Fast Folk 4/4
I FEEL PRETTY Pull Waltz 3/4 / Slow 3/4
I FEEL THE EARTH MOVE Slow Bass 4/4 / Fast Latin 4/4
I GET A KICK OUT OF YOU Fast 4/4 / Fast Folk 4/4
I GOT A WOMAN Fast Rock 4/4 / Percussive Rock 4/4
I GOT YOU BABE Arpeggiated Triplet 4/4 / Pinch Blues Triplet 4/4
I HAD ONE LOVE Moving Bass Pull Folk Greek 7/8
I HEARD IT THROUGH THE GRAPEVINE Slow Bass 4/4 / Fast Latin 4/4
I JUST WANT TO CELEBRATE Fast Rock 4/4 / Fast Bass Hard Rock 4/4
I KNOW WHERE I'M GOING Slow 4/4 / Slow Syncopated 4/4
I LEFT MY HEART IN SAN FRANCISCO Slow Bass 4/4 / Slow Bass Pull 4/4
I LOVE PARIS Pull 4/4 / Fast 4/4
I LOVE YOU Fast 4/4 / Slow Bass Pull 4/4
I NEVER WILL MARRY Pull Waltz 3/4 / Slow 3/4
I ONLY HAVE EYES FOR YOU Fast Folk 4/4 / Slow Bass Pull 4/4
I REMEMBER APRIL Fast 4/4 / Fast Folk 4/4
I REMEMBER YOU Fast 4/4 / Fast Latin 4/4
I RODE MY BICYCLE PAST YOUR WINDOW LAST NIGHT Slow Bass 4/4 / Fast Latin 4/4
I SHOULD CARE Slow 4/4 / Slow Bass Pull 4/4
I SHOULD HAVE KNOWN BETTER Fast Rock 4/4 / Percussive Rock 4/4
I STOLE ME SE OZEN (Bulgarian) Moving Bass Pull Folk Greek 7/8
I WALK THE LINE Fast 4/4 / Snap Back Carter Style 4/4
I WANT TO HOLD YOUR HAND Fast Rock 4/4 / Fast Latin 4/4
I WISH I KNEW HOW Fast Rock 4/4 / Fast Latin 4/4
I WISH YOU LOVE Slow Bass 4/4 / Slow Bass Pull 4/4
I'D LIKE TO TEACH THE WORLD Slow Syncopated 4/4 / Snap Back Folk 4/4
IF I FELL IN LOVE WITH YOU Slow 4/4 / Slow Bass 4/4
IF I HAD A HAMMER Fast 4/4 / Fast Folk 4/4
IF I SHOULD LOSE YOU Slow 4/4 / Slow Bass 4/4
IF I WERE A CARPENTER Slow Bass 4/4 / Moving Bass Pinch Ballad 4/4
IF I WERE A RICH MAN Pull 4/4 / Pull Folk Chasidic 4/4
IF THIS ISN'T LOVE Fast 4/4 / Moving Bass Arpeggiated Calypso 4/4
IF WE ONLY HAVE LOVE Arpeggiated Triplet 4/4 / Arpeggiated Double Bass Triplet 4/4
I'LL BE SEEING YOU Fast 4/4 / Fast Folk 4/4
I'LL CLOSE MY EYES Slow 4/4 / Slow Bass Pull 4/4
I'LL CRY INSTEAD Fast Folk 4/4 / Travis Pattern Picking 4/4
I'LL NEVER FALL IN LOVE AGAIN Fast 4/4 / Fast Folk 4/4
I'LL NEVER FIND ANOTHER YOU Fast 4/4 / Fast Folk 4/4
I'M A RAMBLER I'M A GAMBLER Fast 3/4 / Snap Back Carter Style 3/4
I'M GONNA GET MARRIED Fast 4/4 / Fast Folk 4/4
I'M HAPPY JUST TO DANCE WITH YOU Fast Rock 4/4 / Fast Latin 4/4
I'M IN LOVE AGAIN Fast Rock 4/4 / Slow Bass 4/4
I'M JUST A GIRL WHO CAN'T SAY NO Pull 4/4 / Fast 4/4
I'M OLD FASHIONED Slow 4/4 / Slow Bass 4/4
I'M ON MY WAY Fast 4/4 / Fast Folk 4/4
I'M SO GLAD Fast Rock 4/4 / Fast Bass Rock 4/4
IMAGINATION Slow 4/4 / Slow Bass 4/4
IMPOSSIBLE DREAM Arpeggiated Triplet 4/4 / Arpeggiated Double Bass Triplet 4/4
IN CONTEMPT Slow 4/4 / Slow Bass 4/4
(THE) IN CROWD Fast Latin 4/4 / Percussive Bass Note Rock 4/4
IN MY LIFE Slow 4/4 / Slow Bass 4/4
IN THE EVENIN' WHEN THE SUN GOES DOWN Slow Bass 4/4 / Percussive Bass Blues 4/4
IN THE HEAT OF THE SUMMER Travis Pattern Picking 4/4 / Snap Back Carter 4/4

IN THE STILL OF THE NIGHT Arpeggiated Triplet 4/4 / Arpeggiated Double Bass Triplet 4/4
INCHWORM Pull Waltz 3/4 / Slow 3/4
INDIANA Fast 4/4 / Fast Folk 4/4
IRENE Pull Waltz 3/4 / Slow 3/4
IRISH BALLAD Pull 4/4 / Slow Syncopated 4/4
IRISH JIG Pull 4/4 / Arpeggiated Triplet 4/4
ISLAND IN THE SUN Moving Bass Arpeggiated Calypso 4/4 / Fast Calypso 4/4
IT WAS A VERY GOOD YEAR Slow 4/4 / Slow Bass 4/4
I'VE GOT A LOT OF LIVIN' TO DO Fast 4/4 / Fast Folk 4/4
I'VE GOT NEWS FOR YOU Fast Rock 4/4 / Percussive Bass Blues 4/4
I'VE GOT TO GET A MESSAGE TO YOU Slow 4/4 / Slow Bass 4/4
I'VE GOT TO KNOW Fast 3/4 / Snap Back Carter Style 4/4
I'VE GROWN ACCUSTOMED TO HER FACE Slow 4/4 / Slow Bass 4/4
I'VE JUST SEEN A FACE Fast 4/4 / Snap Back Folk 4/4
JAILHOUSE ROCK Fast Rock 4/4 / Fast Folk 4/4
JAMAICA FAREWELL Moving Bass Pinch Ballad 4/4 / Moving Bass Arpeggiated Calypso 4/4
JERUSALEM OF GOLD (Hebrew) Slow 3/4 / Arpeggiated 3/4
JESSE JAMES Fast 4/4 / Snap Back Carter Style 4/4
JESUS CHRIST SUPERSTAR (EVERYTHING'S ALL RIGHT) Pull Jazz 5/4
JOEY Fast 4/4 / Fast Folk 4/4
JOHN HARDY Fast 4/4 / Snap Back Carter Style 4/4
JOHNNY B. GOODE Fast Rock 4/4 / Percussive Rock 4/4
JORDU Fast 4/4 / Fast Rock 4/4
JOSHUA Fast 4/4 / Fast Folk 4/4
JOY TO THE WORLD Fast Rock 4/4 / Percussive Rock 4/4
(THE) JOYS OF LOVE Slow 3/4 / Arpeggiated 3/4
JUMPIN' WITH SYMPHONY SID Fast 4/4 / Fast Folk 4/4
JUNE KNIGHT Fast 4/4 / Slow Bass Pull 4/4
JUST A CLOSER WALK WITH THEE Slow Bass 4/4 / Fast Folk 4/4
JUST FRIENDS Fast 4/4 / Fast Folk 4/4
JUST LIKE A WOMAN Slow 4/4 / Slow Bass 4/4
KANSAS CITY Fast Rock 4/4 / Fast Rhythm And Blues Shuffle 4/4
KATY CRUEL Slow 4/4 / Slow Bass 4/4
KAZEH (Japanese) Arpeggiated 4/4 / Slow Bass Pull 4/4
KEEP ON THE SUNNY SIDE Fast 4/4 / Snap Back Carter Style 4/4
KILLING ME SOFTLY Moving Bass Pinch Ballad 4/4 / Slow Bass Pull 4/4
KING OF THE ROAD Fast 4/4 / Fast Folk 4/4
KISS OF FIRE Moving Bass Pull Spanish 4/4 / Rasgueado Tango 4/4
KISSES SWEETER THAN WINE Slow Syncopated 4/4 / Snap Back Double Bass 4/4
KODACHROME Fast Rock 4/4 / Fast Latin 4/4
KUMBAYA Slow 4/4 / Slow Bass 4/4
(THE) L AND N DON'T STOP HERE ANY MORE Travis Pattern Picking 4/4 / Snap Back Carter Style 4/4
LA BAMBA Fast Latin 4/4 / Percussive Rock 4/4
LA COMPARSITA (Spanish) Rasgueado Moving Bass Pull 4/4 / Rasgueado Tango 4/4
LA CRUZ MERANGUE Moving Bass Pull Spanish 4/4 / Fast Merangue 4/4
LA FIDOLERA (Spanish) Fast 3/4 / Snap Back Carter Style 3/4
LA LLORONA (Spanish) Rasgueado Pull 3/4 / Rasgueado Huapanga 3/4
LA MARSEILLAISE (French) Slow Syncopated 4/4 / Fast 4/4
LADY OF SPAIN Pull Waltz 3/4 / Rasgueado Pull 3/4
LASS FROM THE LOW COUNTRY Slow 3/4 / Arpeggiated 3/4
LAST NIGHT I DIDN'T GET TO SLEEP Slow 4/4 / Slow Bass 4/4
LAST TANGO ON CANAL STREET Moving Bass Pull Spanish 4/4 / Rasgueado Tango 4/4
THE LAST THING ON MY MIND Fast 4/4 / Snap Back Carter Style 4/4
LAST TIME Fast 4/4 / Percussive Rock 4/4
(THE) LAST TRAIN TO CLARKSVILLE Fast Rock 4/4 / Percussive Rock 4/4
(THE) LAST TRAIN TO SAN FERNANDO Moving Bass Arpeggiated Calypso 4/4 / Fast Calypso 4/4
LAURA Slow Bass 4/4 / Slow Bass Pull 4/4
LAY LADY LAY Fast Latin 4/4 / Slow Bass 4/4
LEAN ON ME Slow Bass 4/4 / Fast Latin 4/4
LEAVING ON A JET PLANE Fast 4/4 / Travis Pattern Picking 4/4
LEMON TREE Fast 4/4 / Slow 4/4
LET IT BE Slow Bass 4/4 / Fast Back Beat Rock 4/4
LET IT BE ME Slow 4/4 / Arpeggiated 4/4
LET THE GOOD TIMES ROLL Fast Rock 4/4 / Slow Bass 4/4
LET THE SUN SHINE Fast Rock 4/4 / Fast Latin 4/4
LET'S TWIST AGAIN Fast Rock 4/4 / Fast Twist 4/4
THE LETTER Fast Rock 4/4 / Percussive Rock 4/4
LIGHT MY FIRE Fast Latin 4/4 / Percussive Rock 4/4
LIKE A ROLLING STONE Slow Bass 4/4 / Fast Latin 4/4
LIKE SOMEONE IN LOVE Slow 4/4 / Slow Bass 4/4
LIMBO ROCK Fast Latin 4/4 / Fast Calypso 4/4
(THE) LION SLEEPS TONIGHT Fast 4/4 / Fast Folk 4/4
LISTEN TO THE FALLING RAIN Fast 4/4 / Snap Back Carter Style 4/4
LITTLE BOXES Pull Waltz 3/4 / Slow 3/4
LITTLE DARLIN' PAL OF MINE Fast 4/4 / Travis Pattern Picking 4/4
LITTLE GIRL BLUE Slow Bass 4/4 / Arpeggiated 4/4
LITTLE GREEN APPLES Slow Bass 4/4 / Arpeggiated Bass 4/4
LITTLE MAN YOU'VE HAD A BUSY DAY Slow 4/4 / Slow Bass 4/4
LITTLE MOSES Fast 3/4 / Snap Back Carter Style 3/4
LITTLE SEA Moving Bass Pull Folk Greek 7/4
LIVERPOOL LULLABY Slow 4/4 / Slow Bass 4/4
LOLLIPOPS AND ROSES Slow 4/4 / Slow Bass 4/4
(THE) LONESOME DEATH OF HATTIE CANOL Fast 3/4 / Snap Back Carter Style 3/4

LONESOME VALLEY Fast 4/4 / Snap Back Folk 4/4
LONG AGO AND FAR AWAY Fast 4/4 / Slow 4/4
LONG CHAINS Fast Rock 4/4 / Percussive Pinch Rock 4/4
(THE) LONG LONESOME ROAD Fast 4/4 / Snap Back Carter Style 4/4
LONG TIME MAN Fast 4/4 / Travis Pattern Picking 4/4
LONG TRAIN COMIN' Fast Rock 4/4 / Percussive Rock 4/4
LOO V'HEE (Hebrew) Slow Bass 4/4 / Pull Slow Bass Rock 4/4
LOOK FOR THE SILVER LINING Fast 4/4 / Fast Folk 4/4
LOOK WHAT THEY'VE DONE TO MY SONG Fast 4/4 / Snap Back Nashville Style 4/4
LOOKIN' OUT MY BACK DOOR Fast 4/4 / Fast Folk 4/4
LOS CONTRABANDISTOS DE RONDA (Spanish) Rasgueado Mexican 3/4 / Percussive Tambor 3/4
LOS CUATRO GENERALES (Spanish) Pull Waltz 3/4 / Rasgueado Mexican 3/4
LOTS OF LOVE Fast 4/4 / Percussive Fast 4/4
LOUIE, LOUIE Fast Rock 4/4 / Percussive Rock 4/4
LOVE ALONE Moving Bass Arpeggiated Calypso 4/4 / Fast Calypso 4/4
LOVE IS BLUE Slow 4/4 / Slow Bass 4/4
LOVE LETTERS Arpeggiated 4/4 / Slow Bass Pull 4/4
LOVE ME OR LEAVE ME Fast 4/4 / Fast Rock 4/4
LOVE MINUS ZERO Slow Bass 4/4 / Arpeggiated 4/4
LOVE STORY Slow Bass 4/4 / Arpeggiated 4/4
LOVE THEME FROM ROMEO AND JULIET Slow 3/4 / Arpeggiated 3/4
LOVE THEME FROM THE GODFATHER Slow 4/4 / Slow Bass 4/4
LOVE WALKED IN Slow 4/4 / Fast 4/4
LOVER Pull Waltz 3/4 / Slow 3/4
LOVER COME BACK TO ME Fast 4/4 / Fast Folk 4/4
LOVER MAN Slow 4/4 / Slow Bass 4/4
LULLABY OF BIRDLAND Fast 4/4 / Fast Rock 4/4
LULLABY OF THE BELLS Arpeggiated Triplet 4/4 / Arpeggiated Double Bass Triplet 4/4
LULLABY OF THE LEAVES Fast 4/4 / Slow Syncopated 4/4
LUSH LIFE Slow 4/4 / Slow Bass 4/4
MACHAR (Hebrew) Pull 4/4 / Fast 4/4
MACK THE KNIFE Fast 4/4 / Percussive Fast 4/4
MAGGIE MAY Fast 4/4 / Travis Pattern Picking 4/4
MAGGIE'S FARM Fast 4/4 / Fast Rock 4/4
MAKE ME A PALLET ON THE FLOOR Fast 4/4 / Inflected Pattern Picking 4/4
MALA FEMINA (Italian) Moving Bass Pull Spanish 4/4 / Rasgueado Moving Bass Pull 4/4
MALAGUENA SALEROSA (Spanish) Rasgueado Mexican 3/4 / Percussive Tambor 3/4
MAME Fast 4/4 / Fast Folk 4/4
MAN OF CONSTANT SORROW Arpeggiated 4/4 / Travis Pattern Picking 4/4
MAN SMART, WOMAN SMARTER Moving Bass Arpeggiated Calypso 4/4 / Fast Calypso 4/4
MANGWAINI MAPULELI (African) Fast 3/4 / Fast Rock 3/4
MANTECCA Fast Latin 4/4 / Percussive Rock 4/4
MARAKESH EXPRESS Fast 4/4 / Travis Pattern Picking 4/4
MARCHING TO PRETORIA Pull 4/4 / Fast 4/4
MARIA Slow 4/4 / Slow Bass 4/4
MARY IN THE MORNING Arpeggiated 4/4 / Slow Bass Pull 4/4
MARYANNE Moving Bass Arpeggiated Calypso 4/4 / Fast Calypso 4/4
MASOCHISTIC TANGO Moving Bass Pull Spanish 4/4 / Rasgueado Tango 4/4
MATCHMAKER Pull Waltz 3/4 / Snap Back Carter Style 3/4
MAXWELL'S SILVER HAMMER Slow Syncopated 4/4 / Snap Back Folk 4/4
MAYBE Arpeggiated Triplet 4/4 / Arpeggiated Double Bass Triplet 4/4
ME AND BOBBY McGEE Fast 4/4 / Snap Back Folk 4/4
ME AND JULIO DOWN BY THE SCHOOL YARD Fast Rock 4/4 / Percussive Rock 4/4
ME CABALLO BLANCO (Spanish) Rasgueado Pull 3/4 / Rasgueado Mexican 3/4
MEAN TO ME Slow 4/4 / Slow Bass 4/4
MEDITATION Slow Bass Pull 4/4 / Pinch Bossa Nova 4/4
MELLOW YELLOW Fast Rock 4/4 / Slow Syncopated 4/4
MIAMI BEACH RHUMBA Moving Bass Pull Spanish 4/4 / Rasgueado Moving Bass Pull 4/4
MICHAEL ROW THE BOAT ASHORE Fast 4/4 / Snap Back Carter Style 4/4
MICHELE Slow 4/4 / Slow Bass 4/4
MIDNIGHT HOUR Fast Rock 4/4 / Percussive Rock 4/4
MIDNIGHT SPECIAL Fast 4/4 / Fast Rhythm And Blues Shuffle 4/4
MINER'S LIFE Fast 4/4 / Travis Pattern Picking 4/4
MISERLOU (Greek) Pull Mid-East 4/4 / Moving Bass Pull Spanish 4/4
MISSION IMPOSSIBLE Pull Jazz 5/4
MR. BIG SHOT Fast Rock 4/4 / Fast Latin 4/4
MR. BO JANGLES Slow 3/4 / Inverted Pattern Picking 3/4
MR. TAMBORINE MAN Fast Folk 4/4 / Travis Pattern Picking 4/4
MRS. ROBINSON Fast Rock 4/4 / Fast Folk 4/4
MISTY Slow 4/4 / Slow Bass 4/4
MOCKINGBIRD HILL Pull Waltz 3/4 / Snap Back Carter Style 3/4
MONDAY, MONDAY Fast Rock 4/4 / Fast Latin 4/4
MONEY IS KING Moving Bass Arpeggiated Calypso 4/4 / Fast Calypso 4/4
MOON RIVER Slow 3/4 / Arpeggiated 3/4
MOONLIGHT IN VERMONT Slow 4/4 / Slow Bass 4/4
MORE Slow 4/4 / Moving Bass Pull Spanish 4/4
MORNING MORGANTOWN Arpeggiated 4/4 / Arpeggiated Bass 4/4
MOSCOW NIGHTS (Russian) Slow 4/4 / Slow Bass 4/4
(THE) MOST BEAUTIFUL GIRL IN THE WORLD Pull Waltz 3/4 / Slow 3/4
MOUNTAIN DEW Fast 4/4 / Snap Back Carter Style 4/4
MOVE Fast 4/4 / Fast Folk 4/4
MUSTAFA (North African) Pull Mid-East 4/4 / Moving Bass Pull Spanish 4/4

MY CREOLE BELLE (French Creole) Travis Pattern Picking $^4_4$ / Extended Complex Pattern Picking $^4_4$
MY FATHER Slow $^3_4$ / Arpeggiated $^3_4$
MY FAVORITE THINGS Pull Waltz $^3_4$ / Pull Jazz $^3_4$
MY FOOLISH HEART Slow Bass $^4_4$ / Arpeggiated Bass $^4_4$
MY FUNNY VALENTINE Slow $^4_4$ / Slow Bass $^4_4$
MY SWEET LORD Fast Rock $^4_4$ / Fast Folk $^4_4$
NAD ELAN (Hebrew) Pull Mid-East $^4_4$ / Slow Bass $^4_4$
NAVA Slow Bass Pull $^4_4$ / Accented Pinch Bossa Nova $^4_4$
THE NEARNESS OF YOU Slow $^4_4$ / Slow Bass $^4_4$
NEVER BEEN TO SPAIN Slow Bass $^4_4$ / Pull Slow Bass Rock $^4_4$
NEVER ON A SUNDAY Fast Latin $^4_4$ / Rasgueado Moving Bass Pull $^4_4$
NIGHT BOAT Slow Bass Pull $^4_4$ / Pinch Bossa Nova $^4_4$
NIGHT IN TUNISIA Moving Bass Arpeggiated Calypso $^4_4$ / Fast Calypso $^4_4$
(THE) NIGHT THEY DROVE OLD DIXIE DOWN Slow Bass $^4_4$ / Fast Latin $^4_4$
NIGHT TRAIN Fast Latin $^4_4$ / Fast Rhythm And Blues Shuffle $^4_4$
NIGHT WINDS Slow $^4_4$ / Slow Bass $^4_4$
NINE HUNDRED MILES Fast $^4_4$ / Snap Back Carter Style $^4_4$
NOCHES DE LUNA (Spanish) Rasgueado Mexican $^3_4$ / Percussive Tambor $^3_4$
NORWEGIAN WOOD Fast $^3_4$ / Fast Rock $^3_4$
NOWHERE MAN Slow $^4_4$ / Fast Latin $^4_4$
NUMBER TWELVE TRAIN Slow Syncopated $^4_4$ / Percussive Bass Blues $^4_4$
O GOUSO (Brazilian) Slow Bass Pull $^4_4$ / Pinch Samba $^4_4$
O PATO (Brazilian) Slow Bass Pull $^4_4$ / Pinch Samba $^4_4$
O SOLE MIO (Italian) Arpeggiated $^4_4$ / Slow Bass Pull $^4_4$
OB LA DI Fast Latin $^4_4$ / Fast Calypso $^4_4$
ODE TO BILLIE JOE Slow Bass $^4_4$ / Pull Slow Bass Rock $^4_4$
OH BABE IT AIN'T NO LIE Travis Pattern $^4_4$ / Full Pattern Picking $^4_4$
OH FREEDOM Fast Rock $^4_4$ / Percussive Rock $^4_4$
OH MARY DON'T YOU WEEP Fast $^4_4$ / Fast Folk $^4_4$
OKLAHOMA Pull $^4_4$ / Fast $^4_4$
OLD DEVIL MOON Moving Bass Pinch Ballad $^4_4$ / Fast Calypso $^4_4$
OLD JOE CLARK Fast $^4_4$ / Snap Back Calypso $^4_4$
ON BROADWAY Fast Rock $^4_4$ / Fast Latin $^4_4$
ON THE STREET WHERE YOU LIVE Fast $^4_4$ / Fast Folk $^4_4$
ON THE TRAIL OF THE BUFFALO Fast $^4_4$ / Snap Back Carter Style $^4_4$
ON TOP OF OLD SMOKEY Pull Waltz $^3_4$ / Snap Back Carter Style $^3_4$
ONCE IN A WHILE Fast $^4_4$ / Slow Bass Pull $^4_4$
ONE HAND, ONE HEART Slow $^4_4$ / Slow Bass $^4_4$
ONE LESS BELL TO ANSWER Slow $^4_4$ / Slow Bass $^4_4$
ONE MAN'S HANDS Fast $^4_4$ / Snap Back Carter Style $^4_4$
ONE MINT JULEP Fast Rock $^4_4$ / Fast Latin $^4_4$
ONE NOTE SAMBA (Brazil) Slow Bass Pull $^4_4$ / Pinch Samba $^4_4$
ONE, TWO, THREE Slow Bass Pull $^4_4$ / Fast Latin $^4_4$
ONLY YOU Arpeggiated Triplet $^4_4$ / Arpeggiated Double Bass Triplet $^4_4$
ORNITHOLOGY Fast $^4_4$ / Fast Folk $^4_4$
OSEH SHALOM Pull $^4_4$ / Fast $^4_4$
OTCHI TSCHORNIA (Russian) Pull Waltz $^3_4$ / Slow $^3_4$
OUR DAY WILL COME Moving Bass Pull Spanish $^4_4$ / Moving Bass Slow $^4_4$
OUR LOVE IS HERE TO STAY Fast $^4_4$ / Slow Bass $^4_4$
OUT OF NOWHERE Fast $^4_4$ / Fast Latin $^4_4$
OUT OF THIS WORLD Moving Bass Pull Spanish $^4_4$ / Slow Bass Pull $^4_4$
OVER THE MOUNTAIN Arpeggiated Triplet $^4_4$ / Arpeggiated Double Bass Triplet $^4_4$
PACK UP YOUR SORROWS Fast $^4_4$ / Snap Back Carter Style $^4_4$
THE PARTY'S OVER Slow $^4_4$ / Slow Bass $^4_4$
PASSIN' THROUGH Fast $^4_4$ / Snap Back Carter Style $^4_4$
PASTURES OF PLENTY Fast $^4_4$ / Snap Back Folk $^4_4$
PAY ME MY MONEY DOWN Moving Bass Arpeggiated Calypso $^4_4$ / Fast Calypso $^4_4$
PENNIES FROM HEAVEN Fast $^4_4$ / Fast Rock $^4_4$
PENNY LANE Slow $^4_4$ / Slow Syncopated $^4_4$
PEOPLE (WHO NEED PEOPLE) Slow $^4_4$ / Slow Bass $^4_4$
PEOPLE GET READY Fast Rock $^4_4$ / Fast Latin $^4_4$
PEOPLE GOT TO BE FREE Fast Rock $^4_4$ / Percussive Rock $^4_4$
PEOPLE WILL SAY WE'RE IN LOVE Fast $^4_4$ / Snap Back Carter Style $^4_4$
PEPPERMINT TWIST Fast Rock $^4_4$ / Fast Twist $^4_4$
PERDIDO Fast $^4_4$ / Percussive Fast $^4_4$
PERFIDIA Moving Bass Pull Spanish $^4_4$ / Rasgueado Moving Bass Pull $^4_4$
PERSONALITY Fast $^4_4$ / Fast Rock $^4_4$
PIECE OF MY HEART Fast Latin $^4_4$ / Fast Back Beat Rock $^4_4$
PLAYBOYS AND PLAYGIRLS Fast $^4_4$ / Snap Back Carter Style $^4_4$
PLEASE DON'T LAY YOUR TRIP ON ME Travis Pattern Picking $^4_4$ / Snap Back Nashville Style $^4_4$
PLEASE, PLEASE ME Fast Rock $^4_4$ / Percussive Rock $^4_4$
POCO PELO Fast Latin $^4_4$ / Percussive Rock $^4_4$
POLKA DOTS AND MOONBEAMS Slow $^4_4$ / Slow Bass $^4_4$
POLLY VON Travis Pattern Picking $^4_4$ / Full Inverted Pattern Picking $^4_4$
POR FAVOR Fast Latin $^4_4$ / Percussive Rock $^4_4$
THE POWER AND THE GLORY Fast $^4_4$ / Snap Back Carter Style $^4_4$
THE PREACHER Fast Latin $^4_4$ / Fast Folk $^4_4$
PROUD MARY Fast Rock $^4_4$ / Percussive Rock $^4_4$
PUFF THE MAGIC DRAGON Fast $^4_4$ / Travis Pattern Picking $^4_4$
PUPPY LOVE Arpeggiated Triplet $^4_4$ / Arpeggiated Double Bass Triplet $^4_4$
PURPLE HAZE Fast Rock $^4_4$ / Fast Bass Hard Rock $^4_4$
PUT YOUR HAND IN THE HAND Fast Rock $^4_4$ / Fast Latin $^4_4$
PUTTIN' ON THE STYLE Fast $^4_4$ / Snap Back Carter Style $^4_4$
QUE BONITA BANDERA Fast Latin $^4_4$ / Moving Bass Pull Spanish $^4_4$
QUIET NIGHTS Slow Bass Pull $^4_4$ / Accented Pinch Bossa Nova $^4_4$
RAD HA LAYLA Pull $^4_4$ / Fast $^4_4$
RAG DOLL Fast Rock $^4_4$ / Percussive Rock $^4_4$
RAGAPUTI RAGA Fast $^4_4$ / Fast Rock $^4_4$
RAILROAD BILL Fast $^4_4$ / Travis Pattern Picking $^4_4$
RAINDROPS KEEP FALLIN' ON MY HEAD Slow Syncopated $^4_4$ / Slow Bass $^4_4$
RAINY DAY WOMAN Fast $^4_4$ / Percussive Bass Blues $^4_4$
REASON TO BELIEVE Slow Bass $^4_4$ / Travis Pattern Picking $^4_4$
RED ROSY BUSH Slow $^4_4$ / Slow Bass $^4_4$
RED RUBBER BALL Fast Rock $^4_4$ / Percussive Rock $^4_4$
REUBEN JAMES Fast $^4_4$ / Snap Back Carter Style $^4_4$
(THE) RIVER OF MY PEOPLE Slow $^3_4$ / Arpeggiated $^3_4$
ROCK AND ROLL MUSIC Fast Rock $^4_4$ / Fast Twist $^4_4$
ROCK AROUND THE CLOCK Fast Rock $^4_4$ / Percussive Rock $^4_4$
ROCKIN' ROBIN Fast Rock $^4_4$ / Percussive Rock $^4_4$
ROCKY RACCOON Slow Bass $^4_4$ / Snap Back Double Bass $^4_4$
ROLL ON COLUMBIA ROLL ON Fast $^3_4$ / Snap Back Carter Style $^3_4$
ROLL OVER BEETHOVEN Fast Rock $^4_4$ / Percussive Rock $^4_4$
ROSA MARINA Slow Bass Pull $^4_4$ / Accented Pinch Bossa Nova $^4_4$
ROSE Slow $^4_4$ / Pinch Slow $^4_4$
'ROUND MIDNIGHT Slow $^4_4$ / Slow Bass $^4_4$
ROUND THE BAY OF MEXICO Fast $^4_4$ / Slow Syncopated $^4_4$
ROZHINKES MIT MANDLEN Pull Waltz $^3_4$ / Slow $^3_4$
RUN COME SEE JERUSALEM Fast $^4_4$ / Snap Back Carter Style $^4_4$
RUNAROUND SUE Fast Rock $^4_4$ / Percussive Rock $^4_4$
RUNAWAY Fast Rock $^4_4$ / Moving Bass Pull Spanish $^4_4$
ST. LOUIS BLUES Fast Rhythm And Blues Shuffle $^4_4$ / Percussive Bass Blues $^4_4$
ST. THOMAS Fast Latin $^4_4$ / Fast Calypso $^4_4$
SAKURA Slow $^4_4$ / Pull Arpeggiated $^4_4$
SAL'S LINE Fast $^4_4$ / Fast Folk $^4_4$
SALTY DOG Fast $^4_4$ / Snap Back Folk $^4_4$
SAMBA DE MINBA TERRA Slow Bass Pull $^4_4$ / Pinch Samba $^4_4$
SAMBA DE ORPHEU (SWEET HAPPY LIFE) Slow Bass Pull $^4_4$ / Pinch Samba $^4_4$
SAMBA DO AVIAO Slow Bass Pull $^4_4$ / Pinch Samba $^4_4$
SAMIOTISSA Moving Bass Pull Folk Greek $^7_8$
SATISFACTION Fast Rock $^4_4$ / Percussive Rock $^4_4$
SAN FRANCISCO (WEAR SOME FLOWERS IN HER HAIR) Fast $^4_4$ / Slow Bass $^4_4$
SAN FRANCISCO BAY BLUES Fast $^4_4$ / Fast Folk $^4_4$
SANTA LUCIA Pull Waltz $^3_4$ / Slow $^3_4$
SATIN DOLL Fast $^4_4$ / Fast Latin $^4_4$
SAVE THE LAST DANCE FOR ME Fast Rock $^4_4$ / Percussive Bass Note Rock $^4_4$
SAY HAS ANYBODY SEEN MY SWEET GYPSY ROSE Fast $^4_4$ / Fast Folk $^4_4$
SCANDAL IN ST. THOMAS Pull Waltz $^3_4$ / Fast $^3_4$
SCARBOROUGH FAIR Slow $^3_4$ / Arpeggiated $^3_4$
SCARLET RIBBONS Slow $^3_4$ / Pinch Slow $^3_4$
SCOTCH AND SODA Slow Syncopated $^4_4$ / Slow Bass $^4_4$
SEALED WITH A KISS Slow $^4_4$ / Slow Bass $^4_4$
SEARCHING FOR THE LAMBS (Greek) Pull Jazz $^5_4$
SECRET LOVE Fast $^4_4$ / Fast Folk $^4_4$
SEE YOU IN SEPTEMBER Fast $^4_4$ / Fast Folk $^4_4$
SEPTEMBER SONG Slow $^4_4$ / Slow Bass $^4_4$
SERENATA Fast $^4_4$ / Moving Bass Pull Spanish $^4_4$
SERMONETTE Fast $^4_4$ / Fast Latin $^4_4$
SH-BOOM Arpeggiated Triplet $^4_4$ / Percussive Bass Blues $^4_4$
(THE) SHADOW OF YOUR SMILE Slow Bass Pull $^4_4$ / Pinch Bossa Nova $^4_4$
SHAKIN' UP THE NATION Fast Rock $^4_4$ / Fast Bass Motown Rock $^4_4$
SHAMBALA Fast Rock $^4_4$ / Fast Latin $^4_4$
SHAREM EL SHEICH (Hebrew) Arpeggiated Triplet $^4_4$ / Arpeggiated Double Bass Triplet $^4_4$
SHE LOVES YOU, YEAH, YEAH, YEAH Fast Rock $^4_4$ / Percussive Rock $^4_4$
SHE PROMISED TO MEET ME Moving Bass Arpeggiated Calypso $^4_4$ / Fast Calypso $^4_4$
SHE'S A WOMAN (W-O-M-A-N) Fast Rock $^4_4$ / Fast Latin $^4_4$
SHE'S LIKE A SWALLOW Slow $^3_4$ / Pinch Slow $^3_4$
SHENANDOAH Slow $^4_4$ / Slow Bass $^4_4$
SHIMMY, SHIMMY KO KO BOP Fast Rock $^4_4$ / Percussive Rock $^4_4$
SHINE Fast $^4_4$ / Percussive Fast $^4_4$
SHIP IN THE SKY Fast $^4_4$ / Snap Back Folk Style $^4_4$
SI TU QUIEROS ESCRIBIR Rasgueado Moving Bass Pull $^4_4$ / Rasgueado Spanish $^4_4$
SILHOUETTES Arpeggiated Triplet $^4_4$ / Arpeggiated Triplet Double Bass $^4_4$
SILVER'S REALLY GREY Moving Bass Pinch Ballad $^4_4$ / Travis Pattern Picking $^4_4$
SINCE I MET YOU BABY Fast Rhythm And Blues Shuffle $^4_4$ / Percussive Bass Blues $^4_4$
SINNER MAN Fast $^4_4$ / Snap Back Carter Style $^4_4$
SISU ET YERUSHALAYIM Pull $^4_4$ / Snap Back Carter Style $^4_4$
SIXTEEN CANDLES Arpeggiated Triplet $^4_4$ / Arpeggiated Double Bass Triplet $^4_4$
SIXTEEN TONS Fast $^4_4$ / Slow Bass $^4_4$
SKILLET GOOD AND GREASY Fast $^4_4$ / Snap Back Carter Style $^4_4$
SLOOP JOHN B Moving Bass Arpeggiated Calypso $^4_4$ / Fast Calypso $^4_4$
SO LONG IT'S BEEN GOOD TO KNOW YOU Fast $^3_4$ / Snap Back Carter Style $^3_4$
SO WHAT Fast $^4_4$ / Fast Calypso $^4_4$
SOCIETY'S CHILD Slow Bass $^4_4$ / Fast Latin $^4_4$
SOMEDAY MY PRINCE WILL COME Pull Waltz $^3_4$ / Pull Jazz $^3_4$
SOMEDAY SOON Fast Folk $^4_4$ / Travis Pattern Picking $^4_4$
SOMETHING Slow $^4_4$ / Slow Bass $^4_4$
SOMETHING BORROWED Pull Waltz $^3_4$ / Pull Jazz $^3_4$
SOMETHING FOR DJANGO Pull Jazz $^5_4$
SOMETHING MUST BE WRONG Fast Latin $^4_4$ / Fast Calypso $^4_4$
SOMETHING'S COMING Fast $^4_4$ / Percussive Fast $^4_4$

SOMETIMES I'M HAPPY Fast $^4_4$ / Fast Rock $^4_4$
SOMEWHERE Slow $^4_4$ / Slow Bass $^4_4$
SOMEWHERE OVER THE RAINBOW Slow $^4_4$ / Pinch Slow $^4_4$
SOUNDS OF SILENCE Arpeggiated $^4_4$ / Slow Bass $^4_4$
SOUTH COAST Rasgueado Pull $^3_4$ / Rasgueado Mexican $^3_4$
(THE) SONG OF THE DEPORTEES Fast $^3_4$ / Snap Back Carter Style $^3_4$
(THE) SOUND OF MUSIC Arpeggiated $^4_4$ / Slow Bass $^4_4$
SPANISH HARLEM Slow Bass $^4_4$ / Fast Latin $^4_4$
SPIKE DRIVER BLUES Travis Pattern Picking $^4_4$ / Complex Pattern Picking $^4_4$
SPINNING WHEEL Fast Rock $^4_4$ / Fast Back Beat Rock $^4_4$
SPLISH SPLASH Fast Rock $^4_4$ / Percussive Rock $^4_4$
SPORTIN' LIFE Arpeggiated Triplet $^4_4$ / Pinch Blues Triplet $^4_4$
SPRING CAN REALLY HANG YOU UP THE MOST Slow $^4_4$ / Slow Bass $^4_4$
STAGGER LEE Fast Rock $^4_4$ / Percussive Rock $^4_4$
STELLA BY STARLIGHT Slow Bass $^4_4$ / Slow Bass Pull $^4_4$
STEWBALL Fast $^3_4$ / Snap Back Carter Style $^3_4$
STOP IN THE NAME OF LOVE Fast Latin $^4_4$ / Percussive Rock $^4_4$
STRANGER ON THE SHORE Slow $^4_4$ / Slow Bass $^4_4$
STRANGERS IN THE NIGHT Slow Bass $^4_4$ / Slow Bass Pull $^4_4$
STRANGEST DREAM Pull Waltz $^3_4$ / Slow $^3_4$
STRING MAN Slow Bass $^4_4$ / Slow Bass Pull $^4_4$
STUDY WAR NO MORE Fast $^4_4$ / Fast Latin $^4_4$
SUBO (Spanish) Rasgueado Mexican $^3_4$ / Rasgueado Huapanga $^3_4$
SUGAR IN THE MORNING Fast $^4_4$ / Snap Back Carter Style $^4_4$
SULIRAM Slow $^3_4$ / Pinch Slow $^3_4$
SUMMER SAMBA (SO NICE) Slow Bass Pull $^4_4$ / Pinch Samba $^4_4$
SUMMER TIME Slow $^4_4$ / Slow Bass $^4_4$
SUNDAY Fast $^4_4$ / Percussive Fast $^4_4$
SUNDAY WILL NEVER BE THE SAME Fast Rock $^4_4$ / Percussive Rock $^4_4$
SUNNY Slow Bass $^4_4$ / Pull Slow Bass Rock $^4_4$
SUNNY GOODGE STREET Slow $^3_4$ / Slow Bass $^3_4$
SUNRISE, SUNSET Pull Waltz $^3_4$ / Slow $^3_4$
SUNSHINE GO AWAY TODAY Fast Latin $^4_4$ / Percussive Rock $^4_4$
SUNSHINE OF MY LIFE Slow Bass $^4_4$ / Pull Bass Note Rock $^4_4$
SUNSHINE OF YOUR LOVE Fast Latin $^4_4$ / Fast Bass Hard Rock $^4_4$
SUPERCALEFRAGELISTICEXPEALIDOTIOUS Pull $^4_4$ / Fast $^4_4$
SURREY WITH THE FRINGE ON THE TOP Pull $^4_4$ / Fast $^4_4$
SUZANNE Arpeggiated $^4_4$ / Moving Bass Pinch Ballad $^4_4$
SWAY Fast Latin $^4_4$ / Percussive Rock $^4_4$
SWEET BABY JAMES Fast $^3_4$ / Snap Back Carter Style $^3_4$
SWEET CAROLINE Slow Syncopated $^4_4$ / Fast Rock $^4_4$
SWEET GEORGIA BROWN Fast $^4_4$ / Percussive Fast $^4_4$
SWEET MELISSA Slow Bass $^4_4$ / Pull Slow Bass Rock $^4_4$
(THE) SWEETEST SOUNDS Fast $^4_4$ / Percussive Fast $^4_4$
SWING LOW SWEET CHARIOT Fast $^4_4$ / Fast Folk $^4_4$
(THE) SWINGING SHEPHERD BLUES Slow Syncopated $^4_4$ / Fast Latin $^4_4$
TAKE A WHIFF ON ME Fast $^4_4$ / Snap Back Carter Style $^4_4$
TAKE FIVE Pull Jazz $^5_4$
TAKE GOOD CARE OF MY BABY Fast $^4_4$ / Fast Folk $^4_4$
TAKE ME Moving Bass Arpeggiated Calypso $^4_4$ / Fast Calypso $^4_4$
TAKE THIS HAMMER Pull Bass Note Rock $^4_4$ / Percussive Bass Blues $^4_4$
TAMMY Pull Waltz $^3_4$ / Slow $^3_4$
TANGERINE Fast $^4_4$ / Percussive Fast $^4_4$
TANGO DELLA GELOSIA Fast Latin $^4_4$ / Rasgueado Tango $^4_4$
TARRENTELLE Pull $^4_4$ / Snap Back Double Bass $^4_4$
TAXMAN Fast Latin $^4_4$ / Fast Bass Hard Rock $^4_4$
TEA FOR TWO Fast Latin $^4_4$ / Percussive Rock $^4_4$
TEARS Slow Syncopated $^4_4$ / Fast Rhythm And Blues Shuffle $^4_4$
TEARS ON MY PILLOW Arpeggiated Triplet $^4_4$ / Arpeggiated Double Bass Triplet $^4_4$
TENDERLY Slow $^4_4$ / Slow Bass $^4_4$
TENNESSEE Waltz Pull Waltz $^3_4$ / Slow $^3_4$
TEQUILA Fast Latin $^4_4$ / Percussive Rock $^4_4$
THAT OLD FEELING Fast $^4_4$ / Slow Bass Pull $^4_4$
THAT'LL BE THE DAY Fast Rock $^4_4$ / Percussive Rock $^4_4$
THERE GOES MY BABY Slow Bass $^4_4$ / Fast Latin $^4_4$
THERE WILL NEVER BE ANOTHER YOU Fast $^4_4$ / Slow Bass Pull $^4_4$
THERE'S A KIND OF HUSH Slow $^4_4$ / Slow Bass $^4_4$
THERE'S A NEW WORLD I CAN SEE Fast Latin $^4_4$ / Fast Back Beat Rock $^4_4$
THEY CAN'T TAKE THAT AWAY FROM ME Fast $^4_4$ / Slow Syncopated $^4_4$
THEY LOOKED A LOT LIKE WE Arpeggiated $^4_4$ / Arpeggiated Bass $^4_4$
THIRSTY BOOTS Fast $^4_4$ / Travis Pattern Picking $^4_4$
THIS COULD BE THE START OF SOMETHING BIG Fast $^4_4$ / Percussive Fast $^4_4$
THIS GUY'S IN LOVE WITH YOU Slow Syncopated $^4_4$ / Percussive Bass Blues $^4_4$
THIS LAND IS YOUR LAND Fast $^4_4$ / Snap Back Carter Style $^4_4$
THIS LITTLE LIGHT Fast $^4_4$ / Fast Folk $^4_4$
THIS MAGIC MOMENT Moving Bass Arpeggiated Calypso $^4_4$ / Fast Calypso $^4_4$
THIS TRAIN Fast Rock $^4_4$ / Percussive Rock $^4_4$
THOSE WERE THE DAYS Slow Bass $^4_4$ / Pull $^4_4$
THREE COINS IN A FOUNTAIN Arpeggiated $^4_4$ / Moving Bass Arpeggiated Calypso $^4_4$
THREE SISTERS Moving Bass Pull Folk Greek $^7_8$
THREE YOUNG MEN FROM VOLOS Moving Bass Pull Folk Greek $^7_8$
TICKET TO RIDE Fast Rock $^4_4$ / Fast Back Beat Rock $^4_4$
TILL THERE WAS YOU Slow $^4_4$ / Slow Bass $^4_4$
TIMES A GETTIN' HARD Slow Syncopated $^4_4$ / Arpeggiated $^4_4$
(THE) TIMES THEY ARE A CHANGIN' Fast $^3_4$ / Snap Back Carter Style $^3_4$
TINA (SINGU LAYLA VOOTAYA) Fast $^4_4$ / Snap Back Carter Style $^4_4$
TO SIR WITH LOVE Slow $^4_4$ / Slow Bass $^4_4$

TO TRENO YERMANEO ATHENON Pull Mid-East $^4_4$ / Moving Bass Pull Spanish $^4_4$
TODAY Slow $^3_4$ / Pinch Slow $^3_4$
TOMORROW IS A LONG TIME Arpeggiated $^4_4$ / Full Inverted Pattern Picking $^4_4$
TONIGHT Moving Bass Pull Spanish $^4_4$ / Travis Pattern Picking $^4_4$
TONIGHT, TONIGHT Arpeggiated Triplet $^4_4$ / Arpeggiated Double Bass Triplet $^4_4$
TOP OF THE WORLD Fast $^4_4$ / Snap Back Carter Style $^4_4$
TOPSY Fast $^4_4$ / Percussive Fast $^4_4$
TOSSIN' AND TURNIN' Fast Rock $^4_4$ / Percussive Rock $^4_4$
TRACES Slow Bass $^4_4$ / Slow Bass Pull $^4_4$
THE TREES THEY DO GROW HIGH Slow $^4_4$ / Pinch Slow $^4_4$
TROPICAL MERENGUE Fast Latin $^4_4$ / Fast Merengue $^4_4$
TROUBLE IN MIND Slow Syncopated $^4_4$ / Percussive Bass Blues $^4_4$
TRY TO REMEMBER Slow $^3_4$ / Arpeggiated $^3_4$
TURKEY IN THE STRAW Fast $^4_4$ / Snap Back Carter Style $^4_4$
TURN, TURN, TURN Slow $^4_4$ / Slow Bass $^4_4$
TURTLE DOVE Slow $^4_4$ / Pinch Slow $^4_4$
TWELVE GATES TO THE CITY Fast $^4_4$ / Fast Rhythm And Blues Shuffle $^4_4$
THE TWIST Fast Rock $^4_4$ / Fast Twist $^4_4$
TWIST AND SHOUT Fast Rock $^4_4$ / Fast Twist $^4_4$
TWO BROTHERS Slow $^4_4$ / Slow Bass $^4_4$
UCH MA MAYCHO NAYCI (Bulgarian) Pull Jazz $^5_4$
UM ABRACO NO BONFA Slow Bass Pull $^4_4$ / Accented Pinch Bossa Nova $^4_4$
UMBRELLAS OF CHERBOURGH (I WILL WAIT FOR YOU) Slow $^4_4$ / Slow Bass $^4_4$
UN CANADIEN ERRANT (French Canadian) Slow $^3_4$ / Slow Bass $^3_4$
UNA TARDE FRESQUITA DE MAYO (Spanish) Rasgueado Mexican $^3_4$ / Percussive Tambor $^3_4$
UNCHAIN MY HEART Fast Rock $^4_4$ / Fast Latin $^4_4$
UNCHAINED MELODY Arpeggiated $^4_4$ / Arpeggiated Bass $^4_4$
UNDER THE BOARDWALK Slow Bass $^4_4$ / Fast Latin $^4_4$
UNITED NATIONS Pull $^4_4$ / Fast $^4_4$
UNIVERSAL MERENGUE Fast Latin $^4_4$ / Fast Merengue $^4_4$
UNIVERSAL SOLDIER Fast $^4_4$ / Travis Pattern Picking $^4_4$
UNTIL IT'S TIME FOR YOU TO GO Slow $^3_4$ / Slow Bass $^3_4$
URGE FOR GOING Arpeggiated $^4_4$ / Moving Bass Ballad $^4_4$
VENGA JALEA (Spanish) Fast $^3_4$ / Rasgueado Mexican $^3_4$
VENGELIO (Greek) Moving Bass Pull Folk Greek $^7_8$
VIDALITA (Spanish) Rasgueado Mexican $^3_4$ / Rasgueado Huapanga $^3_4$
VINCENT Arpeggiated $^4_4$ / Arpeggiated Bass $^4_4$
VIVA EL MATADOR (Spanish) Fast $^3_4$ / Rasgueado Mexican $^3_4$
VIVA LA QUINCE BRIGADA (Spanish) Rasgueado Spanish $^4_4$ / Rasgueado Moving Bass Pull $^4_4$
VOLARE (Italian) Fast $^4_4$
WABASH CANNONBALL Fast $^4_4$ / Snap Back Carter Style $^4_4$
WAGONER'S LAD Slow $^3_4$ / Pinch Slow $^3_4$
WALK ON BY Slow Bass $^4_4$ / Fast Latin $^4_4$
WALK RIGHT IN Fast Rock $^4_4$ / Snap Back Double Bass $^4_4$
WALK THROUGH THE VALLEY Fast $^4_4$ / Fast Latin $^4_4$
WALTZING MATILDA Slow $^4_4$ / Pinch Slow $^4_4$
WASN'T THAT A TIME Fast $^4_4$ / Snap Back Carter Style $^4_4$
WATCH WHAT HAPPENS Slow Bass Pull $^4_4$ / Pinch Bossa Nova $^4_4$
WATER COME TO ME EYES Moving Bass Arpeggiated Calypso $^4_4$ / Fast Calypso $^4_4$
(THE) WATER IS WIDE Slow $^4_4$ / Arpeggiated $^4_4$
WAVE Slow Bass Pull $^4_4$ / Accented Pinch Bossa Nova $^4_4$
(THE) WAY YOU LOOK TONIGHT Fast $^4_4$ / Travis Pattern Picking $^4_4$
WE ARE CROSSING JORDAN'S RIVER Fast Folk $^4_4$ / Fast Rhythm And Blues Bo Diddley $^4_4$
WE SHALL NOT BE MOVED Fast $^4_4$ / Snap Back Carter Style $^4_4$
WEARY AND A LONESOME TRAVELER Fast $^4_4$ / Snap Back Folk Style $^4_4$
WEDDING BELL BLUES Fast $^4_4$ / Fast Rock $^4_4$
WEDDING SONG Moving Bass Pinch Ballad $^4_4$ / Inverted Pattern Picking $^4_4$
WE'LL SING IN THE SUNSHINE Fast $^4_4$ / Slow Syncopated $^4_4$
WELL YOU NEEDN'T Slow Syncopated $^4_4$ / Fast $^4_4$
WEST COAST BLUES Pull Waltz $^3_4$ / Pull Jazz $^3_4$
WHAT A GRAND AND GLORIOUS FEELING Pull Waltz $^3_4$ / Slow $^3_4$
WHAT I SAY Fast Rock $^4_4$ / Percussive Rock $^4_4$
WHAT KIND OF FOOL AM I Slow $^4_4$ / Slow Bass $^4_4$
WHAT NOW MY LOVE Slow Bass Pull $^4_4$ / Fast Latin $^4_4$
WHAT THE WORLD NEEDS NOW Pull Waltz $^3_4$ / Pull Jazz $^3_4$
WHATEVER LOLA WANTS Fast Latin $^4_4$ / Rasgueado Tango $^4_4$
WHAT'S NEW Slow $^4_4$ / Slow Bass $^4_4$
(THE) WHEEL OF LIFE Travis Pattern Picking $^4_4$ / Inflected Pattern Picking $^4_4$
WHEN A MAN LOVES A WOMAN Arpeggiated Triplet $^4_4$ / Arpeggiated Double Bass Triplet $^4_4$
WHEN I FALL IN LOVE Slow $^4_4$ / Slow Bass $^4_4$
WHEN I WAKE Fast $^4_4$ / Travis Pattern Picking $^4_4$
WHEN I WAS A COWBOY Fast Rock $^4_4$ / Snap Back Nashville Style $^4_4$
WHEN I'M GONE Arpeggiated $^4_4$ / Moving Bass Pinch Ballad $^4_4$
WHEN SUNNY GETS BLUE Slow $^4_4$ / Slow Bass $^4_4$
WHEN THE IDLE POOR BECOME THE IDLE RICH Pull $^4_4$ / Fast $^4_4$
WHEN THE SAINTS COME MARCHIN' IN Fast $^4_4$ / Fast Folk $^4_4$
WHEN YOU WISH UPON A STAR Slow $^4_4$ / Slow Bass $^4_4$
WHERE ARE YOU GOING Slow $^3_4$ / Slow Bass $^3_4$
WHERE CAN I GO WITHOUT YOU Slow $^4_4$ / Slow Bass $^4_4$
WHERE DOES IT LEAD Slow $^4_4$ / Slow Bass $^4_4$
WHERE HAVE ALL THE FLOWERS GONE Slow $^4_4$ / Arpeggiated $^4_4$
WHERE OR WHEN Slow Bass $^4_4$ / Travis Pattern Picking $^4_4$

WHISPERING Fast $\frac{4}{4}$ / Percussive Fast $\frac{4}{4}$
WHISPERING BELLS Fast $\frac{4}{4}$ / Percussive Fast $\frac{4}{4}$
WHITER SHADE OF PALE Arpeggiated Triplet $\frac{4}{4}$ / Arpeggiated Double Bass Triplet $\frac{4}{4}$
WHO CAN I TURN TO Slow $\frac{4}{4}$ / Slow Bass $\frac{4}{4}$
WHO DO YOU LOVE Fast Rock $\frac{4}{4}$ / Fast R and B Bo Diddley $\frac{4}{4}$
WHO WILL BUY Pull $\frac{4}{4}$ / Fast $\frac{4}{4}$
WHO'S GONNA SHOE YOUR PRETTY LITTLE FOOT Fast $\frac{3}{4}$ / Snap Back Carter Style $\frac{3}{4}$
WHY DO FALLS FALL IN LOVE Fast Rock $\frac{4}{4}$ / Percussive Rock $\frac{4}{4}$
WILDWOOD FLOWER Fast $\frac{4}{4}$ / Snap Back Carter Style $\frac{4}{4}$
WILL THE CIRCLE BE UNBROKEN Fast $\frac{4}{4}$ / Snap Back Nashville Style $\frac{4}{4}$
WILL YOU STILL LOVE ME TOMORROW Slow Bass $\frac{4}{4}$ / Arpeggiated Bass $\frac{4}{4}$
WIMOWEH Fast $\frac{4}{4}$ / Fast Latin $\frac{4}{4}$
(THE) WIND CRIES MARY Slow Bass $\frac{4}{4}$ / Percussive Bass Note Rock $\frac{4}{4}$
WINDMILLS OF YOUR MIND Slow $\frac{4}{4}$ / Pinch Slow $\frac{4}{4}$
WITCHCRAFT Slow Bass $\frac{4}{4}$ / Fast $\frac{4}{4}$
WITHOUT A SONG Fast $\frac{4}{4}$ / Travis Pattern Picking $\frac{4}{4}$
WIVES AND LOVERS Pull Waltz $\frac{3}{4}$ / Pull Jazz $\frac{3}{4}$
WOKE UP THIS MORNING Fast Rock $\frac{4}{4}$ / Fast Back Beat Rock $\frac{4}{4}$
WONDERFUL, WONDERFUL Slow Bass $\frac{4}{4}$ / Fast Latin $\frac{4}{4}$
WONDERFUL, WONDERFUL COPENHAGEN Pull Waltz $\frac{3}{4}$ / Pull Jazz $\frac{3}{4}$
WOODSTOCK Fast Rock $\frac{4}{4}$ / Fast Back Beat Rock $\frac{4}{4}$
(THE) WORD Fast Rock $\frac{4}{4}$ / Fast Bass Hard Rock $\frac{4}{4}$
WORK SONG Fast Rock $\frac{4}{4}$ / Percussive Rock $\frac{4}{4}$
WORRIED MAN'S BLUES Fast $\frac{4}{4}$ / Snap Back Carter Style $\frac{4}{4}$
WOULDN'T IT BE LOVERLY Pull $\frac{4}{4}$ / Slow Syncopated $\frac{4}{4}$
YA, YA Slow Bass $\frac{4}{4}$ / Fast Latin $\frac{4}{4}$
YELLOW BIRD Moving Bass Arpeggiated Calypso $\frac{4}{4}$ / Fast Calypso $\frac{4}{4}$
YERAKINA Moving Bass Pull Folk Greek $\frac{7}{8}$ / Moving Bass Pull Spanish $\frac{4}{4}$

YES INDEED Fast Rhythm And Blues Shuffle $\frac{4}{4}$ / Percussive Bass Blues $\frac{4}{4}$
YESTERDAY Slow $\frac{4}{4}$ / Slow Bass $\frac{4}{4}$
YESTERDAY ONCE MORE Slow Bass $\frac{4}{4}$ / Arpeggiated Bass $\frac{4}{4}$
YESTERDAY WHEN I WAS YOUNG Slow Bass $\frac{4}{4}$ / Slow Bass Pull $\frac{4}{4}$
YESTERDAYS Arpeggiated $\frac{4}{4}$ / Fast $\frac{4}{4}$
YISMACHU Pull $\frac{4}{4}$ / Fast $\frac{4}{4}$
YIVERRECHECHA Pull $\frac{4}{4}$ / Fast $\frac{4}{4}$
YOU GO TO MY HEAD Slow $\frac{4}{4}$ / Slow Bass $\frac{4}{4}$
YOU KEEP ME HANGIN' ON Fast $\frac{4}{4}$ / Fast Back Beat Rock $\frac{4}{4}$
YOU MAKE ME FEEL SO YOUNG Slow Syncopated $\frac{4}{4}$ / Fast Rhythm And Blues Shuffle $\frac{4}{4}$
YOU STEPPED OUT OF A DREAM Moving Bass Pull Spanish $\frac{4}{4}$ / Fast Calypso $\frac{4}{4}$
YOU WERE ON MY MIND Fast $\frac{4}{4}$ / Travis Pattern Picking $\frac{4}{4}$
YOU WON'T SEE ME Fast Rock $\frac{4}{4}$ / Fast Latin $\frac{4}{4}$
YOUR CHEATING HEART Fast $\frac{4}{4}$ / Snap Back Carter Style $\frac{4}{4}$
YOUR MOTHER SHOULD KNOW Slow Syncopated $\frac{4}{4}$ / Snap Back Double Bass $\frac{4}{4}$
YOU'D BE SO NICE TO COME HOME TO Fast $\frac{4}{4}$ / Slow Bass Pull $\frac{4}{4}$
YOU'RE A THOUSAND MILES AWAY Arpeggiated Triplet $\frac{4}{4}$ / Arpeggiated Double Bass Triplet $\frac{4}{4}$
YOU'RE DRIVING ME CRAZY Fast $\frac{4}{4}$ / Percussive Fast $\frac{4}{4}$
YOU'RE SO VAIN Fast Rock $\frac{4}{4}$ / Fast Latin $\frac{4}{4}$
YOU'VE GOT A FRIEND Slow $\frac{4}{4}$ / Slow Bass $\frac{4}{4}$
YOU'VE GOT TO HIDE YOUR LOVE AWAY Fast $\frac{3}{4}$ / Fast Rock $\frac{3}{4}$
YOU'VE LOST THAT LOVIN' FEELIN' Slow Bass $\frac{4}{4}$ / Fast Latin $\frac{4}{4}$
ZING WENT THE STRINGS OF MY HEART Fast $\frac{4}{4}$ / Percussive Fast $\frac{4}{4}$
ZOG NIT KEINMOL Slow Syncopated $\frac{4}{4}$ / Percussive Bass Blues $\frac{4}{4}$
ZORBA Pull $\frac{4}{4}$ / Snap Back Carter Style $\frac{4}{4}$
ZUM GALI GALI Pull Folk Chasidic $\frac{4}{4}$ / Fast $\frac{4}{4}$

Index of Songs Appearing In This Book

Abe and Malká

Apart from their separate, musical backgrounds and years of teaching experience, Abe & Malká have been performing as a duo for nearly 4 years. A good part of their material is sung in over a dozen languages, so it isn't surprising that their music is called "International Folk-Rock and Jazz."

Abe & Malká lived and performed abroad for over a year. Most of that time was spent in Israel, where they entertained in night clubs, concert halls, open-air festivals and on radio and television shows. They continued their work through Europe and Scandinavia, performing mostly on TV programs.

More recently, they've been working New York clubs, coffee houses, cable TV shows and City sponsored and college concerts. Their 4-part concert series was funded by a cultural grant from the Bronx Council on the Arts and the Parks Recreation Department. They've also performed widely for organizational centers, hospitals and correctional/rehabilitation centers.

They've just returned from a summer in Japan, where they did TV shows and concert work. Their first record has just been released by Open Door-Records.